The Lovely Ambition

*Novels by Mary Ellen Chase*

# THE *Lovely Ambition*

## A NOVEL BY
### *Mary Ellen Chase*

**W · W · NORTON & COMPANY**

*New York · London*

Published simultaneously in Canada
by Penguin Books Canada Ltd,
2801 John Street, Markham, Ontario L3R 1B4

A small portion of this book, contained in Chapter 22 of Part IV,
appeared in *The Atlantic Monthly*, May, 1932.

"I Think Continually of Those Who Were Truly Great" is quoted
from *Poems* by Stephen Spender, copyright 1934 by The Modern
Library, Inc., and is reprinted by permission of Random House, Inc.

First published as a Norton paperback 1985

Library of Congress Cataloging in Publication Data
Chase, Mary Ellen,. 1887–1973.
The lovely ambition.
I. Title.
PS3505.H48L6    1985    813'.54      85-2952

W.W. Norton & Company, Inc.
500 Fifth Avenue, New York, N.Y. 10110
W.W. Norton & Company Ltd.
37 Great Russell Street, London WC1B 3NU

ISBN 0-393-30234-2

PRINTED IN THE UNITED STATES OF AMERICA

1  2  3  4  5  6  7  8  9  0

*This book is dedicated to*
*NORA KERSHAW CHADWICK*
*in admiration, and in gratitude for my life in*
*England, especially for Cambridge and Bury St. Edmunds*

# Contents

# *I Think Continually of Those Who Were Truly Great*

I think continually of those who were truly great.
Who, from the womb, remembered the soul's history
Through corridors of light where the hours are suns,
Endless and singing. Whose lovely ambition
Was that their lips, still touched with fire,
Should tell of the spirit clothed from head to foot in song.
And who hoarded from the spring branches
The desires falling across their bodies like blossoms.

What is precious is never to forget
The delight of the blood drawn from ageless springs
Breaking through rocks in worlds before our earth;
Never to deny its pleasure in the simple morning light,
Nor its grave evening demand for love;
Never to allow gradually the traffic to smother
With noise and fog the flowering of the spirit.

Near the snow, near the sun, in the highest fields
See how those names are fêted by the waving grass,
And by the streamers of white cloud,
And whispers of wind in the listening sky;
The names of those who in their lives fought for life,
Who wore at their hearts the fire's centre.
Born of the sun they traveled a short while towards the sun,
And left the vivid air signed with their honour.

*Stephen Spender*

ONE · The
Dream

*I DREAMED* last night again about Mrs. Gowan. She was as real in my dream as she was fifty years ago in our Maine orchard. There she sat beneath the apple trees, weaving and plaiting or intertwining with bits of string and thread those absurd wreaths for our heads—for my father's and my mother's, for my sister Mary's, for my twin brother Ansie's and mine, and even for Mrs. Baxter's severe, tightly arranged hair. There she sat, telling us all in her new, intoxicating freedom about Mr. Wheeler, Mrs. Nesbit, and Charley Bright and asking my father with some anxiety about the Grace of God, more for Mrs. McCarthy's sake, she said, than for her own. Her eyes widened in exactly the way they always used to do when we in our turn told her about the Suffolk harvest fields, and when Ansie, whom she especially loved, made her see the red poppies among the waving grain.

I suppose, in point of fact, that I am beginning to write this story mainly because of these recurring dreams. I am no authority whatsoever on the nature or source of dreams and am more than willing to yield to the famous psychologists who are. Even the most harrowing anxiety nightmares may, for all I know, be closely related to one's conscious or subconscious wishes and, in spite of their hideous and often humiliating distortions, be truly interpreted as a fulfillment of one's most ardent desires, whether recognized or hidden. And yet

I am inclined to wonder, merely on the basis of experience, if certain dreams, especially as one grows older, may not conceivably be the grateful evidence of truth and reality in one's past life.

At all events, Mrs. Gowan's frequent presence in my sleep at night has prompted me to write these chapters, not only about her, but also about our life as a family in both Old England and New. She has been dead for half a century, yet in both my memory and my dreams she is still true to her merry, sometimes confused, but always resilient sense of life. Perhaps she returns to assure me of the certainties of that Other World toward which she was hastening when we knew her at nearly eighty years old, or perhaps to reassure me of the verities of this one in which we all lived with her for three brief seasons. She kept so close a vigil with me last night after my dream that, when a December snowstorm began on a rising wind just before dawn to beat against my windows, I more than half expected to hear her scratching at a pane and demanding shelter as Mr. Lockwood heard the ghost of Catherine Linton in *Wuthering Heights*.

As to our life as a family, I feel so fortunate because of it that I think it may hold some interest and perhaps even some value, at least for those who still believe that in the character of families lies our chief hope, or despair, for the redemption of this erring, perplexed, and overburdened world. Of course we, the Tillyards, can contribute little to divert, or amuse, or warn, or reassure in comparison with the immortal families, the Forsytes or the Jellybys, the Ramsays or the Bennets or the Marches. Nevertheless, it is possible that my father at least may afford something of hope. Hope was a favourite word of his, just as it was the glowing Reality which made his life.

My father never forgot Mrs. Gowan. He had often talked of her, my mother told me, when I went back to England to see her before, between, and after the two tragic World Wars. Whenever anything of especial importance to him had happened—a Danish or a Roman coin which he had dug up in his garden, baby mallards reluctantly following their mother over a slow Suffolk stream, skylarks soaring out of sight into the close February skies and endlessly singing there, the birth of lambs in a lambing meadow on a clear, cold winter night —he always wished for Mrs. Gowan to share his delight. And since the bitterness of old woes and griefs loses its sharpness with time and merges into limitless, even healing compassion, my mother, too, had come to wish for her and, like my father, to be grateful for her.

# TWO · *Saintsbury, Cambridgeshire*

$M$Y FATHER was born in Suffolk, that East Anglian shire of weavers, incredible fields of buttercups, brooding, cloud-filled skies, beautiful Perpendicular churches, and small, placid rivers, the Stour, the Waveney, the Lark, and the Little Ouse. There are numberless streams, too, in addition to the rivers, gentle lines of water that seem to be flowing nowhere in particular; and there are ditches as well, which in the more level land of this undulating countryside often take the place of hedges in separating field from field. All these quiet waterways encourage the tangled growth of rose willow herb, white cow parsley, and red campion; in the early spring, primroses clothe their banks with sheets of pale gold; the red-billed moor hen and the mallard duck find homes among their reeds and sedges. So, alas! do the water rats.

My mother in frequent moments of extreme irritation attributed my father's slowness to the influence of these Suffolk streams. She came from the North of England where people in contrast are active and impatient. He always told her, however, with unfailing good nature that she was quite mistaken. People in Suffolk were slow, he said, first because of the bitter east winds which, with no considerable hills between all East Anglia and the Russian steppes to temper their force, had an inevitable way of retarding everyone in whatever he might be doing. Then, too, there was the mud, so heavy in the winter and the spring that farmers in particular were constantly delayed in all their work. The heaviest Suffolk mud is known as *slud*, a word which, he said, might well be an apt combination of *slow* and *mud*.

He was the son of a yeoman farmer, James Tillyard by name, who o /ned some one hundred acres of arable land between the old towns of Bury St. Edmunds and Long Melford, and not far from the village of Lavenham with its rows of timbered houses built centuries ago by the weavers. The farm had been in the freehold possession of my father's family for many generations. The house, of generous dimensions, had been framed in the late seventeenth century of stout oak timbers filled in with red brick; but so many repairs and additions had been given it through the years by so many succeeding Tillyards that its walls contained all manner of other material, plaster, flint, wattles, and a goodly supply of native clunch, that compound of chalk and small stones often seen in old East Anglian buildings and an attractive feature of many of its churches. The upper storey of the house overhung the lower; and its latticed windows, which in the summer were flung wide open to the sun and air (and to thousands of wasps as well) and in the winter were never tight enough to keep out the wind from Russia, sloped and leaned at such sharp angles and in such precarious positions that as a small child visiting my grandparents I always feared a sudden collapse of the whole superstructure. My grandfather, however, reassured me in his slow, uneven East Anglian speech.

"Nawthen," he said, meaning *nothing*, "moves oak timbers. They be for good and all."

The great old barn also was made strong with oak stanchions and rafters, some black and shining, others silvery grey and cut with narrow slits where the wood had slowly separated through the centuries. There was stone, too, in its construction together with clunch, brick, and plaster; and some of its narrow windows were lined and even arched with cut stone like those in a church. When years afterward I read about the sheep-shearing barn in Hardy's *Far from the Madding Crowd*, I remembered my grandfather's barn in Suffolk. Beyond stretched the sheep folds and the enclosures for cattle and for the ubiquitous Suffolk pigs, which frightened me by their size and seeming ferocity.

When I look back upon our visits to the Suffolk farm, I remember most keenly the cold of its low bedrooms in winter and the sound of the wind smiting their loosely fitted windows in mighty gusts during the night. It was quite cold enough, to be sure, in our Cambridgeshire parsonage, for the same east winds did not spare the fens; but my mother filled stone jars with boiling water at bedtime and, moreover, we always undressed before my father's study fire, a pleasant custom which she did not feel free to introduce into set Suffolk ways.

I remember our evening walks after tea along the drift, which in Suffolk means a narrow lane between fields, or a cartway given to the passage of farm carts painted blue or red or yellow, or of cattle, or of labourers going home from work. My grandfather's drift was bounded by high banks, which in the spring were white with traveller's-joy and with elder. Sometimes, when my feet grew tired from the uneven ground or shadows began to darken the drift, my father lifted me to his shoulders where I rode happily over the stone stiles, along the footpath, and home.

I suppose I do not actually remember the names of my grandfather's fields, but only think that I do because of my father's frequent recounting of them in later years. They fascinated him by their suggestions of happenings long since forgotten in the passage of time, perhaps even of centuries. One was called Hangman's Field; another Lost Lena's Meadow; a third, more happily, the Shoulder of Mutton; and a fourth, Dead Boy's Pightle.

I am sure I remember my grandmother's word for the see-saw which my father made for us in an open space among the drooping, lacy willow trees by one of the small slow streams. She called it a *teetermatawter*. The first two syllables of this odd word apparently meant rising in the air; the last two were, I gathered, descriptive of the bump experienced when one hit the ground at the end of the downward passage. Later, when we went to America, I introduced the word to the children of our Maine parish. Perhaps it still survives there.

### 2

My grandparents were elderly, kind, taciturn people who were intensely proud of my father, their only son and the child of their middle age, and of the advantages they had given him. Unlike most of their neighbours, they were by stout descent if not as stout desire Nonconformists, in the local term "chapel" rather than Church, being Wesleyan by inheritance. When my father had completed the village school, they sent him, how-ever, to a public school at Bury St. Edmunds, a strictly Church foundation, where he so distinguished himself as a potential scholar that they determined to manage three years for him at Clare College in Cambridge only some thirty miles west-ward.

I think my father remained firm toward his Wesleyan tra-dition and heritage partly because he felt that he had disap-pointed his parents in other ways. He was clearly no farmer either by inclination or by fitness. When as a young boy he scared rooks from the fields by shaking a wooden rattle de-signed for that purpose, he was always conning some book and forgetting the job at hand; when he grew older and cul-tivated the barley or the wheat, he carried Horace or Plato in his pocket and snatched too many minutes with them at the end of the long grain rows. Once I had begun the study of Latin and Greek in the Maine academy of our transplanted home, he used to tell me of those Suffolk days and of the sea gulls from the coast swooping above his head as he stumbled unwillingly among the furrows.

There were, as a matter of fact, only two occupations in farm life which he loved. One was lambing; the other, the weekly market. He used to spend night after night in the lambing meadow when the young lambs began to come in through December and January. There he stayed in a curious small hut placed on wheels and containing, together with a tiny stove which always bore a can of milk on its black top, country nostrums in the shape of salves, oils, disinfectants, and ointments needed for the care of newly born lambs before they were strong enough to be returned to their mothers. When he heard the bleating of some ewes in labour under the rude thatched hurdles placed for their protection about the field or surmised from the jangling of their bells that they were restless in their shelters, his business was to stride with his lantern to the birthplaces, give any assistance he could to the quivering creatures, and then return to his hut with the long-legged young in his arms. To these he gave warm milk, medical or simple surgical treatment if necessary, and some warmth on blanketed heaps of straw by his fire before he carried them back to nuzzle and feed from their mothers under the winter skies. This task was so pleasing to him, partly perhaps because of its primitive association with early ages in which a goodly portion of his nature always lived, partly because he liked caring for the young and helpless, that he spared his father the night wages of a shepherd during many of his winter holidays from Cambridge.

The weekly market for the region was held in Bury St. Edmunds on Saturdays. My father as a boy, when he was not in school or often when he was, always went with my grandfather to help with the stock, carted or driven up for sale along the winding Suffolk roads, the garden produce and flowers, the lengths of wool woven by my grandmother, or the various other pieces of her handiwork in knitting or crochet. On such days from dawn till dark what bustle and commotion rent the air of that ancient town! Cattle, sheep, poultry, and pigs jostled one another, bellowed, bleated, squawked, squealed, and grunted in a hundred enclosures; farmers in worn corduroy and fustian stamped about in their heavy, mud-caked boots, caring for their animals or their garden stuff and constantly calling out the superior excellencies of both; labourers of every sort, thatchers, shepherds, hedgers, ditchers, sought to better their present wages by interchanges of confidences with one another or by judicious approaches to some prosperous farmer, known to be hiring; children screamed from mere excitement or from noisy slaps administered by tired or outraged mothers; hawkers, whose business it was to journey day by day from one market town to another, mingled with the crowds and yelled out the charms of their wares, which they bore on wide trays suspended from their shoulders or secreted in capacious bags around their waists. These included gimcracks and gewgaws of every description, cheap jewellery, brooches, beads, bangles, ribbons, hair ornaments, small tools, and toys; all manner of remedies, tinctures, liniments, cough syrups, freckle removers, toothache cures, plasters for corns and bunions, poultices for croup, salves for bee stings; and, always a popular item, fortune-telling books equally dependable, they claimed, for gentry or for common folk.

I am sure it was not the market itself which endeared Bury St. Edmunds—or Bury, as the old town was locally known— to my father. He was forever straying away from Butter

Market Hill, that slight elevation which only in East Anglia could be termed a hill at all, and going to the sloping square in front of the Angel Inn and opposite the gate of the Benedictine Abbey where he was well out of the confusion, could wander about the abbey ruins and gardens, or bend over the cases of antiquities in the nearby museum. Nor was Bury as the site of his school, for which he retained no particular affection, his lodestone. None of us, indeed, ever clearly understood why Bury St. Edmunds had so captivated my father's imagination as a boy that he was all his life to look upon it as his Earthly Paradise.

"Perhaps it's Mr. Pickwick," my brother Ansie said, when we had all returned one December evening to the parsonage after yet another day's outing to Bury and after my father had gone to talk with the shepherd in a Cambridgeshire lambing meadow beyond our garden hedge. Ansie's idea sprang, of course, from our frequent readings of Dickens and his recollection of Pickwick at the Angel Inn.

My mother said nonsense to that suggestion as she warmed up some scones and set the kettle boiling for our tea. Mr. Pickwick alone, she felt sure, could never explain my father's passion. Afterward, as we sat around the study fire in our flannel nightgowns eating scones and honey and drinking far too many cups of hot tea, she told us not to try to understand my father's love for Bury St. Edmunds. It might, of course, lie deep in Saxon history, or in the bones of St. Edmund, the Martyr, once King of East Anglia, or in the Museum of Antiquities, or in the ancient abbey ruins above the river Lark; but she was inclined to believe it lay just in the peculiar spirit or the soul of Bury, which was doubtless compounded of all these things and yet was suffused by some mysterious essence beyond them. Certain places, she said, possessed these singular spirits, which they disclosed to certain people in a strange, yet very real way and even went so far as to cast a spell over them.

I knew then, as I was to know many times afterward, that she was forestalling any irritation which we might feel against my father. When he came in an hour later, drenched from a sudden gust of rain and sleet, she helped him out of his wet clothes and made him a pot of tea all on his own, without the least suggestion that she had found the long day at Bury worn to shreds and tiresome as well. He was jubilant over twin lambs just dropped by one of the ewes and now in the shepherd's hut on a pile of straw.

"Such long legs you never saw," he told us, "and the smaller one as black as a piece of this coal."

As for me, I rather shared the hold which Bury St. Edmunds had upon my father even though I could not fathom it. I am sure my eyes were never so eager as those of Mary and Ansie when my mother fervently proposed a day at Felixstowe, where we could play upon the beach or perhaps even bathe; or among the Roman ruins at Colchester; or at Flatford Mill, where, beneath the willows of the Stour, we might well see some rare water birds; or even at Ely, so close that on extra-clear days we could see the great tower and lantern of its cathedral rising dimly above the trees on the horizon. My father was always courteous toward these suggestions and seemed amenable, though they seldom in the end influenced him. Most of our single holidays began and ended at Bury.

Once in the abbey gardens there—it was the spring when Ansie and I were ten and only a few months before our departure for America—I found among the stone ruins which marked the site of the abbot's kitchen a tiny shoe belonging without doubt to some little girl's doll. It was made of pale-blue felt and had an ankle strap decorated with a jaunty miniature rosette. It lay on the green grass among the old stones and rubble as out of place there as some silly bit of finery on someone who is dead.

"There it is," my father said. "What a symbol of the past and the present together! It's just as that dour old Scot has written in his torrent of words about Bury."

I was overjoyed by my find and fearful all the rest of the day lest its owner might be discovered. For whenever we met any women with children, my father kept asking in his slow Suffolk voice, "Has your little girl by any chance lost her dolly's shoe?" Fortunately for me no little girl claimed my treasure, and I was allowed to keep it.

When in late August we all went aboard the ship in Southampton, stumbling in a daze of unreality up the ribbed and slippery gangway, my father suddenly asked me if I had brought along that little blue shoe. He seemed relieved and pleased when I assured him that I had.

### 3

My mother, whose maiden name was Oldroyd, came, as I have said, from the North of England. Her father was not only sound Church, but an archdeacon in the East Riding of Yorkshire. He was a tall man with a long, thin face and long, spindly, rather bowed legs in black gaiters. He always wore a black shovel hat; and since his neck, too, was long and thin, there was a quite considerable space left vacant around his white clerical collar. He had somewhat mellow, protruding brown eyes under drooping lids, critical rather than kind eyes, and he scanned us children with them on his infrequent visits as though he were surprised that the children of a chapel parson could be in general so presentable and well-behaved as we were.

"Frankly," said my sister Mary, who loved to begin sentences with adverbs, "he gives me the creeps. Candidly, I prefer Grandfather Tillyard."

Whenever my grandfather Oldroyd came to see us, which he always carefully arranged to do in the middle of the week so that the problem of Church versus chapel should not actively arise as it would have been bound to do on Sundays, he spent a great deal of time studying the trefoiled windows and the old brasses in the chancel of our beautiful fourteenth-century parish church of St. Peter the Apostle. He saw also a great deal of the vicar, a short, round-faced, placid man, who loved antiquities of every sort and had an honest, even zealous admiration for my father. We did not in the least object to my grandfather's occupations, since they not only established his immovable Anglican position to his own satisfaction but also made him cognizant that my father was held in high regard by the vicar, a fact which he was reluctant to concede.

Up to the final weeks before my parents' marriage he had never relinquished the consuming hope (granted, of course, that he could be consumed by any hope) that his prospective son-in-law would abandon his Wesleyan adherence and read decently for Orders in the Church of England. That my father had not done so remained to him a source of both bewilderment and bitter resentment. If he had felt merely regret, my mother might have been able to share it, for she truly loved her Church inheritance and found numberless things about chapel difficult to bear; but his resentment only kindled her anger, which she was not always able or, for that matter, eager to conceal. Whenever my grandfather, perhaps in an honest attempt to lighten the heavy atmosphere in our parsonage which his presence there invariably engendered, praised us children, Mary's command of language, Ansie's knowledge of music, and my rather quick and retentive memory, she was given to a reply which, in the kindest terms, was little better than a retort.

"I'm quite sure they get everything of any distinction from

their father," she would say. "I certainly can't trace their talents to our side of the family."

My grandmother Oldroyd was not of much help in making their brief stays with us any easier for anyone. She was a short, plump, talkative woman with round, calm, very blue eyes, like my mother's in colour, but in neither shape nor expression. She always seemed to be swathed in a lot of extra material, her dresses pleated or gathered, smocked or flounced in an unnecessary way and one unfortunate for her type of figure even in an era of superfluous yardage in ladies' costumes; and she spent a great deal of time, whether she was sitting or standing, in pinching or patting or poking or smoothing these various furbelows. Perhaps, to do her justice, she felt ill at ease. She took cues readily from my grandfather, even stopping her flow of talk when he began to cross and recross his long, gaitered legs and to fidget about in his chair at teatime. She always said, "Thank you, my dear child," whenever we passed the crumpets or seedcake or brought her a fresh cup of tea, a phrase which grew annoying from sheer repetition. She had the reputation, often verbally re-established by my grandfather, of being the perfect wife for an archdeacon, since she was never perturbed by any number of vicars or curates dropping in for counsel or conferences, or by accompanying her husband around his diocese on his tours of inspection to the most remote Yorkshire parishes. My mother rather unreasonably held it against her that she "dearly loved" to teach in the Church school, which she carefully never called Sunday or Sabbath school after the Wesleyan manner.

### 4

Perhaps the marriage of my father and mother *was* a singular union, for it surely represented a combination of diverse traits and dissimilar backgrounds. They had met in the early eighteen-eighties at Cambridge, where they were both under-graduates, my mother at Newnham College, that recent and deeply suspected institution for the higher education of women, my father at Clare. Their romance—for it remained a romance to the end of their days together with all its ups and downs—started at the home of one of the university dons, a rugged, untidy, gruff, and most learned Yorkshireman named Bentley, who because of his eminence had been appointed to a professorship, a rare distinction even at Cambridge. Professor Bentley was a linguist, particularly in Anglo-Saxon, an historian, an archaeologist, an antiquarian, and, quite on his own, an ornithologist and a botanist. He was as well the most charming and humane of men, admired and even adored by his undergraduates. Rumour had it that he had been married in a rather soiled and tattered mackintosh in an hour snatched from his college supervisions—or seminars, in the American term; and that once the ceremony had been performed he had hastily returned to his teaching together with his bride, who was, in fact, one of his students.

During their last year at Cambridge John Tillyard, my father, and Hilda Oldroyd, my mother, who had been named for the famous and learned Abbess of Whitby in the seventh century, spent much time with the Bentleys both in the pursuit of scholarship and on various expeditions about East Anglia in search of common interests. They boated down the river toward Ely; bicycled across Newmarket Heath to Bury St. Edmunds; explored the old town of Norwich; or walked along the chalky crest of that ancient Saxon earthwork known as the Devil's Dyke, which tumbles for seven miles from the village of Reach to that of Wood Ditton, between what was a thousand years ago the fenland and the forest. My father planned all his life to write a book about the Devil's Dyke. The book was not completed, for he had a way of never actually completing his plans and projects. His hours were his sole accomplishments. He was a genius at filling and finishing each and all of those.

The Bentleys without doubt furthered my parents' love for each other if, indeed, any furtherance was necessary. They knew a great deal about the companionship of minds, for they richly experienced it with their own. I doubt if they ever worried or even thought much about the sectarian vexations and problems which might presumably arise even from the marriage of two young people so clearly congenial and so well-matched in intelligence and common interests. They themselves were deeply religious or, perhaps more accurately, spiritual by nature; yet they gave allegiance to neither Church nor chapel. They had, to be sure, both sprung from northern Wesleyan stock, which background was in itself somewhat an anomaly in Cambridge University circles around the turn of the century; but, as all know, to be "chapel" in the thriving and wealthy industrial towns of the North or of the Midlands was, and still is, quite a different matter from professing the same adherence among the small villages of the largely agricultural Eastern and Southern counties.

Just why my father clung to his Wesleyan tradition has always remained something of a mystery to me. He loved tradition, it is true, and yet he was singularly free from its hold in any number of other ways. The idea that he had disappointed his parents in becoming a university scholar rather than assuring them of the continuance of the Suffolk farm, which idea without doubt had its influence upon him, was surely not strengthened by any tangible pressure from them. When Ansie and I were nearly seven years old and Mary nine and we were all settled in our Cambridgeshire village of Saintsbury, they sold the farm and moved to a modest house on the outskirts of Cambridge where they had a few bits of land to plant and care for, a small, slow stream to enjoy, and plenty of space for gardens. They seemed very happy there. They could go to the Market Place on market days, wander along the Backs to watch the carpets of purple and yellow crocuses give place to thousands of daffodils, roam among the quadrangles of one college after another, and swell with pride over the advantages which their thrift and ambition had made possible for my father. Not for a moment did they clearly fathom the intricacies of a "double First in the Tripos" which he had achieved; but for all their lack of comprehension they were the most satisfied pair of elderly parents in all Cambridge when each June they scanned the long white degree lists on the Senate House, in a dozen other conspicuous places about the town, and even in the London *Times*, and realized how few graduates of any college had reached their son's distinction a dozen years earlier. No, one must look elsewhere than to his parents for the cause of my father's stubborn decision to spend his days as a Wesleyan parson. It is not inconceivable, indeed, that they might have welcomed an Anglican career for him in spite of the fact that they felt awkward and out of place with the Oldroyds whenever it seemed inevitable that our combined grandparents should meet together.

Nor were the Bentleys in the least influential in my father's making this singular choice of a way of life. They were, in fact, quite the opposite. Their fervent and repeatedly expressed desire had been that, after more time spent in study and research, he should teach undergraduates, lecture, perhaps even at Cambridge, or Oxford (as a second choice, of course, but a tolerable one), write learned books, live, in short, a scholar's life. There were not many young men, they knew, with my father's selfless devotion to learning; and, if they had been consulted in time, which they probably were not, they would certainly have deplored the waste of such gifts in a

Wesleyan country parish.

Had my father been of a different nature, more perhaps like my mother, he might well have stuck to his odd resolve simply to flout the archdeacon, who, once he had been apprised of the incredible, even disastrous determination of his daughter to marry a Wesleyan parson, straightway did his utmost to put a stop to such madness. But revenge of any sort was totally omitted from my father's make-up, though I have never felt entirely sure that it did not play its part in my mother's decision. She loved my father beyond a doubt, his gentleness, his quick sympathy, his enthusiasms, his simplicity, his obvious admiration for her; yet I suspect that these qualities steadily increased in value as she continued to receive vituperative and warning letters from Yorkshire. Her naturally fiery nature was only refuelled by any attack against my father; and like all girls in love she was not inclined, or perhaps even able, to look far into the future or seriously to consider consequences.

## 5

As I grew older and learned more about those tenets upon which various religious persuasions are based, I often wondered what part theology or practices arising from it had played in my father's mind. I am inclined to think almost no part at all. Except for long, heated, and rather humorous disputations with the vicar whenever he came for tea and perhaps also when they went fishing or pedalled off together to study some Saxon remains in a country church, I don't think he gave much thought to pure theology or cared a whit about it. He was, instead, consumed by other matters of far greater importance to him than the Thirty-nine Articles, the doctrine of the Trinity, or the Communion of Saints. As to those practices encouraged or expected by stouter Wesleyans than he, he disliked and even deplored them; and he often insisted that in this point of view he was but echoing the great John Wesley himself, who had had his fears lest the Society founded by him might lose its dignity in unrestrained emotionalism. My father suspected revivals, abhorred "love feasts," considered most extemporary prayers awkward and embarrassing, as well as an insult to the language, and, whenever he was able, avoided the use in his congregation of lilting, sentimental hymns such as "Bringing in the Sheaves." He was as negligent as he dared to be, small villages being what they were, about family prayers, partly because they were discomfiting to us all, largely because it took my mother fully an hour to recover from her irritation over them.

In the place of abstruse theological speculations and noisy indulgences in chapel practices in general, my father possessed a consuming and invincible love of God, Who, he believed, knew "no variableness neither shadow of turning" and Who had formed us all to fear Him, to worship Him, and, in so far as each was able, to work out His purposes for all men upon the earth. He was not interested in trying to prove God's existence, which, he said, was impossible and, therefore, a foolish waste of time, or in defining Him, which had been attempted not very successfully through the centuries only by human beings like ourselves. He simply staked all that he had, and was, on a tremendous gamble that God lived and moved among us and that His active concern for His world and for all His creatures was constant, invulnerable, and unfailing. When the exciting question had arisen as to a name for my brother Ansie, my father insisted on calling him Anselm after a saint, who, he claimed, had done more for his peace of mind and ways of thought and action than had any other philosopher or teacher throughout all recorded time. This St. Anselm had contended and taught that a simple belief in God would in the end bring some understanding of Him; indeed, that no understanding whatever was possible without an initial and perhaps even reckless casting aside of all one's unanswerable questions, doubts, and fears.

My father was aware to a high degree of what he always termed the "miraculous" on the earth and in the skies. He took unquenchable pleasure in watching an amber ladybird crawling up a stalk of grass, swans taking suddenly into the air, planets and constellations blazing in the heavens, ants busily at work bearing burdens twice their size. These were all wonders which he gratefully accepted together with their healing mystery.

His love of God extended quite naturally to a love and concern for all men, and especially for the humble and undistinguished among them. Candidly, to use my sister Mary's early mania for prefatory adverbs, I think that this love for just ordinary people, this faith in their limitless possibilities, was, more than any other reason, at the root of his going to Manchester, after he had left his double First at Cambridge, and studying in a seminary there for his ordination in the Wesleyan ministry. He had been deeply distressed as a schoolboy by stories of the lamentable and hideous conditions of the poor in London and in the great industrial centres, concerned as a young man with trade unionism, the warfare for the extension of the franchise, and with those social and economic reforms in which Methodism in general had been sincerely and even rampantly engaged in the second half of the nineteenth century.

He had a genius for getting inside the minds of quite simple men and women, nor did he ever assume, as did many pastors of many diverse flocks, that they had no minds to enter. He loved watching thatchers carefully spreading their yellow straw upon brown, huddled ricks, or hedgers in their canvas aprons by their solitary bonfires of the blackthorn, or holly, or beech which they had cleared away for burning. He could speak the language of shepherds and smiths, field labourers, and girls who worked at digging swedes or at milking cows in meadow bartons. Nor was he ever above using his country knowledge to help them at their tasks.

He had, of course, most trying qualities. Those few persons who at least *seem* to know where they are going are often exasperating to the many who are not at all sure concerning their journey through life. My mother used to say that, if only he would rely less on God and consider carefully his modest salary, we should all be better off in every way than we ever were. When, in fact, I recall after all this time the many things so alien and hateful to her that my mother had to put up with for the sake of my father for thirty years, both at home and in America, I still marvel at her powers of endurance, resilience, and restoration. There were, to name but a few, his annoying slowness; Bury St. Edmunds; those sometimes inescapable extemporary prayers and revivals; the problem of Ansie's school; the Plimsolls on the steamship; Mrs. Gowan and our other strange guests; and always without end the mediocre, wearisome round of life in ugly, inconvenient parsonages and in uglier chapels. My mother was lively and beautiful, whimsical and imaginative. She was made to grace other circles than those of unimportant and shabby village parishes.

She was flint to my father's sober steel, and myriads of sparks resulted when these were struck together by her anxiety or impatience. Sometimes at night in Saintsbury I awoke in my room across the narrow hall from theirs, conscious of her expostulations and even anger and of his quiet rejoinders. They made it a custom after one of these collisions of minds to creep down the stairs to the kitchen for a healing cup of tea. I am sure that the security and happiness of my English childhood owe much to Mazawattee or to the more expensive brew of

Thomas Lipton, drunk happily in the dead of night by a hastily replenished fire.

At all events I can recall few family breakfasts when quickening devotion to my father did not light up my mother's face.

6

In this mid-twentieth century it is difficult if not impossible to realize the almost impassable gulf which existed at its beginning between Church and chapel, or the condescension and disrepute which were the lot of chapelgoers, especially in distinctly rural communities in the East or South of England. These absurd humiliations had little or nothing to do with one's social and economic position as such. Dozens of labouring families in our rather remote Cambridgeshire village had been Church for untold generations. Their grubby, ill-nourished little boys sang in the choir of St. Peter's in blue cassocks and starched white Elizabethan ruffs; their weatherworn husbands and fathers, trudging to Matins at eleven o'clock in their best suits and celluloid collars, might well be sidesmen who took up the contribution, showed rare strangers to seats, and, as well, sat on the Church Council. Far more village families, indeed, were Church rather than chapel. So also were unattached household servants like our cook, Katie Lubbock.

Katie was Church to her backbone; and many of her fellow parishioners wondered why she worked for us. Her explanation was twofold. In the first place, she liked us far better than she liked "most Church folk"; and, in the second place, my mother had not the slightest objection to her laundering the vicar's surplices, for which she felt herself wellpaid at sixpence each. The sight of them billowing in the wind on the clothes ropes in our back garden lent us all a bit of status perhaps; and the pennies helped to swell her slender wages, not to mention the satisfaction she felt when she saw on Sundays her starched and spotless handiwork on the vicar in the chancel.

In my English childhood you belonged to chapel usually and often only because some forebear of yours, perhaps a full century ago, had come in contact in some field or on some hillside with an evangelist who had touched his heart or made him feel sure, as Wesleyan evangelists were skilled in doing, that the Church with all her tradition and "Establishment" was not ministering to his needs as a human soul, humble perhaps in terms of this world's goods, yet dear and valuable to God Himself. Regardless of God, however, you would have been dearer and more valuable to your neighbours in villages such as ours had you been safely born, baptized, and in due course of time confirmed, married, and finally buried under the protection of the Church of England, in all that decency and quiet dignity which she bestowed upon her own. There was rarely a shred of unkindness shown you either from neighbours or from the Church; there was merely a somewhat intangible, though inescapable attitude compounded of perplexity, self-satisfaction, surprise, and at least a tinge of patronage. Surprise was perhaps the strongest element, for it seemed more than a little strange that you should be willing to bear the responsibility of your own salvation when the Church through her sacraments had been designed to arrange such matters for you, to see that all was managed in security, order, and complete decorum.

All chapelgoers were not necessarily Wesleyans. Occasionally a Baptist chapel intruded itself even upon Southern communities; and in the North there were as well Independents, or Congregationalists, and some rare Presbyterians leaking in from Scotland. In general, however, the few chapels in our region were Wesleyan, nor were we often called Methodists unless we belonged to the Primitive variety, adherence to which fifty years ago required even more social fortitude than plain Wesleyans possessed.

Few of the so-called neighbourhood or country "gentry," a word widely used in England half a century ago and by no means obsolete today, were chapelgoers. In our Cambridgeshire parish where I lived between the ages of six and ten years, there was literally not one. My father's congregation of some forty or fifty souls was formed entirely of labourers and small tradesmen, the butcher, the saddler, the cobbler, the ironmonger, a few tenant farmers, and dayworkers of several sorts. Most of these good and worthy people lived among rows of old cottages, inhabited also by their strictly Church neighbours, cottages which were set behind hedges and tiny, well-kept gardens along the single village street or along lanes leading from it. With their timbered and plastered sides and their thatched roofs such houses were undoubtedly picturesque; yet no one could be quite sure, my mother said, that beneath the thatch and around the timbers they were not the homes also of numberless other inhabitants of an active and decidedly voracious character.

7

No feat or even flight of the imagination could discover any attraction for our Wesleyan chapel in Saintsbury, Cambridgeshire. It stood just outside the village proper on the long road leading toward the open country. It was a small, square building framed of brick with stone uprights at its four sides, double oaken doors stained a dingy yellow, and a rather squat steeple of the same red brick. It was surrounded by a meagre bit of ground and enclosed by a privet hedge. My mother tried to brighten up its ground by planting a few hardy garden shrubs, hydrangea, laurustinus, lad's-love, and forsythia, but without marked success. It did not seem to welcome any such adorn-ment.

Inside it consisted mainly of one sizable room with perhaps twelve pews of the same golden oak on either side of its one aisle, a communion rail, and a pulpit enclosure raised two or three steps above the level of the floor. Within this enclosure, behind the pulpit itself and beneath a rather depressing window of stained glass depicting Christ blessing little children, stood two straight-backed chairs. My father sat in one of these for a few minutes before the service began; the other was reserved for any rare visiting minister or for a returned Wesleyan mis-sionary, usually, it seemed, from darkest Africa. There were no seats for any choir, which was just as well since we dealt entirely in congregational singing; but just below the pulpit platform and in front of the pews on the left side there was a small organ, or harmonium, which, considering its age, size, and general condition, was quite admirably played by Mrs. Rowley, the stout, rosy wife of the ironmonger.

To the right, off the pulpit enclosure, was a tiny room where my father donned his black gown with white neck-bands which he always wore after the manner of John Wesley. The same space on the left was used in the afternoon for the infants' Sunday school. We children, together with the few others relatively of our age, held our Sunday school in the basement, a cold, cheerless room with uncomfortable chairs, dingy small windows, and a brass petroleum lamp hanging from the centre of the low ceiling. On dark autumn or winter days when there was heavy cloud or fog this lamp was lighted; but it had a sinister way of increasing rather than brightening the gloom of the room.

On Sunday mornings when the bell ringers of St. Peter the Apostle began their work upon the ropes, and the peals, clangs, and jangles sounded across the low, flat fields to mingle with those of other churches in villages not far distant, and most of our neighbours were passing through the old lych gate and over the churchyard grass toward the ancient porch, we left the parsonage, which was but a stone's throw away, and went to chapel. My father always left home a quarter of an hour ahead of us in order to prepare his mind and to get into his gown and bands. The four of us sat in the front pew on the right, since this was always set aside for the pastor's family.

I cannot say that I recall vividly any of my father's sermons during my English childhood, although I am sure he was an excellent preacher. We were taught never to take our eyes from his face, partly as an example to others, my mother said, but largely to encourage him. This polite attention was not difficult as he was always fervent and simple in whatever he said, and, unlike those of most Wesleyan parsons of that time, his sermons were never long. He looked dignified and handsome, too, in his black gown. He always placed his rather long, thin hands over the edge of the big chapel Bible on the top of the pulpit and never moved them as he spoke. Several of his flock would, I daresay, have preferred more action, even drama, in his sermons; but once they grew used to his quiet manner they seemed satisfied. Several, too, if not all, were puzzled by his prayer which always preceded the sermon, for it was far less extemporaneous, colloquial, and familiar than most chapel petitions. It was often interspersed by phrases and sentences from the Book of Common Prayer, which he admired and deeply reverenced: . . . *O God, Who art the author of peace and lover of concord, in knowledge of Whom standeth our eternal life, Whose service is perfect freedom . . . Therefore with Angels and Archangels and with all the company of heaven, we laud and magnify Thy glorious Name . . .* Whenever one of these wise borrowings occurred, I always stole a glance at my mother and saw beneath her bowed head the smile which curved her lips.

What I do most clearly and closely remember about our Sunday mornings in chapel is my brother Ansie's singing, especially when, like me, he was around nine or ten years old. In contrast to many if not most small boys, Ansie was rarely awkward or self-conscious. He was, instead, frank and friendly, sure and easy in his ways, and not often boisterous or noisy. He had a high, clear soprano voice, and he dearly loved to sing. He always stood at the end of our front pew, next the single aisle, his broad white collar glistening with starch above his short black Sunday jacket, his thick, unruly yellow hair plastered down with soapy water, his blue eyes, so like my mother's, shining with pleasure. Only infrequently, and always at the request of members of the congregation, my father allowed him to sing by himself the first verse of a hymn, "Jerusalem the Golden," perhaps, or "Ten Thousand Times Ten Thousand," for, as tenaciously as he could, my father stuck to the old, tried hymns. Once Ansie had received Mrs. Rowley's amiable nod, his voice rose and filled that bare, ugly room like motes and beams of sunlight. And it still continued to rise above the others, the cobbler's sepulchral bass, the uncertain tenors, Mrs. Rowley's robust alto, the shrill tones of the children, even after the congregation had joined in the following verses.

## 8

Our parsonage, although it was plain enough externally, became really a pleasant house. Like the chapel it was built of red brick and was a fairly large, boxlike structure with neither form nor age to improve it. When my mother first saw it in the autumn of 1897, she flopped down on a hideous dull-green sofa in its small drawing-room and burst into tears. She could safely give way to that luxury at the moment, for my father had gone out at once to become acquainted with his human charges and to ascertain if what looked like a lambing meadow beyond our garden was really dedicated to that purpose; and we three children, unable to cope with her distress and feeling not too far from tears ourselves, were only too glad to take ourselves out of her sight as she rather angrily ordered us to do.

Her outburst of despair, if intense, was brief. A visit of inspection from her father, the archdeacon, was imminent, she feared; and she did not want ill-concealed pity from him. Within a matter of days she had performed miracles upon the permanent Wesleyan furnishings and with the help of a few possessions of our own had completely transformed our new home. Although my father was quite manually ineffective when it came to the renovation of a house, he was only too pleased with the fresh paint and wallpaper which she put on herself with some help from willing workers in the neighbourhood. Nor did he utter more than a weak protest when a large and bad print of the Royal Family, which had dominated the drawing-room, was removed to the outlying coal shed together with a larger and worse one of Susannah Wesley patiently teaching too many of her nineteen children to read from the Book of Genesis.

"There is no woman I admire more than Susannah Wesley," my mother said, "but I can't have her reproving me every day at teatime."

Our drawing-room was an entirely different place after my mother's feverish activities were spent in its behalf. So was my father's study behind it with its books and open grate for our evening fires. The study and the dining-room opposite looked out upon the garden, which when the spring came, my father said, and he had set to work with plants and seeds, would blossom like those solitary waste places of the prophet Isaiah.

My mother deplored, on the principle of household privacy, a kitchen which faced the street, but Katie loved it since with no extra steps she could keep closely in touch with our small outside world. The five cold bedrooms upstairs were more than sufficient for our needs; indeed, my mother with her Yorkshire parents in mind or the descent upon us of an occasional missionary regretted the fifth, which was set aside as a guest-room and upon which, from pride rather than desire, she expended her many talents.

The Wesleyan housewives in Saintsbury, once they became accustomed to my mother's energy and to her strange notions about homes, which at first they said were "proper upsetting" and "fair twizzled up their insides," were vastly proud of the parsonage in its new freshness. Curiosity finally conquering shyness and even dread, they came to tea in safe twos and threes and were made to feel so much at ease that they recovered from their "twizzling" and by November were running in and out with the last of their garden produce and the best of their jellies and conserves.

"Her might as well be a vicar's wife," they confided to their Church neighbours. "Us chapel folks ain't used to a woman like she."

The thought of the Royal Family in the coal shed weighed a bit heavily on my father's mind, although he made no plea for the restoration of Susannah Wesley. One night just before Christmas, while Katie and my mother were making preparation for the waits with their carols (perhaps the single village custom in which Church and chapel happily joined), he went outside with his lantern and rescued them from their ignominious banishment. They did not, to be sure, return to the drawing-room wall, but he found a place where they could be clean and dry, as well as quite out of sight, behind his study desk.

## 9

It was at school that we children were most conscious of our chapel status; and this consciousness was a prolonged one since except for Christmas and Easter holidays school consumed eleven months of any given year. For us to go elsewhere, that is, to preparatory school as always the sons and often the daughters of the gentry did, would be most unwise, my father said, for children of the chapel parson, even if we could have afforded it. The free elementary school, fostered as many such schools were at that time by the Church, was our inescapable lot.

The school, which stood almost in the centre of the village and just beyond the village green, was a plain brick one-storey building of two rooms, one for the so-called infants, the other for children between eight and eleven or twelve years old. One might, of course, stay on until fourteen, the English age then for leaving school, unless one had been bright enough or possessed of sufficient means at eleven or twelve to move on to a secondary or grammar school. Near it, surrounded by a scrap of lawn and a hedge, was the schoolhouse where lived the two women who taught us, sternly perhaps but thoroughly, and doubtless as well the unlikely human material afforded them made possible.

School began promptly at nine o'clock for us all except on Thursdays when chapelgoing children convened an hour later. On Thursday mornings the vicar appeared for his weekly drilling of his flock in the Creeds and the Collects of the Prayer Book, in Church hymns, and in stories and precepts from the Scriptures. Chapel children were not in any sense banned from these sessions; in fact, I am sure the vicar would have been glad of our presence. It merely seemed the unalterable custom that we were to arrive at ten on Thursdays.

Just before that hour we straggled along the village street, ten or twelve of us in number, and waited in the playground until the vicar, sent on his way by a lusty "Thank you, sir, good morning, sir" from his spiritual charges, emerged from the entrance. He always greeted us in a kindly, benevolent fashion, and we were quick to remember our manners toward him as the one really important personage in our little world. Then we took our places in the schoolroom, boys on one side, girls on the other, and began the long day. Vicar's Day always resulted in confusion, for an hour had already gone from our usual educational routine. On ordinary days we merely mumbled the Lord's Prayer, which was generously conceded to be the property of us all, regardless of Church or chapel, and sang a hymn.

Sums always came first. On Thursdays these were often accompanied by tragedy since, once solved in record time, they had to be copied in ink, and too many blots or smears might well result in the painful application of the mistress's cane across blundering palms and fingers. English history required the memorizing with their exact dates of all our sovereigns from William the Conqueror to our new king, Edward VII, who, though anything but a shadowy figure as he looked down at us from the wall above the teacher's desk in the spring of 1901, still seemed unreal after our long familiarity with Queen Victoria. Geography rarely strayed from the British Isles and our far-flung colonial possessions, our Empire on which the sun never set. I do not recall many references to the United States of America in either history or geography. We did learn that its eastern shores known as *New* England had been settled by some undeniably brave men and women called Pilgrims and Puritans, who had left their homeland because of mistaken ideas of their right to worship God as they chose; and we did know that we had unfortunately lost America from our Empire through a rather stupid and equally mistaken Revolution. But to most of our school America meant Red Indians, who were seemingly still occupied in a unique and gory exercise known as *scalping*. When my sister Mary denied this hotly and bolstered her denial by unwelcome information concerning the now-peaceable Indians, she did not add to her popularity. What we three children knew about the "States" we learned not in school but at home from my father's profound interest in them.

Penmanship seemingly governed most of our afternoons at school. If we wrote laborious essays, which we sometimes did, they were judged more from their outside appearance than from their content. Inkpots and long quill pens were our smudgy, postprandial lot. We copied numberless aphorisms, warnings, and Scriptural or Prayer Book passages set for us in flowing script within green, pasteboard-covered exercise books; and since our school was under the aegis of the Church, many of these quite naturally savoured of that firm Establishment: *The Glorious Company of the Apostles praise Thee . . . My soul doth magnify the Lord . . . The Holy Church throughout all the world doth acknowledge Thee.*

### 10

I do not think that my brother Ansie and I minded this not always tacit suggestion at school that we were outsiders so much as did my sister Mary. She was of a rebellious nature like my mother; and since she possessed a quite unusual facility in the use of language, an incendiary sense of justice, and an eager readiness for conflict, she was well equipped to maintain her own rights as well as the more halfhearted ones of the chapel children as a group. These assets were in no way diminished by the fact that she was by all odds the brightest pupil in our school.

On a morning in May in the year 1901 our ecclesiastical differences caused a memorable explosion on the school playground. This unexpected burst of fury between Church and chapel flamed toward the close of a school year which, since January, had been tense with unusual excitement. Late in that long, cold month we had solemnly elevated King Edward VII to his mother's place of honour and sadly removed the old Queen to a side wall where she looked not only out of place but aggrieved, as, one recalls, she had a way of doing, though over far more momentous matters than the religious atmosphere of our elementary school.

In any other country under the sun except England an all-enveloping and enduring sorrow over the death of any sovereign would be almost inconceivable; but to her subjects, from those on ducal estates to those in the meanest rural cottage, Queen Victoria, whose reign of sixty-four years had encompassed the life span of countless thousands, had been the symbol, even the corporeal reality of human perfection, both in her family relations and in the high concerns of State. Her virtues as a devoted wife, mother, grandmother, and great-grandmother were dwelt upon tearfully at every tea table and by every hearthstone; her stable, unquestioning religious faith was echoed and re-echoed; her picture in a hundred newspapers and magazines was studied reverently and tacked upon numberless walls; each sombre detail of her death and burial was rehearsed daily for months, together with all available bits of information about her life at Balmoral, Windsor, Osborne, and Buckingham Palace, from her pony cart to the ribbons on her bonnets, from her unmended heart over the death of her beloved consort to her dancing a polka with her great-grandson, Prince Edward. From John of Groats to the Channel a veritable orgy of grief had subdued, and vastly entertained, an entire population; and our school was a tiny but integral part in this general upset. Every child, including the smallest infants, wore mourning during the long period prescribed for that seemly observance, armbands, sashes, or neckties if black frocks and jackets were not possible. Our teachers likewise dutifully and more completely assumed that melancholy garb. In short, after four months of a cataclysmic change in history and of lesser, but more intimate changes in our emotional climate both at home and at school, we were ripe and ready for any other excitement that might present itself.

Then there was the influence of the spring upon us, which after weeks of its usual hesitancy had at last reached its fulness. The month of May is a perilous, even shattering season for the human heart in England, for nowhere else is winter quite so sullen or borne with such stoicism. Mists and heavy fog, endless days of driving rain, early darkness and late dawns, bitter winds from northern seas, sodden, dripping hedges, an all-pervading chill that reaches to the marrow of one's aching bones—these all take their toll of endurance and fortitude. In school at long last the languid and unsuccessful fires in our two small stoves were quenched for the remainder of the term. Chilblains were gone for six full months; our itching, purple elbows no longer demanded savage rubbing. The three free days at Whitsuntide, for once benign and beautiful, were over; and summer holidays were but eight weeks away. The cuckoo, already on the eve of his departure, sounded his persistent, spendthrift call from copse and spinney; may trees were masses of red or white blossom; the golden chains of the laburnum hung above the hedges or glowed in cottage gardens; the Whitsun candles of the chestnuts stood fragrant and upright upon the branches of the great trees before the parish church; buttercups filled the meadows, and kingcups, the marshes; the blackbird whistled from the tree-tops, the rooks flapped and squawked above their high, untidy nests in the elms, and the missel thrush trilled and warbled for hours on end among the garden shrubs. With all this madness without, we squirmed on our hard benches within, hated our teachers, thought only of gathering cowslips, feeding swans, fishing in every stream, and playing cricket in the long, bright evenings.

I do not, of course, lay the responsibility for my sister Mary's disgraceful conduct in the school playground either upon the death of the old Queen or upon the spring; yet each had indirectly done its part in engendering the restlessness which goaded her and which quivered within us all. The direct cause of outbreak was St. Peter the Apostle, whose day fell on June 29. Since he was the patron saint of our parish church, this date was always celebrated by an early-morning service and later in the day by a village fête or festival, to which chapel folks were always welcome but in which they usually took no active part since all arrangements for it were made by the vicar, his sidesmen, his teachers, his council, his church-wardens, and his choir.

Our headmistress and the teacher of our room, Miss Caxton, doubtless beside herself from the general feverishness with which she had to cope and longing for a change from the usual turgid round of sums and history, announced on this fatal morning a surprise for the vicar as well as a contest for us. We were all to copy in our best script the Collect for St. Peter's Day, or even to print it in fine block letters if we felt sure enough of our talents to do so. She promised that she would place the best copy in a frame so that the vicar might actually read from it as he stood at the altar in the early morning. In further desperation she overwhelmed us all by offering a prize of half a crown for the winning production.

We were not at all averse to escaping our usual dull routine; and the very notion of half a crown, which meant affluence beyond description, fired us to unprecedented zeal. For two hours we dipped and scratched as we strove to fit the collect upon the single sheet of lined paper. Meanwhile Miss Caxton, giving herself up gladly to the spring, gazed from our murky windows in more peace than she had known for months.

At promptly eleven o'clock, the time for playground games and exercise, our creations were demanded and brought to Miss Caxton's desk, from which they were propped against the blackboard for the judgement of us all. In this judgement Miss Hawes, the infants' teacher, joined, bringing along her twelve infants, who, although they were allowed no power of choice, gazed with awe upon the results of our corporate genius. These ranged widely both in quality of work and in cleanliness. Some bore smudges, blots, and misspellings; others were incomplete; several scribes had failed in apportioning the necessary words to the space allotted them. My own copy was clearly a mess since I had too lavishly filled my pen for both "God" and "Bishops" with awful results; and Ansie's was little better, for he at the very start had put an extra *l* in "Almighty," which, he told me later, had so unnerved him that all the following words trembled on his paper.

Actually no formal judgement was necessary. Common consent prevailed. Mary's copy stood so above all the others that with one reluctant accord we awarded her signal honour and half a crown. She had printed the Collect in really beautiful block letters and had so carefully arranged her spacing that the "Amen" was quite alone by itself on the next to the lowest line. There was not the faintest suggestion of a smear, let alone a blot or a smudge. Her clear black lettering on the clean white paper was a triumph both of extreme care and, in our inexperienced eyes, of distinguished talent.

Her cheeks grew very red as she walked forward amid applause to receive her prize. It was a trifle disappointing, to be sure, to be given a shilling and three rather tarnished sixpences instead of the big, round piece of silver itself. Miss Caxton had obviously conceived the contest on the spur of a disheartening moment and had left home unprepared in proper coinage. Still, though thus dismantled, it *was* half a crown.

When the winner had returned to her bench, which she shared with Susan Pratt, the daughter of the proprietor of our one public house, The Green Man, and Miss Hawes had departed with the impressed infants to her side of the partition which separated our two rooms, yet another triumph followed for my sister.

"I think it might be helpful for us all," Miss Caxton said, standing at her desk in her worn grey dress with her pale-grey eyes blinking behind her gold-rimmed spectacles, "if Mary would tell us just how she went about her work to produce so splendid a result."

Mary rose to her feet amid wiggling and scuffling, for we were eager to get out into the playground. With all her distinction and the four coins in the pocket of her pinafore, she was modest in her explanation.

"I counted the words first," she said, "so that I'd know how many to put on each line. The Collect has sixty-three words, and there were twelve lines on the paper. So I just reckoned as well as I could with the short words and the long ones. I thought it would be nice if I could save one line just for the 'Amen' by itself."

"Admirable," Miss Caxton said. "I'm sure we can all profit from Mary's care before she even began to copy. I know the vicar will be delighted; and you can all see the Collect in its nice frame on the altar on St. Peter's Day."

Her final statement was, of course, unfortunate, but it might well have passed unnoticed had it not been for Susan Pratt.

Susan's resentment of Mary's success was deepened both by daily proximity with a seatmate brighter than she and by the recognition that her own copy was indescribably bad, and unfinished as well. Her resentment, of course, might have been fed by the Collect itself, which, as all familiar with the Book of Common Prayer know, is somewhat more closely tied than others to the Church in view of the fact that St. Peter had been declared its foundation. It is doubtful, however, that Susan was intelligent enough to be bolstered by that knowledge. Now, to our collective amazement, she rose to her feet, without even raising her hand for permission, and faced Miss Caxton.

"Her won't see it," she said, "because her's chapel. I think myself, miss, the 'alf a crown belongs to a proper Churchgoer. Chapel folks knows nothin' about collects or saints."

The silence which followed Susan's remarks was ominous. We were all so stunned that we ceased our hitching about. It was incredible that a schoolmistress could be thus taken to task and especially by so soggy and stupid a child as Susan Pratt with her short, fat legs and her stringy hair.

Miss Caxton, taken aback though she was, rallied well.

"That will do, Susan," she said sharply. "The contest had nothing to do with Church or chapel. Please sit down. Now, children, playtime, and remember your manners in the future."

We all rushed for the door and the healing sunlight. Miss Caxton and Miss Hawes, instead of deciding which should remain with us for purposes of supervision as was their custom, started for the schoolhouse to make a calming cup of tea. They looked as though they were in huddled, outraged confidence as they moved toward the opening in the hedge.

Susan's round, rather flat face was crimson and her eyes were blazing. With her Whitsuntide Confirmation by the great Bishop of Ely himself in his mitre and his embroidered robes doubtless lending her courage, she dragged Mary, who was not in the least disposed to resist her, toward the corner of the playground farthest from the schoolhouse. I am sure that Mary had not imagined actual physical combat. Perhaps she had relied upon her superiority over Susan in the use of words. She recovered herself quickly, however, once she realized the nature of the onslaught, but not before Susan had dealt a telling blow upon her nose with her right fist which was instantly followed by some scratchings on her face. Then, injustice blazing within her and all seemliness cast to the winds, she sprung into delayed, but vigorous action. She was taller and more agile than Susan, and in a matter of minutes or even seconds she had mauled her antagonist's face in generous return and so expertly managed a tripping movement upon one of her legs that Susan was screaming and writhing on the gravel of the playground.

As onlookers the thirty or so of their schoolmates were quite useless. We were all too horrified to intervene or to range ourselves on one side or the other in terms of loyalty. Even the older boys did nothing but cry "Coo!" in amazement as they witnessed the brief conflict. Two infants ran bawling toward the schoolhouse. Our teachers lost no time in reaching the scene. Both combatants were summarily sent to their homes; Miss Hawes gathered the terrified infants together and administered pacifying sweets; Miss Caxton herded the others of us inside, where we were too subdued and cowed even to listen to her furious upbraidings.

I caught a glimpse of Mary as she moved homeward down the village street. I must confess to a measure of admiration for her because she carried her head and shoulders high, although the blood flowing from her nose required constant and rather undignified attention. Ansie was clearly crushed. He kept stealing desperate glances at me from his side of our room, and I could see that he was striving to keep back his tears.

The aftermath of this event has perhaps remained with me in more concrete detail than the event itself. In the early evening Mr. Pratt came down our road from The Green Man leading his daughter by the hand. He was a tall, large, rather shambling man with a kind, florid face. He had dressed up for the occasion in his black suit and a stiff white collar with a black bow tie set a bit crookedly upon the collar stud. Susan was in a clean pink frock, an ill-chosen colour since one of her eyes was completely sealed by a deep purple lump, the size and hue of an Easter egg. She looked bedraggled and miserable as they neared our hedge. My mother's heart warmed toward her, and she hastily asked Katie to get together some biscuits and some lemon squash.

My father went out to meet them while we children in acute embarrassment waited in the doorway for their entrance. Mr. Pratt was a solid though quite passionless Churchman; and my father and he were friends. He was too bald at the top of his head to have any hair to pull after the country manner; but he carefully touched his forehead, together with removing his hat.

"I'm 'ere to apologize, sir," he said while Susan sniffled in her handkerchief. "I don't holds with such goin's-on, nor do me wife. All this ol' nonsense ower Church nor chapel ain't nothin' to me. I serves both an' looks on both equal long's them pay their reckonin's. Susan, speak yer piece."

"I'm sorry," mumbled Susan from her dripping handkerchief.

"More, me girl," her father said sternly. "That ain't all you was to say."

"That's quite enough, Susan," my mother said, for she had now joined my father at the hedge. "Please don't make her say any more, Mr. Pratt. Mary is sorry, too. She behaved very badly, and we're all ashamed. It's quite too silly for us to remember. Let's go into the garden for a nice talk."

Mr. Pratt held his ground.

"Sorry, ma'am," he said, "but her has to say it all. Her mum's waitin' at 'ome to hear. Now, Susan, the finish."

"I didn't ought to do it," managed Susan. "'Twan't right, an' I knows it now. I've brung Mary my best marble. No one tol' me to do it, neither."

The visit in our garden was not too successful as a purely social affair. My father and Mr. Pratt sat by a table and drank some ale which my mother brought them. My father thought a pipe each would help out matters and fetched Mr. Pratt a fresh clay one from his study since Mr. Pratt had left his at home. They talked about the weather; the prospects for an early harvest; the incalculable loss to England of the old Queen; and how only a first-class thatcher could make crosspieces and braids on ricks and roofs. Mary and Susan sat a short distance away, gurgling lemon squash and munching biscuits, saying nothing. The marble was a large and beautiful one of transparent glass with a tiny white bear ingeniously placed inside. I felt sorry for Susan's sacrifice and thought that Mary had done rather well for herself, what with the marble and half a crown. The late sun still shone brightly, and the cries of some boys at cricket drifted back from a nearby field. Ansie and I soon escaped to the back garden where we aimlessly knocked some croquet balls about.

Sometime in the night I awoke in the bed which I shared with Mary to hear her sobbing into her pillow. Then I knew that she was wretched, beyond any cure from a marble, half a crown, or even victory in battle. I ached to comfort her, but I said nothing at all. For I suddenly understood in that clear perception sometimes granted to children that her sorrow was too deep for any shallow comfort of mine. It went

far back, quite out of sight for both her and me, to those days
in Suffolk when my father, following the furrows, had made
up his stubborn mind to stick closely to John Wesley, whatever the heavy cost.

## 11

If this unfortunate episode had occurred a year or even several months earlier, it might have exerted some slight influence
on our decision to go, or, as my father invariably said, to
*emigrate* to America; but, as it happened, our plans were already nearing completion. For several years there had been
strong motives for emigration at work in my father's mind,
among which were his new literary enthusiasms, his exalted
conception of American democracy, and the problem of Ansie's school. Of all these the last-named was the first in importance.

In England at the turn of the present century the question
of a school for a young boy was perhaps the weightiest question to be answered, at least among families which were determined, for social or educational reasons, upon a good school
for their sons; and even today it still engages and requires a
great deal of attention. Then it made little difference whether
or not a boy went on to the Universities; but his parents' choice
of a school for him was of primary and vital importance to
his future well-being and happiness, even to his success in life.
In our family it seemed, at least to Mary and me, as though
our parents talked about little else during our four years in
Saintsbury except about what should be done with Ansie. Mere
girls did not matter so much in those days. If they were ex-
traordinarily bright and promising, they might, given daring
and emancipated parents, dream of the still-new colleges for
women at Oxford and Cambridge after some years at boarding
school. If they were only average and pleasant girls, they re-

mained at home after seventeen or eighteen, contributing to the enjoyment and comfort of their families until marriage mercifully rescued them; or, if they did not marry, they might be sure that in course of time they could spend the rest of their lives in looking after one or two aged parents. The problem of Mary and me, therefore, although it may have existed in some dim recesses of my parents' minds, was as nothing in comparison with their concern over Ansie; and as we approached our tenth birthday, an age when many boys were already in preparatory schools with "public" ones but three or four years away, this problem increased to enormous size and weight. To it was firmly attached beyond any hope of severance the added problem of pounds, shillings, and pence.

The solution of a school for Ansie might have been easier could it have been confined to our own immediate family, but that seemed impossible. First of all the vicar (whose name was Mr. Read though some of the more "advanced" among the gentry in his flock called him "Father," to his discomfiture, since he was quite safely Low Church) intruded himself into our deliberations. Because of Ansie's voice and his ability to read even difficult music, Mr. Read wanted him to try for the King's College choir in nearby Cambridge. He felt quite sure, he said, that Ansie would win out there, and, if he did, he would be assured of a practically free education at the Choir School in return for his singing in King's College Chapel. The vicar further generously declared that it didn't make a whit of difference, or wouldn't with *his* backing, whether Ansie stemmed from Church or chapel. All that mattered was his voice.

Mary and I loved to think of Ansie in the King's Choir School. Once there he would wear grey knee socks with a band of purple, a purple jacket, and a black cap with a white fleur-de-lis on it. In the great, dim chapel he would sing in a

red cassock, his high clear soprano echoing among the vault-
ing, fan-shaped arches of the fifteenth-century ceiling.

" 'Music lingering on as loth to die,' " my father said, quot-
ing Wordsworth, and yet he was disinclined toward the Choir
School for Ansie. He thought, and perhaps with good reason,
that such a solution of Ansie's problem would be unwise, and
even far-reaching in its consequences, in view of his own position in Saintsbury. My mother tolerantly voiced no opinion
on this matter, although I am sure that, like Mary and me, she
had her exciting moments of seeing Ansie in his purple school
coat or in his red cassock.

She was, however, not at all silent when her father, the archdeacon, offered his advice as to Ansie's education. He made
several visits to our parsonage to discuss it and wrote numberless letters as well. It was his well-considered opinion, he said,
both orally and in writing, that Ansie should come to Yorkshire. There in ancient King Edwin's School at York, which
dated as far back as the days of Alcuin in the eighth century,
Ansie might be assured of a most superior training in the Clas-
sics and, he felt sure, be granted as well the inestimable priv-
ilege of singing in York Minster. He would be assured, too, of
a real home with his grandparents during his briefer holidays.
Finally, as my grandfather's most telling inducement, he offered to bear all expenses for Ansie at King Edwin's School.

My father was understandably hesitant in view of this overwhelming generosity in the matter of fees, for with Ansie's
future at stake he was willing to set aside his stalwart pride;
but my mother was as immovable as God Himself.

"He can go to any grammar school in England," she said
to my father one day upon the receipt of a rather peremptory
letter from the archdeacon. "Or he can stay right here with
Miss Caxton until he's fourteen. He shall never go to Yorkshire. Now that's that, and there's an end of it."

Even Katie had had her say about Yorkshire. One evening, following a visit from my grandfather Oldroyd, when she was giving Ansie and me some teacake in the kitchen after we had been playing late at jackstones in the garden, she put her arms akimbo and glared at us both as we perched on her clean table.

"I hope I knows me place," she said, "but I can't thole York for you, me boy. Namin' no names, of course, York would be a fair awful place for the likes o' you. You crawl right under your mum's wings, who knows what's what about that school up north, old though it may be."

In all this confusion and indecision Ansie felt, he said, like some cricket ball with half the stuffing out being batted unmercifully about; but after my mother's ultimatum he took heart, at least about York. He had dreamed one night that he was singing in the Minster when, catching sight of the archdeacon in one of the high chancel stalls, he lost all control of his voice which went off into so many forbidden flats and sharps that he was dragged from the choir by the hair of his head in the outraged hands of the choirmaster. When he told his dream at breakfast, my mother gave my father such a look that he left the table. We were finally convinced then that the awful spectre of King Edwin's School was "laid and staked," in Katie's words, for good and would never rise again.

My father meanwhile had been doing a good bit of reading about American schools, and we all, of course, shared his researches into them.

"It seems that there are these academies in the towns and even small villages all over the States," he said. "In some districts they favour the term 'high school.' 'Academy,' I take it, is used mostly in New England. They are free schools, too—anyone can go to them; in fact, most boys, and girls too, do go. They are prepared for college there, and they can live at home with their parents. Can you imagine it, my dear?"

"I can imagine anything after thirteen years with you," my mother said. But she said it merrily, and she kissed my father before she gathered up her trappings for an unwelcome jumble sale to help swell the meagre resources of the Chapel Women's Fund.

## 12

When my father was not viewing, or hunting for, antiquities, with or without the vicar, or talking over back fences with his parishioners, or spending winter hours in the lambing meadow with the shepherd, or pottering about our garden, or journeying to Bury St. Edmunds, he was reading. Like most men of his make-up he found in books men of larger stature than he found in life outside them, not to mention the thoughts he discovered there. He was inclined, like many avid readers, to be consumed with one passion for a season before the next claimed his mind and heart. During our years in Saintsbury, perhaps from the idea of America sitting uneasily in his consciousness or actively nagging at him, he eagerly surrendered himself to two writers, Alexis de Tocqueville and Henry David Thoreau.

When we pooled our combined resources to give him *Democracy in America* on his thirty-eighth birthday, he was so overcome with delight at the two fat volumes which he could now mark up as he liked that he paid scant attention to Katie's birthday cake, topped with thick almond paste and lurid with pink icing. She presented this marvel to him at tea, and we all had to atone for his wan enthusiasm over it. He clearly could not wait to sink into his old leather chair in his study and review what Tocqueville had said about America. Needless to say, we were subjected to this discerning Frenchman for months thereafter, for now that my father actually possessed him for his own he could be more sure of the accuracy of quotations from him.

"It's extraordinary," he said one bitter Saturday evening in November when the wind from the Russian steppes and the North Sea was battering the parsonage, "that a young man just turned thirty could grasp as he did the essence and spirit of another country. Ansie, you can surely spare a moment from your stamps. I want all of you to listen to this:

In the United States the more opulent citizens take great care not to stand aloof from the people; on the contrary, they constantly keep on easy terms with the lower classes: they listen to them, they speak to them every day. They know that the rich in democracies always stand in need of the poor, and that in democratic times you attach a poor man to you more by your manner than by benefits conferred.

If you should care to memorize that really noble passage, Ansie—verbatim, mind you—I think I could dig up a sixpence as a reward."

"What about me?" I asked, sure that I had as good a memory as Ansie's, if not a better one.

"And me?" Mary echoed.

My father was so eager to rivet Tocqueville firmly upon our minds that he hesitated only for a moment, nor was he slow to seize an opportunity of furthering our acquaintance with him even at considerable cost.

"Very good," he said. "My offer holds. But why not vary the quotations? Here's another fine one:

I have seen no country in which Christianity is clothed with fewer forms, figures, and observances than in the United States, or where it presents more distinct, simple, and general notions to the mind.

And there's another noble statement in the Introduction to the whole work, which shows the religious nature of the author. I mean to use it as the chief part of my sermon on Sunday week. Just listen to this:

I am ignorant of God's designs, but I shall not cease to believe in them because I cannot fathom them, and I had rather mistrust my own capacity than His justice.

Why don't you girls choose those to win your sixpences? And remember, it's verbatim again and an excellent recital, or no rewards."

"Is that man always noble?" asked my mother a bit sharply, since with the early cold and the awful wind she had had an especially trying day.

"By no means," my father said, "but he always seems wise, at least to me. As a matter of fact, there are certain things about American democracy which he mistrusts; but in general he thinks it has a great deal to teach our older civilizations, and I must say I agree with him."

"I can easily see that," my mother answered as she folded her sewing and went toward the kitchen to prepare our tea. "It's just that nobility in large doses gets on my nerves."

With all my father's admiration for Tocqueville, he did not love him as he unquestionably loved Thoreau. His old copy of *Walden* was so thumbed and tattered from being carried in his pocket on a hundred fishing trips and another hundred solitary walks that we all determined on a fresh one for Christmas or another birthday. He thought Thoreau a greater man than Abraham Lincoln; indeed, he held not only that America had never produced his equal but that few if any other countries had done so.

"I'd rather see Walden Pond," he was fond of saying, "than even Delphi or the Roman Forum."

My mother always looked alarmed at this statement since she had learned that my father's wishes were not so much mere desires as they were prophecies awaiting only fulfillment.

He loved introducing Thoreau and especially *Walden* to rare bookish friends and acquaintances who were either hazy about the sage of Concord or quite ignorant of his independence, courage, wisdom, and faith. The vicar was among the ignorant.

One afternoon when Mr. Read had come for tea, my father repeated to him one of his favourite sentences from *Walden*:

> I know of no more encouraging fact than the unquestionable ability of man to elevate his life by a conscious endeavour.

"My dear boy," asked the vicar, for to his seventy years my father still seemed young, "do you mean to tell me you really believe that?"

"I not only believe it, sir," said my father. "I stake my life on it, not to say my religion."

"Fancy that," the vicar said, looking a bit uncomfortable at the intrusion of religion. "Of course, it's pure Scripture, too, but I must say my long experience with human minds hasn't often borne it out. What else does this extraordinary fellow say?"

Then my father launched forth happily on Thoreau's retreat to Walden Pond to learn in solitude there what life had to teach him. The vicar listened courteously enough as my father quoted "lives of quiet desperation" which, according to Thoreau, most men live. He became hopelessly bewildered, however, when my father read to him the paragraph about the loss of "a hound, a bay horse, and a turtle dove."

"You wouldn't perhaps think that with all his wisdom, which I wouldn't for a moment disparage, this man was a bit of a zany?" he asked.

"The answer to that," my father said, "depends on just what you mean by a zany."

"Well, in other words, a crackbrain, at least in certain ways. That turtledove for instance. He doesn't even take the trouble to explain that dove."

"He had more sense, not to say more vision, than any man I've ever known," my father said, a trifle hotly, "in books or outside them."

In all his indignation and disappointment, however, he felt called upon to grant that Thoreau *had* been looked upon by many as at least uncommon in his way of life and thought; and the vicar, in his turn, felt relieved that he did not stand quite alone in his opinion.

"But isn't it just these uncommon men," my father persisted, "who have most to say to us? Isn't the Bible itself full of uncommon men?"

"That's undeniably true," the vicar admitted, "but, funnily enough perhaps, in everyday life they don't mix in so well."

"And yet," my father said, seeing that it was prudent to leave the realm of ideas for that of fact, "Thoreau was an extremely practical man as well. He gives here exactly what it cost him in American dollars and cents to live at Walden. He estimates that the total expense was twenty-seven and a half cents a week."

"What's that in English coinage?" asked the vicar.

"A shilling and twopence."

"Quite impossible," the vicar said, "unless, of course, his pond was full of fish and his woods of game."

"He came not to like hunting," my father said, determined to be honest about his idol, "but he did fish. He says Walden Pond was not very fertile in fish, and yet he names several kinds, especially pickerel, which, I take it, is an American variety of pike. There were perch, too, and bream, which are usually called shiners over there. In fact, he says a good bit about fishing in this book."

No information could have raised the status of Thoreau higher in the mind of the vicar; and my father, in view of this new approbation, took on added courage.

"He does say something about fishing in another sense. There's one place here where he says that the streams he mostly fished in were the streams of time and of the sky. What would you say to that, sir?"

The vicar's calm blue eyes became thoughtful then and even a little sad as though at threescore years and ten he feared that his own fishing had perhaps been too much circumscribed.

"I grant you that does take a bit of pondering on," he said. "I'll think on that."

When he started homeward he carried at his own request my father's sole copy of *Walden* under his long black cape. A fortnight later when my father went to the vicarage to reclaim his treasure he was unable to do so since the vicar had taken it on a solitary fishing expedition. We decided then not to wait for Christmas or a birthday, but to give him his present on just an ordinary day, which we straightway proceeded to do, to his amazement and even rapture.

### 13

My brother Ansie's discovery of the words on the Statue of Liberty coincided almost exactly with my father's final decision to emigrate to America. We had, of course, all known of the statue before, largely through my father's frequent references to it; but for some odd reason none of us had been made familiar with its inscription. Only a day after my father had left home in late February of 1901 to meet in London some mysterious American bishop of the Methodist Church, Ansie received a postcard from a visiting missionary who had heard him sing in our chapel and who was travelling about the

United States in the interests of darkest Africa. The Statue of Liberty itself was not on the card, which was given up entirely to the poem.

Ansie was so deeply impressed by its words (as had been kind, fumbling Mr. Grimes, our postman) that he had them all placed securely in his mind hours before my father's excited and exciting return that evening; in fact, he kept repeating them about the house and garden until all of us, including Katie, knew them almost as well as he did and were, I am afraid, growing somewhat weary of them merely from repetition:

> *Give me your tired, your poor,*
> *Your huddled masses yearning to breathe free,*
> *The wretched refuse of your teeming shore,*
> *Send these, the homeless, tempest-tossed, to me:*
> *I lift my lamp beside the golden door.*

Katie had her own reservations about the poem. After my mother had explained to her what *refuse* meant, that it was a noun and not a verb, she resented the idea that any English whatsoever were refuse. "Wretched refuse" only added to her resentment.

"Them Eye-talians, perhaps," she said, "an' maybe gypsies an' sechlike, but not proper English folk. An' us here breathes as free in this old land as in any new one. Us ain't homeless an' us ain't no poorer than the next. But say it to your father, Ansie. I can see it's his proper cuppa tea."

My mother agreed with Katie that the poem was precisely my father's cup of tea; and I think she rather dreaded the effect upon him of Ansie's impassioned recital of it once he had returned from London. I could see the words seething about in Ansie's mind as we all sat in my father's study on that fateful evening when the future loomed before us, not dark per-

haps, but unknown and breath-taking. My father explained
first of all what had happened in London. He spoke slowly
and quietly as though he were thinking over each word as he
uttered it.

This American bishop, who had heard of him from the seminary in Manchester and from other Wesleyan preachers in
England, had urged him to accept a parish in New England, in
a village known as Pepperell in the State of Maine. He might
be called or sent elsewhere after a few years, the bishop said,
since the Methodist Conferences in America encouraged moving about. Moreover, he might well rise far higher in a country where there was no Established Church, where, indeed,
the Nonconformist sects were in the ascendancy. The word
*chapel* was not used in America as it was in England, the bishop
said. There all religious congregations were known as churches
and looked upon quite as equals.

"Did you like this bishop?" my mother asked. She was darning an old red jersey of Ansie's, and the colour looked bright
and warm in the lap of her grey dress.

"Very much," my father said, with only a momentary hesitation which was not lost upon my mother.

Then it became quiet in the study, for we were all busy
with our thoughts. Curiosity, I could see, was deferring even
Ansie's desire to recite his poem. A piece of smoking coal fell
from the grate onto the hearthstone, and my father retrieved
it with the fire tongs. My mother unwound a long strand of
red wool from the ball in her lap, threaded her darning needle,
and began to weave the strand in and out of the frayed elbow
of the jersey. A sprig from the ivy on the wall of the house
began to beat against the window in the rising wind.

"What's this place Pepperell like?" asked my sister Mary
after a few minutes.

"A rather sizable village, I would say," my father said, "perhaps more like a town. This bishop said some two thousand people live there. It's in the eastern part of the State of Maine, not far from the Maritime Provinces. Those provinces belong to Canada and are under our own flag," he explained to us children.

"Maritime means the sea," Ansie said thoughtfully. "Would this village be on the seacoast, then?"

"Yes," my father said. "Men fish there as well as farm and, I gather, build boats in a small way. I grant the sea is a tempting idea. I've always thought I should like to live by the sea."

Mary and I were knitting scarves in bright bits of leftover wool for the summer sale of the Missionary Society; but now in our absorption in my father we stopped our work.

"Is there one of those academies in Pepperell?" I asked him.

"Yes. I found out about that. I told the bishop it was a matter of great moment—this question of a school for Ansie, and for my daughters too. He assured me that all the schools were good and that this academy made one ready for college without leaving home at all. I understand that this academy in Pepperell supplies an education for several other villages rather close at hand."

Then we were all silent again. Mary and I resumed our knitting. We could hear Katie moving about in the kitchen.

"I don't quite have a picture of this bishop," my mother said.

My father shifted his position in his big chair before he answered her.

"He's a big man," he said, "both tall and large, and very friendly in his ways. I would think he would be most able in managing matters, let us say, of a Conference. He's also very persuasive in his manner, I would say almost urgent." He paused. "He seems to think," he added, "that this is a call to me from God."

My mother, still busy with her weaving of the red wool,

did not speak for a few moments. Then she said:

"I'm always a bit skeptical myself about these calls from God."

None of us said anything. In the face of calls from God, the sea, an academy, fishing, and boatbuilding seemed matters too small to pursue.

My father drew his pipe from the pocket of his coat, but he did not fill or light it, only laid it on the table. Then he rose from his chair and stood by the fire. Although he was not an exceptionally tall man, he looked tall standing there. His thick dark hair, rather unruly like Ansie's and already greying at his temples, rose above his deeply lined forehead. His grey eyes were puzzled and even anxious as he looked upon us all. He had been holding some book as he talked about London and the bishop, and now he balanced it against his black waistcoat and placed his hands across it just as he always did in chapel.

"I think we should get this quite straight and clear in our minds," he said. "Your mother is quite right, as she usually is. I don't hold at all with this bishop about direct calls from God. God strengthens and sustains us all. We must never waver from that faith and knowledge. But I've never believed with some men in Church or chapel or among the Romanists that He devises special schemes and plans for men, or even tells them just what to do. His purposes, to my mind, are far higher than mere plans. I think instead that He has given us freedom to make our own decisions as to the way we lead our lives. He means for us to choose as best we know how, and then we pay whatever costs there may be from our own choices. There may, of course, have been these calls, these vocations, for certain gifted men. I wouldn't presume to say there haven't been, only I just don't think along those lines."

He stood by the fire, still holding the book against him. The coals in the grate glowed red and hot, and the sprig of ivy continued to tap and slap against the window.

"It's true that I've come to think of America as a land of promise," he continued. "Perhaps, in fact, I'm more than a bit silly in that thought. And yet I know we'll be giving up many things here that we love. We can't foresee what the costs may be if we decide to go. They might be heavy enough in many ways; but that's just the chance we have to take when we decide anything at all."

My mother's face brightened as she looked at him standing there; but she did not say anything. Nor did Mary and I, though Mary told me later that she couldn't help thinking of Moses or of Joshua leading us through the Red Sea or across the Jordan to our Promised Land. It was Ansie who broke the long silence.

"It might be very nice for you to rise higher," he said thoughtfully. "I'm sure we'd all be proud of that."

My father smiled at him, but made no reply.

"You'd miss Bury St. Edmunds, father," Ansie continued. "Not to go there would be one cost for you."

"Thank you for thinking of that, Ansie," my father said. "Yes, I should miss Bury sadly, I'm afraid."

"Still, I hope we shall go to America," Ansie said. "I'm sure we'd all be willing to help you pay any other costs there might be."

My mother's eyes filled suddenly with tears. She let the red jersey fall into her lap, and her ball of wool rolled to the floor. My father stooped to pick it up for her, and with that simple action the spell which had held us all seemed to break and allow us to be again in the familiar parsonage, ready for our evening tea.

"I think, Ansie," my mother said, her voice shaking a little, "that it's time now for you to say your poem."

"Poem?" asked my father, just as though he had never been

in London or met a bishop from America. "Poem? What poem?"

"Ansie will tell you," my mother said.

"I'd like to ask Katie in to hear it," said Ansie. "I think she'd like to."

"By all means ask Katie," my father said.

Katie looked pleased, if a bit flustered, when she came from the kitchen. She had hastily tied her white apron over her black dress and pinned her white cap on so quickly that one of its black ribbons in the back had got caught behind her left ear where it dangled across her cheek. My father offered her his chair; but she declined that honour, preferring to remain standing by the door. She whispered something to Ansie before my father went back to his chair and just before Ansie took his place to stand in front of the fire.

"Katie thinks I should explain first about the Statue of Liberty before I say the poem," Ansie said, "just in case I might possibly be asked to recite it in school."

"Very good," my father said.

Then Ansie began his prefatory speech. His eyes were shining as they shone in chapel and his yellow hair, unconfined by soapy water as on Sundays, was rumpled and untidy. He smiled at my mother as he took his place by the fire as though he and she already felt sure of my father's surprise and pleasure.

"The Statue of Liberty," he said, spacing his words carefully and making each round and clear, "is on an island in the harbour of New York City. Ships which bring strangers to America are bound to pass near it so that all can see it. It is over three hundred feet high, and it is made of a woman holding a torch high in her hand. She is the symbol of liberty to all these strangers. Her head is so large that forty people can stand inside it. This statue was given to the people of America by the people of France. It was placed in New York harbour in the year 1886. I hope someday to see this Statue of Liberty. There is a poem printed on the pedestal of the statue. This is the poem."

We all listened carefully as Ansie recited the poem. He took great pains with its every word. Katie stood in the doorway, her round face flushed with pride and wonder. She forgot all the indignation she had felt in the morning about the *refuse*. I knew then that she loved Ansie more than any other one of us.

When Ansie had finished, my father said:

"If you are willing, Ansie, I'm sure we should all like to hear the poem again."

Ansie was quite willing. His second rendering was even more fraught with excitement and meaning than the first had been. Katie did not stay for the second recital. She had left her handkerchief in the kitchen and was obliged to use her apron to wipe her eyes and to blow her nose.

## 14

Katie did not shed a tear, however, when she came to Southampton with our Suffolk grandparents to see us all embark for America. My mother was vastly proud of her, for she knew that Katie had been steeling herself for weeks to be stalwart and even gay over our departure. My father was proud of her, too, and grateful as well, for upon her own suggestion she was now to live with his mother and father and see that all went right with them. To leave them behind was a mighty wrench for him, perhaps the heaviest among those costs of our decision to emigrate, although they themselves had been eager and even urgent that he should go. Like Ansie they were proud in the thought that he might "rise higher" in a land where chapel was every whit as respectable as Church.

My grandfather, though nearing eighty, was still strong and straight in spite of years of Suffolk wind and mud; and my grandmother, only a little younger, seemed anything but frail and old. They had all manner of plans for their land and gardens which Katie would now help to make possible. We were never to give them so much as one anxious thought. And who could tell, my grandmother said, with life being as unpredictable as it was and surprises around every corner of it, that they might not be boarding a ship themselves before too long to come to visit us?

I knew I should always remember them standing there on the bustling, noisy, misty pier among other old parents, voicing without doubt similar cheerful myths. Katie stood between them, short and solid in her shabby brown coat and her old tan straw hat, with a rakish bunch of red cherries just in front of its high crown. We had seen those cherries every Sunday for four years, which span of time, Katie had assured us, was but a fraction of their actual age. I knew, too, that I should sadly miss the cherries.

"I hope you'll come, Katie," Ansie said, just at that point in all leave-takings when nothing whatever remains to be said.

He stood in front of Katie in his black jacket and his broad white collar. He had his cricket bat in one hand and in the other a satchel of heavy grey wool which she had fashioned for him to stow away his special treasures, his coins and stamps, his marbles, and bits of rock from this place and that which he valued.

"There's travellin' folks an' waitin' folks, Ansie," Katie said. "I'm one o' them as waits. I'm for old lands, not new. Only six or seven years an' you'll be comin' back a young gentleman from one o' them respectable academies to go to your father's college at Cambridge. I'll be 'ere waitin' to keep you starched up an' stuck close to your books. An' don't you go plasterin' your hair down with too much soap, Ansie. For meself, I fancy it risin' up, natural like."

Our Yorkshire grandparents did not come to see us off. The archdeacon wrote my mother a letter which arrived on the day before our departure for Southampton. When Mr. Grimes had left it at the door, said goodbye and God bless you to us all in a rather tremulous voice and thanked Ansie for the Statue of Liberty poem, which was a farewell gift, my mother stuck the letter beneath the Royal Family, whom we had returned to the drawing-room wall. She was quite too flustered, she said, with packing all our boxes which were strewn about the floor to open it at the moment. She had quite enough on her mind what with finding a place for Tocqueville and Thoreau, both of whom my father had insisted must be easily accessible on the ship, instead of being sent on ahead with his other books, to be able to endure any more confusion. The letter stayed there all day, its unknown and perhaps menacing contents concealed beneath Queen Victoria and an almost unbelievable number of descendants grouped respectfully around her ornate chair.

My mother read it aloud to us after we had been well stayed by our evening tea in my father's dismantled study with the last of the long summer twilight darkening the garden. Although he was naturally consumed by distress, my grandfather Oldroyd wrote, certain most important, in fact imminent affairs in his diocese would prevent his journeying so far south to bid us Godspeed; but we must be assured that his prayers were always with us. All the tired lines left my mother's face as she folded the letter and smiled at my father.

"I'm beginning now to believe in the mercies of God," she said. "And just to prove what a really good wife I am to you,

I won't say another word about your carrying that wretched *Walden* in your pocket though it does sag your jacket."

My father laughed as he had not laughed for weeks; and Ansie ran to the kitchen to tell Katie the good tidings from Yorkshire.

THREE · *The Voyage*

WHENEVER we reviewed our voyage of ten days on the *Empress of Austria* as we often did not only in the weeks and months immediately following it, but in years afterwards, we always remembered the Plimsolls above every other feature. They blotted out all the other astonishments or at least effectively obscured them. It seemed a sacrilege that Mr. Plimsoll, moving constantly about among our motley fellow passengers in his worn black frock coat and his frayed felt shoes, could quench our wonder over the long succession of completely windless days when the sea was as still as some slow Suffolk stream, my father said, and the great ship cut through the silvery expanse of pale-green water with as little disturbance as a swan floating beneath the willows of the Lark at Bury St. Edmunds. Or that he and his incredible family could dull our sorrow when a drunken Rumanian wrung the neck of a canary which an old Bohemian woman had smuggled on board as her greatest treasure and which had enraged the Rumanian by perching on his shoulder as it darted and fluttered about the crowded deck. Or that our amazement over them all could minimize our horror when two young Italians drew knives against each other in a fight over a Greek girl, the magnet to most of the men in our quarters except, of course, to Mr. Plimsoll, who in a noble attempt to separate the Italians received such blows from them both that he was hurtled across the deck like some piece of worthless baggage, and not, I fear, to the deep regret of anyone.

My mother, who declared soon after our embarkation that the "huddled masses" in the Statue of Liberty poem could never again be any mystery to her, kept reminding us a dozen times during our memorable crossing of the Atlantic that, had we accepted the archdeacon's generous offer of funds, we should forevermore have been deprived of the Plimsolls. The archdeacon for purely social reasons, my father said, and therefore unimportant and extremely distasteful, if not abhorrent to him, had volubly objected to our travelling as steerage passengers. The very thought, he wrote, kept him from sleep by night and from peace of mind by day. If to travel first class were out of the question, we must at least manage second, which management he would be glad to make possible from his own slender purse. My mother, in a weak moment, might have accepted her father's proposal on the theory that families who had little or nothing to offer in terms of emotional and spiritual gifts should be allowed to contribute material necessities whatever motive prompted their willingness; but my father was invulnerable and perhaps even a bit shocked by her disconcerting realism. Not only was he determined to shoulder his own responsibilities, he said, but he also eagerly welcomed the opportunity to travel as an emigrant among his fellow men, regardless of their race or their colour or their poverty. They were all men of good hope seeking to better their lot in a new land. Why should he who shared their common lot and believed devoutly in their dignity and value as human souls accept or even expect greater comfort than they were able to obtain for themselves and their families?

Whether my father ever wavered in his infinite faith in human worth and aspiration, or upon occasion questioned his exalted idea of human personality, he carefully never divulged to us; and, so far as was possible for her, my mother kept her opinions to herself during our days at sea with some nine hundred other pilgrims bound, like us, for a more abundant life. Most of these had boarded the ship in Hamburg and generously represented several Southern European countries. Those who had embarked in Southampton were few in number and, to use a kindly and inclusive adjective, distinctly *different* in background. Whenever the din and confusion on our deck, which was at the stern of the ship and open to the sky, became unbearable or Mr. Plimsoll too fervent and ubiquitous, my father went to the tiny cabin which he shared with Ansie where he could sit on the edge of his narrow bunk, read his Thoreau, and meditate upon, or perhaps even recapture, his faith in that dignity and value of the human spirit under whatever guise these qualities seemed to be quite successfully concealing themselves on our steamship.

## 2

My mother said that the very presence of the Plimsolls was a mystery, for, had they all been on the dock in Southampton, we could never have avoided seeing them. Ansie grieved that Katie had not seen them, since he felt sure that the daily journal of our voyage which he was keeping to send to her could never do justice to them all or take the place of Katie's own startled observation. Our sensible conclusion, of course, was that they had been hustled on board early, once the embarkation officials had recovered from their surprise. At all events, when we had reached the crowded deck, there they all were, gathered at the rail, Mr. and Mrs. Plimsoll, three pairs of twins, one baby in a battered pram, a younger in its mother's arms, and the six other assorted Plimsolls who completed the family circle of sixteen in all, not to mention the obvious prophecy of a seventeenth to be fulfilled before many weeks had passed.

Although the Plimsolls claimed most of our thoughts and many of our hours on board ship in much the same manner as they seized the attention of everyone else from harassed stewards to derisive or infuriated passengers, they vanished completely from our knowledge once we had reached New York and departed on our separate ways. The vastness of the Dakotas toward which they were journeying to engage in missionary labour on the limitless prairies of those still-new states seemed to have absorbed them all, erased them, swallowed them up. My mother sent Mrs. Plimsoll a present for the forthcoming baby more out of curiosity than kindness, she admitted, but no news of its arrival ever reached us; nor did Moses Plimsoll, who was Ansie's age and had aroused Ansie's sympathy because of his lame leg and the tragic fate of his rabbit, ever reply to Ansie's postcards. Still we never forgot them all or the extraordinary mixture of emotions which they aroused within us.

They had their more practical uses, too, for during Mrs. Gowan's visits to us, whenever she was about to enter her Betsy Ross world and cause us confusion, she could usually be deterred if one of us offered quickly enough to tell her about the Plimsolls. They never ceased to entertain her. Moreover, in their amusing or their pathetic aspects, they tended helpfully to dim the resentment and even bitterness which she had felt with good reason toward all Methodists until she had met my father.

### 3

The Reverend Abraham Plimsoll was a Primitive Methodist parson from a small village on the coast of North Cornwall; and he richly possessed and exhibited all the extreme and sensational habits which had marked that sect for nearly a hundred years before his day. He was a tall man and almost unbelievably thin. He had thin, reddish hair, a drooping moustache of the same colour and thinness, and a sparse goatee which could not hide his receding chin. His eyes were pale blue and blazed beneath their reddish brows with an almost frightening fervour. His high cheekbones blazed, too, with flushes of bright red, which disturbed my mother, although perhaps they were merely the result of the fire that burned within him and of his perpetual and frenzied tearing about. He wore always a long frock coat which hung from his shoulders and flapped about his legs. Both the coat and the trousers beneath had once been black, but were now almost green from wear and age. Two buttons were missing from the coat probably because of Mr. Plimsoll's agitated twirling of them. These Mrs. Plimsoll planned to replace if ever she could salvage a few minutes from her constant knitting.

The name Abraham had been given to Mr. Plimsoll by his mother, who had, he told my father, received it in a trance as a direct command from God. This trance was of continual inspiration to him since it undeniably placed his mother among similarly gifted Biblical characters such as Elijah, Balaam, the apostle Paul, and the father of John the Baptist. My father's one contribution to Mr. Plimsoll's busy days aboard ship was his explanation that the word *Abraham* in Hebrew meant "the high father of a people," which, since Mr. Plimsoll knew no Hebrew, came to him not only as a pleasant surprise but as an added assurance of his mission in life; and my father was charitable enough not to suggest his own amused application of it only to the size of the immediate Plimsoll family.

In general Mr. Plimsoll suspected my father, his lack of missionary zeal, upon which Mr. Plimsoll had unwisely counted, his quiet faith in mankind, his dislike of "love feasts" and camp meetings, which were Mr. Plimsoll's meat and drink, and, above all, his university training. To Mr. Plimsoll's explosive evangelism any learning valued for its own sake was but a stumbling block to the saving of souls. The Lord, he insisted, had carefully chosen the unlettered to carry His Gospel throughout the world; and he himself took as great pride in his own humble origin as a Cornish miner's son and his almost total lack of education as he took in the fact that the Primitive Methodists had been founded by a joiner and a potter, who were determined to preserve the "original zeal" of the Methodist movement. Once he and my father discovered, after several heated sessions on our first days at sea, that their respective understandings of this original zeal were quite contrary to each other and that their ideas about John Wesley were different, not to say disparate, they forbore further argument, Mr. Plimsoll with unconcealed contempt, my father with intense relief.

There was, however, little relief for anyone travelling steerage on the *Empress of Austria* from Mr. Plimsoll's constant presence. He was like some vulture flapping about among us all. The confusion of language on the ship like that at Babel or in Jerusalem on the day of Pentecost did not in the least deter or discourage him. Once he had discovered the possession of even a few words of English by any of his many-tongued brethren on board he attached himself like a leech to the possessor and began to unload upon his victim all the terrifying tenets of his cramped and ugly theology. In the early morning he gathered his family in a corner of the deck to lead them in prayer and in the singing of revivalistic hymns; at meals from the well-filled Plimsoll table in the centre of our crowded, untidy dining-room, he enforced upon us all unwilling thanksgiving for our tasteless food; at sunset he again held devotions in the midst of his cowed, submissive brood, delighted when the circle was increased in circumference by those who from mere astonishment watched and listened. He delighted, too, in the persecutions which he willingly endured and which included not only scorn and derision but upon occasion unsavoury and well-placed missiles aimed at him in fury by various young unregenerates from southern climes. Perhaps his one annoying source of suffering came from two Roman priests who refused to talk with him and who calmly read their breviaries in the midst of the hubbub of the deck, their dark thin faces clothed in sardonic indifference.

My father said that Mr. Plimsoll almost equalled St. Paul in the number and nature of the indignities heaped upon him with the exception of shipwreck and imprisonment. Indeed, he narrowly escaped the latter fate when some outraged ship's officers, descending on the fifth day into our chaotic midst, warned him that unless he ceased from his rantings he might find himself placed in confinement well below the deck. This threat may have slightly modified his zeal, though not too noticeably, for doubtless he was aware, as were we all, that steamship officials during those years of mass emigration did not overly concern themselves with the human freight which on every voyage crammed their steerage quarters.

4

It was impossible to feel any emotion whatever about Mrs. Plimsoll, except perhaps a satiated wonder, since she herself betrayed not the slightest awareness of her peculiar situation in life. So far as one could gather from her manner, her behaviour, or her rare conversation, she felt neither pride in her husband nor embarrassment over his antics. She took charge of her many children, all of whom were clean and decently behaved, but without any visible vestige of affection or concern. She managed to hold her youngest in her arms and keep her two-year-old beside her in his pram, to attend to their needs, and to quiet their frequent wailings; but she did all these things as though she were attending to extraneous pieces of furniture. My mother wondered if she knew that her fifteenth child was clearly imminent, might, it seemed, arrive at any hour, but of that she gave no sign. At their long table in our close, ill-ventilated dining-room, where children screamed in a dozen languages and stewards in soiled white coats commanded and cursed, where my father's fellow men snatched greedily at food and raucous shouts of laughter mingled with unpleasant smells, she sat, silent and imperturbable, seeing to the wants of her family like some machine stocked with necessities and emitting each as needed or desired. She sang at family services in a high, true voice, but with no change of expression, if, indeed, her sharp, thin face could be said to have an expression. She simply sat among her family like some extra piece of luggage which has been filled with unnecessary pieces and brought along in the thought that its contents might someday prove useful. She was apparently neither in a daze nor, perhaps unhappily for her, in a dream; she did not invite pity or anxiety; she rarely smiled and seldom spoke; she was merely there.

She was a small woman with dark straight hair drawn neatly back and coiled in a severe knot. Her eyes were small, dark, and lustreless. She wore every day a neat grey dress, the skirt of which was covered by a wide black sateen apron with a capacious pocket. In this pocket she carried her knitting. This knitting was the one evidence of any animation about her except for a nervous twitching in her right cheek which made its skin quiver as a still pool quivers from the sudden impact of a stone. She literally never ceased from knitting except at mealtimes or when one of the two babies demanded that she free her hands for necessary services. She kept her needles clicking even while she was singing at devotions. Her sole output was socks, which was understandable considering the number of her children; and she was so quick that she could turn out a pair a day whatever the size. The colour of these was of no importance at all to her. She had clearly never wasted a strand of wool since she had begun to knit. When one colour from the odds and ends in her pocket gave out, she simply used any other which came to her hand so that her finished products, at least, were gay and lively.

My mother, when she was finally convinced that Mrs. Plimsoll welcomed neither sympathy nor any form of assistance, was absorbed by curiosity concerning her and used her knitting as a means of satisfying this. When she had gotten together a quite generous supply of wool from our luggage in the cabin which she shared with Mary and me, she took it to Mrs. Plimsoll in the hope of engaging her in conversation. The conversation, however, was a disappointment. Beyond thanking my mother for the wool, Mrs. Plimsoll said nothing at all except, in rather a defensive way, that she did plan to restore Mr. Plimsoll's missing buttons once she could take time from her socks.

5

The fourteen Plimsoll children, who could not fail to appeal to our imaginations as to just what might prove to be their mission in the Dakotas except to provide a ready-made Sunday school there, were all named from the Old Testament. This fact, in turn, engrossed my father's curiosity, for, given Mr. Plimsoll's mania for spreading the Gospel, it seemed odd that he had bestowed upon his children Hebraic rather than Christian names. Since an impassable gulf had early separated him and my father, there seemed no way to solve this mystery; and my father had to content himself with the assumption that somewhere deep within Mr. Plimsoll's attenuated frame there glowed passionate memories of the patriarchs fleeing from false gods to pitch their tents in a forbidding land; or of Moses before the Burning Bush; or of the fury of Elijah by the river Kishon; or of the unspeakable sins of Sodom and Gomorrah. Or perhaps he was merely recognizing the ancient promise made to the original Abraham that his seed should be as the stars in number.

The Plimsoll family began with twin sons, Adam and Amos, who were tall, sober boys of fifteen. Two more pairs of twins followed them after the single births of Asenath, who was fourteen, and Rebekkah, who was twelve. Elijah and Elisha were eleven, Isaiah and Isaac nine, and in between came Moses, who was an undersized, pale little boy with puzzled, frightened eyes and a crutch, for he was lame from a shrunken leg. Below the latest twins were five other small Plimsolls ranging in age from eight to one. Each pair of twins was of the identical variety so far as one could determine; and all the fourteen, ten of whom were boys, resembled their father in features and colouring except Moses, who was like none of his brothers or sisters and totally unlike either parent. Mrs. Plimsoll had bequeathed nothing of her own appearance to any of her children. Indeed she seemed as nonexistent in them as in herself.

It was difficult to discover what the Plimsoll sons thought or felt about their father or just what they were actually like in themselves. In the intervals between their revivalistic services they wandered around the crowded deck usually in pairs and almost always silent. Adam and Amos were invariably kind to Moses, whom they often carried between them in a sort of sling made of a square of canvas gathered at two sides; and the eleven-year-old twins occasionally shared this responsibility. My mother was delighted one morning to see Elijah and Elisha engaged in a wrestling match, umpired by their older brothers. The match, however, could hardly be termed exciting and came to an abrupt close as soon as other boys on board who had gathered to see the fun began in a medley of tongues and a series of rough gestures to instruct the wrestlers in more violent tactics than they were clearly in the habit of employing against each other.

The Plimsoll daughters, Asenath and Rebekkah, were more loquacious and sociable than their brothers. They also offered more to their father, for they were either willing or eager to shout ejaculations in the family hymn singing and at intervals during his exhortations. "Glory, hallelujah!" Asenath would cry, and Rebekkah in obedience to a signal from her sister would add somewhat less stridently her "Amen" or "Jesus saves." They often attached themselves to Mary and me, perhaps out of genuine loneliness or the bond of a common language, or perhaps from curiosity in us as Methodists of a different sort from themselves. Asenath in particular concerned herself with the state of our souls; but when she discovered that such concern only made Mary nervous and tearful and me rude and stubborn, she contented herself with the story of her own and Rebekkah's conversion at a Cornish camp meeting, at which, we gathered, most of the Plimsolls above the age of nine had been likewise redeemed.

In the afternoons when many of our fellow travellers were sleeping in their bunks below or stretched out snoring in the sun and it was possible to find a clear space on the deck, my mother read aloud to us for an hour. Moses Plimsoll at Ansie's invitation joined us from the beginning; and after a few days the others of the flock, except the youngest who kept close to their impassive mother, came also. Adam and Amos perched self-consciously on the outside of the circle

on the folding canvas chairs provided us in the steerage and
stared at my mother as though she were some creature from
another planet. Asenath and Rebekkah sat on their chairs also
and knitted almost as swiftly and skillfully as their mother.
The younger twins drew nearer day by day, sitting on the
ends of their bony spines on the deck flooring and hugging
their thin knees above their multicoloured socks. On the second
day my mother impulsively took Moses on her lap, a place
which, once he had recovered from his astonishment, gave
him both pride and pleasure and which he shyly expected and
claimed on all following days. If Mrs. Plimsoll, knitting on
the opposite side of the deck and attending desultorily to the
needs of her five youngest, observed him, she gave no sign;
and his father was too immersed in his Bible or too agitated
over the many sinners among us to pay the slightest attention
to our occupation.

I think the Plimsolls really enjoyed our reading hours as
the fine weather miraculously held and the ship moved onward over the calm sea in the hot sunshine. None of them,
to be sure, was so entranced as Moses, whose big brown eyes
began to lose their fear and to glow with delight and wonder;
but even Adam and Amos brightened occasionally, and the
younger twins rocked back and forth on the hard deck boards
with excitement. *The Jungle Book* was obviously a new
world to them all: Mowgli and his foster parents, the Wolves;
the valiant mongoose, Rikki-tikki-tavi; Toomai and his ele-
phant, Kala Nag.

My mother, her curiosity about them all still prodding
her, used her reading as a means of appeasing it; and in this
she was ably seconded by Ansie, who sought more material
for his journal to Katie.

"Doesn't your mother read to you?" he asked one day,
addressing this question to any Plimsoll who might be dis-

posed to answer him.

"She don't have time," Rebekkah said.

"And if she did," Asenath added sharply, "she wouldn't read heathen books like that one. She'd read the Bible."

"Shut up, Asenath," Isaiah Plimsoll said, to my mother's relief and amazement.

"We read the Bible, too," Mary said, with more than a trace of anger in her voice.

Asenath clicked her needles furiously after darting a vengeful glance at Isaiah and a scornful one toward Mary. Ansie attempted to lighten the atmosphere.

"I don't think there are cobras like Nag and Nagaina on the prairies in America," he said, "but I'm sure there are rattlesnakes. They don't live in New England, where we are going, but they do in the Dakotas. My father has told me about them. You hold their heads down with a forked stick, and then you beat them to death."

"I hope I don't ever see one," Moses said with a shiver of fear.

"They mean to warn you in time," Ansie said with scant comfort. "They have rattles on their tails to warn you with."

"We'll take care of you, Moses," Amos said quickly. "Don't you go to worrying. We'll see that you don't see no snakes."

"God will protect us all," Asenath said with unctuous and repulsive piety. "We're going to do His work way out there, and He'll look out for us." She looked up from her knitting to shoot a mean glance at Moses. "Only maybe not you, Moses, to pay you for disobeying father about your rabbit."

"Leave him alone, Asenath," Adam said. "Keep your mouth shut!"

My mother, seeing that Mary was about to pounce upon

Asenath with a hot flow of words and that I was ready to lend her any amount of assistance, hastily swung the conversation to more general information.

"What town are you going to live in?" she asked the family at large.

The boys left the reply to their sisters, and since Asenath was sulky over Adam's rebuff, Rebekkah answered.

"In a place near Fargo in the State of North Dakota," she said. "I don't remember its name. Does anyone remember?"

Apparently no one did; but my mother, encouraged, continued her questions.

"What will you do there? I mean, will your father preach in a chapel of his own?"

"No," Asenath said, now sufficiently recovered to take on her position as spokesman for the family. "He'll hold camp meetings on the prairie for hundreds and hundreds of people who don't know nothing about Jesus. He'll ride a horse miles and miles; and we four oldest will likely ride horses too. In just a few more years," she finished proudly, "I shall be a missionary on my own. My father says so. I've had a call to preach the Gospel, and Rebekkah may have one, too, when she's as old as me."

Rebekkah had the grace to look at that moment as though such a call would be most unwelcome to her; and we warmed a bit toward her and toward each pair of twins as we sensed their combined filial hatred of Asenath.

6

My father never joined our reading circles. He confided to my mother that the very sight and sound of the Plimsolls was unnerving to him and that any closer contact with them would be devastating. Whenever he was on the deck he spent most of his time standing in the farthest corner of the stern and watching the shining swells of the ship's wake roll together until they again quieted into the flat expanse of still water. My mother felt anxious about him, for she feared that his thoughts were tumultuous and troubling. She was pleased when he occasionally talked with a rabbi, who had come from Warsaw and was going to New York to make his home with his son, a tailor there.

This rabbi was a frail old man with a long white beard, a sharp nose, and great, sorrowful dark eyes. He wore a small black skullcap on his bald head and even on the warmest days wrapped himself in the folds of a black shawl. He was very learned, my father said, and had borne many sufferings for the sake of his faith. He seemed completely unaware of the hubbub and uproar which surged about him. He sat in the midst of it all as though he dwelt in some closely encompassing world of sacred scrolls and the holy utterances of prophets and the ancient griefs of all mankind. Almost no one spoke to him although he knew many languages; yet all, even the most uncouth among us, felt an awed respect for him sitting there on the low roof of our main companionway, strangely alive in his own Realities. Whenever my father drew near to sit down beside him, he raised his right hand from his black shawl and said: "*Shalom*, my brother."

Although my father deplored all the Plimsolls except Moses and, after his initial arguments with Mr. Plimsoll, kept his distance from them in so far as it was possible to keep one's distance from anything or anybody in the steerage of the *Empress of Austria*, he was not in the least averse to hearing about them. As soon as Ansie at his request had gotten all their names from Moses and copied them for him on a sheet of paper, he went one afternoon to his cabin and amused himself for fully an hour by making them fit into classical metre. My mother said that if there were ever a perfect instance of a collision of worlds, it was exemplified by the Plimsolls, on the one hand, and Latin hexameters, on the other; but my father was proud of his accomplishment, which we all memorized and which remained in our minds long after the Dakotas had engulfed the Plimsolls:

> Adam, Asenath, Isaiah; Isaac, Rebekkah, Elijah.
> Amos, Naomi, Ruth, Seth; Aaron, Elisha, Job, Moses.

When later I began to scan my Vergil, the names of the fourteen Plimsolls were forever ousting those of Aeneas and Dido, old Anchises, and young Ascanius from the pages.

### 7

Moses Plimsoll called his rabbit Brownie. It was a baby rabbit, which his brother Amos had caught perhaps unwisely on some Cornish moor or heath and given to Moses only a short time before their departure for America. Moses had never before had a pet of his own. Since he could not bear to leave it behind, he had somehow managed to bring it with him, whether or not with the connivance and assistance of Amos we were never able to learn, but surely with neither the knowledge nor the approval of his father. Brownie was not born to thrive in any sort of captivity, and that of a stuffy berth on the *Empress of Austria* did not encourage its slender chance of life.

Moses kept his rabbit in a box at the foot of his bunk, which with fifteen other identical ones in a long row formed the sleeping quarters of the Plimsolls, quarters far less comfortable than ours and situated two decks lower down and well below the water line. Brownie cowered and quivered in his box for most of the day, though Moses and Ansie did their utmost at frequent intervals to make him hop about the bunk or nibble at some sorry vegetables which they managed to salvage at mealtimes. At night Moses held him close, in his arms, beneath his blanket.

Sometimes Ansie fetched him from Moses' bunk and carried him in his box to his and my father's cabin where there was more light and air, but he did not improve noticeably in activity; and Moses never ventured to take him to the open deck where both he and Brownie would be bound to suffer the venom of Asenath and likely as well to incur the pious wrath of his father. Moses felt sure that, once they had reached the Dakotas, his pet would flourish in an environment not unlike his native one, wax fat and merry; and Ansie carefully refrained from any further mention of rattlesnakes, which, he had rightly gathered, were able and eager to swallow rabbits as small and apathetic as was Brownie.

The struggle for Brownie's fragile existence was in vain. On the fifth morning at sea Moses awoke to find him motionless and quite stiff in his arms. When Adam and Amos, who went each morning to get Moses ready for breakfast, discovered what had happened, they did their utmost to dispose of Brownie after the manner of all worthless things aboard a ship and to accomplish this without the knowledge of the rest of the family or of the steward in charge of their location. That hard-faced German, however, appearing suddenly upon the scene, was so overcome by pity for Moses that he impulsively parted with his own penknife together with a dozen assorted picture postcards of the city of Berlin in an effort to make things more bearable for him. For in spite of the fact that after years of a thankless job he, like most stewards, cherished little sentiment toward human freight in general, he had been genuinely stirred by the thought of a child like Moses in the inescapable midst of the Plimsolls and had purposely made himself blind to Brownie's forbidden presence.

Ansie worried because Moses did not cry as he himself would have done over a similar loss; but apparently tears were a weakness neither encouraged nor assuaged by the Plimsolls. Moses merely looked more puzzled and frightened than before, as though this latest offering of life were quite beyond his comprehension, even if in keeping with his brief experience. My mother held him more closely now during our reading time, and my father often gave up his books or his staring at the sea to play draughts or dominoes with him and Ansie. We all waited and hoped for the look in his eyes to become once again less questioning and fearful; but in that we were disappointed.

8

Anxious as my mother was over the effects which, she feared, our passage might have upon my father's peace of mind and his ways of life and thought, she was troubled, too, about us children and especially perhaps over Ansie and me, whose knowledge of human experience, hitherto discreetly limited, had been suddenly and immeasurably widened and deepened by the unfamiliar sights and sounds on board ship. Our somewhat dim memories of stays on the Suffolk farm or those common occurrences in animal behaviour which surround all country children had heretofore made small impression upon us and had never been translated in our imaginations into human terms. Now on the teeming deck where people swarmed about in the sun we could hardly fail to become acutely aware of passions and greeds, desires and ferments, the existence of which we had never realized in our circumscribed decade of life. The Greek girl who shamelessly bared her breasts and offered her full lips to any one of a dozen men struggling to lie beside her; the half-clad children who were reluctant to go below decks when the trough by the rail offered a convenient toilet; mothers nursing babies in any available spot; boys and even men scrambling like so many dogs after fruit and confections which from time to time were thrown down by first-class passengers from the decks far above; fights and cursings, overlong pulls at jugs and bottles, blows and consequent yells, throwing of dice and of filthy cards, drunkenness, stupors, and snorings; the despair and discomfort of the old carried along by their families like extra and unwanted bales and boxes, or journeying alone to join sons and daughters in a strange new world—all these stamped their rude marks upon our minds. Mary, wiser in the ways of the world than we and at nearing thirteen far more sensitive to human conduct at its worst, was swept by such disgust and loathing that she often resorted to tears whereas we were consumed largely by surprise and shocked curiosity.

My father characteristically left all necessary explanations to my mother; and she was hampered by that reticence common to most mothers fifty years ago whatever their background or training, and especially to English ones. Nor was she able to glean much commiseration and understanding from other outraged women of her own land and language. For few of those who had boarded the ship at Southampton, except for the Plimsolls and a smattering of northern farmers bound for the wheat fields of Canada, had shared my father's desire for any close association with all sorts and conditions of men. Most of them were instead decently housed in second-class quarters and thus far removed from our maelstrom.

"See that steward kicking that girl lying on the deck," Ansie said. "Why does he do that? Men don't kick women and girls."

"I hope he kicks her some more," Mary said. "She's horrid

and filthy. I hate her. I hate everybody on this ship. I hate all the horrid men and all the dirty babies, and I hate Asenath Plimsoll worst of all. I wish we were all back home."

"Well, we're not," my mother said. "We're right here together, and there are only three days more. We'll forget all these unpleasant things before very long."

"I shall never forget them," Mary said. "Never, all my life."

Ansie returned to his question.

"Why does he kick her like that?" he asked my mother.

"I suppose because he wants her to get up."

"Why is she always lying down like that?"

"Ask your father. He knows as well as I do."

"I did ask him. He said he didn't know. I asked him why she let all those men kiss her. He doesn't know that either."

"If he doesn't know, why do you expect me to?"

"Because you're always better at answers than he is. Besides, he's all shut up in his own thoughts."

"I'm afraid he's disappointed," my mother said. "I'm afraid all these people are different from what he hoped they'd be."

"He told me last night," Ansie said, "that we must believe America has better things for them. He said that perhaps right here on this ship there are future great musicians, like that Italian boy who plays his violin. He said you should never judge people just by what they look like and do when they are all crowded together like this. Do you believe that, too?"

"I suppose so," my mother said. "I suppose I *have* to believe it if I'm to go on living with your father. Why don't you fetch your marbles, Ansie, and show them to Moses? I'm sure he'd like seeing them. Or your stamps? Or your lead soldiers? Or—well, just anything!"

"Not me," Ansie said. "These kids grab things, and I

don't know how to tell them to give them back to me. Besides, Moses doesn't want to play. Adam said so. He's lying in his bunk, and it's smelly down there."

"You're not thinking of ever *not* living with father, are you?" I asked, for my mother's comment had struck fear to my heart in this world of arrant confusion.

"Don't be silly!" she said. "We're all of us getting too silly for words. We'll be just plain potty if we don't take care."

"Who wouldn't be potty on this crazy old ship?" Mary said. "Positively now, just who wouldn't?"

"Look!" Ansie whispered, his eyes big and shining. "That girl's running downstairs with that gypsy man chasing her. What's she going downstairs with him for? I'm going down and see what they're up to."

"You stay precisely where you are, Ansie," commanded my mother. "Why don't you say a poem for us or sing a hymn? You haven't sung once since we left Southampton."

"Frankly, Ansie, I'm sick and tired of you," Mary said. "You get more revolting by the hour. Why don't you go and sing with those odious Plimsolls? They're getting ready for another meeting right now."

Ansie looked as insulted as he felt.

"Do you think I'd sing those crazy hymns with them? I'm sorry for all those twins. They're not bad chaps. They're not like Asenath." He lowered his voice. "Their steward says Asenath is a filthy little bitch. Just what is a bitch, mother?"

"Ansie!" cried Mary. "Mother, make him stop using such words!"

My mother at that moment looked as though she were completely done for, crushed to bits, even her love for us all crumbling to nothing.

"Well, he did," Ansie persisted before she could recover

herself. "He said that very thing, and he called her a monster as well. He even thinks she may have sneaked to Moses' bunk and done something to Brownie to make him die sooner."

"Now, Ansie," my mother said, "that really will do for you. Asenath has quite enough sins against her as it is. She's not a murderer—at least not of rabbits. You can either say decent and pleasant things or else go straight to your cabin. And don't speak another word to that steward. If you do, I'll just have to consult your father."

"Here he comes now," Ansie said, chastened but by no means silenced. "They've driven him away from his place so that they can hold their horrid old meeting. Mrs. Plimsoll can hardly waddle, she's so fat. Do babies always make their mothers as fat as that?"

"Yes, they do," my mother said, watching my father weave his way toward us across the deck in his mussed old grey suit.

"Ansie!" cried Mary again. "You're only a child. You're not supposed to know about such things!"

"I know a lot more than you think I do, Miss Caxton," Ansie said loftily.

I drew near my mother and whispered in her ear.

"Were you big like that before Ansie and I were born?"

"Far bigger," my mother said gaily, as she put her arm around me and drew me close to her.

"Well, and how's my family?" my father asked, seizing an unoccupied camp stool and sitting down beside my mother.

"We're all fine," my mother said, though Mary was close to tears, and I was bewildered and unhappy, and Ansie was clearly the unrepentant culprit.

My father seemed unaware of any such convulsions among us.

"I can't get over the miracle of this weather," he said. "It demolishes all I've ever heard about an ocean crossing. Seven days and all fair and still! How fortunate we are! Fancy what it would be like if it were raining on this deck! I almost came to fetch you an hour ago, Ansie. There was a school of porpoises rolling in and out just beyond the stern."

"Why don't you have a few words with the old rabbi?" my mother suggested. "He's been sitting there quite alone all the morning long."

"That's precisely what I was aiming to do," my father said.

### 9

The fine weather changed on the day before we reached New York. There was neither rain nor wind, but instead a heavy, hot mist enveloped us, blotting out the sun and the sea, swathing us all in obscurity. Even the outlines of the steamship became invisible. No great stacks bellowing brown smoke upward, no broad upper decks where people laughed and loitered, not even rails and bulwarks could any longer be seen. We were as though on a mysterious phantom ship slipping alone and shapeless through some strange, dim realm of greyness and gloom. Our fellow travellers became vague, ghostly shadows, dark as they loomed near us, thin and pale as they vanished into distance.

Such a sunless dwelling place called for silence; but there was no silence. The wails of frightened children, lost in the thick, enfolding cloud, quavered and echoed through the motionless air. Shouts and curses and nervous laughter came from indistinct, hulking, colliding forms as they strove to find their way toward hidden doors and stairways or to discover those who had once belonged to them. The melancholy blast of the ship's foghorn was clamorous and constant.

An equally enveloping nameless dread seemed to be enclosing us all. This strange, smothering mist had in some indefinable way wrought a peculiar transformation in the very nature of all those embarked upon our common pilgrimage. A multitude of human beings, few of whom had enlisted sympathy or inspired respect among their companions, had suddenly become a host of helpless and forsaken souls, each uttering his own singular burden of sorrow.

In the afternoon, when the impenetrable haze still showed no signs of lightening and the boards of the deck were becoming wet and slippery, my father groped his way among the throngs of restless ghosts to help the rabbi to his berth below. When they emerged together from the mist and passed us huddled around my mother in a damp, silent half circle, we heard the old man say:

"It's like the darkness of Sheol or the black groves of Avernus; but there must be a golden branch among the shadows."

"What did he mean?" Ansie asked. "What's a golden branch among the shadows?"

"It's a talisman," my mother said. "It's a promise that all will come out right in the end."

## 10

Our motley collection of voyagers was curiously grave and silent during our last evening on the *Empress of Austria*. Perhaps the wraiths of fog, drifting below and dimming the lights in the dining-room, sobered them; perhaps their best clothes which all had donned for landing on the morrow made them self-conscious and uncommunicative; perhaps the nearness of an unknown land smote upon them with unanswerable questions and forebodings. From a noisy assemblage, bent on raucousness and crude manners, blatancy and clangor, they had become a company of anxious, homesick strangers. The many children, sensing the mood of their parents, were subdued, wondering, and diffident. Even the most voluble among the younger men and women said little, ate hastily, and left the long, untidy tables early to deal with the packing of their multifarious goods and chattels.

Mr. Plimsoll for the first time either forgot or forbore to ask a blessing for us all upon our food. Was he perchance finding his rampant faith wobbling, incompetent to deal with the practical necessities of the future? Or had he, perhaps, during that baffling, mist-hung day caught a fleeting glimpse of the sorrows of men, erasing for the moment, even in his taut and imprisoned mind, their many sins, their unrepentance, and their danger? His family surrounded him, restless within themselves, dumb, frightened. The quiver in Mrs. Plimsoll's cheek increased. For the first time we felt sorry for them all, not alone for Moses.

When we left our table, my father stopped for a moment at theirs.

"I want to wish you well, sir," he said to Mr. Plimsoll.

For an instant Mr. Plimsoll was too astounded to reply. One could see his amazement mounting within his old frock coat, upon which Mrs. Plimsoll had somehow managed to replace the missing buttons, until it reached his narrow, troubled eyes. Then he managed to rise from his chair above the clutter of the table. He extended his bony hand.

"And you, too . . . sir," he said to my father.

We went early to our cabins. Dank and dim as they were, they seemed a shelter from the still fog-enveloped deck or from our one inadequate, redolent common room. Moreover, my mother had our packing to do. She made Mary and me undress and climb into our narrow upper bunks under the low ceiling in order to be out of her way while, moving

from my father's cabin to ours, she attempted to stow away
our belongings in our many bags and boxes. She banished
my father to the deck, but she allowed Ansie to collect
his own belongings in the bag which Katie had made for
him, warning him only to keep strictly out of her sight if
he knew what was good for him.

Mary and I lay quiet in our bunks. I had the feeling
that she was even more unhappy and homesick than I. The
foghorn still sounded its long, mournful hootings, like the
owls, I thought, in the spinney behind the parsonage or like
the bellowings of the cattle, moving along the high-banked
Suffolk roads toward the market at Bury St. Edmunds. Bury
was at once a soothing and a sad memory. When, I wondered, should we ever go to Bury, my father and I eager
for the abbey ruins, my mother, Mary, and Ansie wishing
for Flatford Mill or for Ely, where at the Lamb Inn we
always had tea and sugar cakes? On a tiny shelf above my
bunk I had placed a few of my treasures. The little blue
shoe was there, and I had a sudden impulse to hold it close
in my hand. It was, I thought, my talisman, my golden
branch among the shadows, my promise that all would come
out right in the end.

I must have dropped off to sleep early in spite of my
sad thoughts, for when I awoke the cabin was dark. Only
the light from the curtained doorway showed a huge pile of
luggage, strapped and ready, piled high on the extra lower
berth. The ship seemed still. There was no racketing about
as there had been on all the other nights. I could hear Mary
and my mother whispering together below me; and I realized
that Mary was in my mother's berth and that she was crying.
I heard her ask: "Why does it all have to be so hateful and
horrid?" and my mother say, "It's not really hateful and
horrid. It's only new and strange. It will all be different

when we have a home again."

"It won't be like our old home," Mary said.

"Yes, it will. We'll make it just the same, perhaps even better."

"How do you know we will? Maybe everyone is bad and sinful just as Asenath Plimsoll said. Maybe God punishes us all. How do we know He doesn't?"

"It's hard to know much of anything," my mother said. "I daresay we know just because your father knows so well." She laughed in the darkness. "Just think what it would be for us all if father were like Mr. Plimsoll!"

Mary managed a broken little laugh then, and I knew that things were better. After a few minutes I heard my mother say:

"Up you go, darling, for the very last night. In no time at all now we'll be having our own tea in our own new home and snuggling down in civilized beds."

We all three lay still, waiting for sleep and for the morning when, the steward had said, we should very early pass by the Statue of Liberty. I still held the tiny blue shoe in my hand.

Then all at once we heard Ansie singing. Perhaps he was making a kind of atonement for all his nagging and annoying questions or for his refusal to sing when my mother had asked him; or perhaps my father, for once discouraged and doubtful, had suggested it to him. Whatever the reason, his voice sounded through the open cabin doors and the thin partition just as it had sounded so many times before:

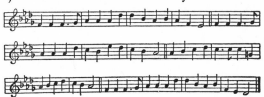

> Through the night of doubt and sorrow
>   Onward goes the pilgrim band,
> Singing songs of expectation,
>   Marching to the promised land.
> Clear before us through the darkness
>   Gleams and burns the guiding light:
> Brother clasps the hand of brother,
>   Stepping fearless through the night.

When he had finished, we all felt immeasurably more happy and safe. I knew that to Mary things did not seem quite so hateful and horrid and that my mother's stifled snifflings just below me came not from sadness, but from pride and pleasure.

Before we had finally drifted off to sleep, my father and Ansie drew our curtain suddenly aside, standing there together in relief against the light, their hair rumpled, their faces smiling.

"We thought we'd best tell the leader of this pilgrim band that the fog is lifting," my father said.

"And we pass the Statue of Liberty at six tomorrow," Ansie added.

"I haven't the faintest interest in that wretched statue," my mother said. "You boys get straight to bed."

FOUR · *Pepperell, Maine*

WHEN I look back beyond these many years to our journey northward to Pepperell, I am still overcome by those first unimaginable wonders of a new land which fifty years of life in America have not been able to lessen or to dim. There were the initial astonishments of things themselves, their number, their variety, above all their length and breadth and height, their very bulk and magnitude. We were like Gulliver in Brobdingnag.

Huge, sweating black men bore our extra pieces of luggage through a mammoth, echoing station, not trundling them on a barrow, but burdened beneath them, on their shoulders, under their arms, in their hands. The locomotive which drew our incredibly high train was a shrieking monster, spouting smoke and flame, capable of consuming three of our tiny English steam engines which in comparison now seemed but snivelling weaklings. The great open coach in which we rode appalled my mother, accustomed as she was to the discreet enclosure of a railway carriage where, at most, eight silent passengers sat behind their newspapers. This long double line of dusty red-plush seats subjected us all to the curious scrutiny of a hundred pairs of eyes.

"You never told us American trains were like this," she said accusingly to my father.

"I didn't know myself," he answered, like some small

boy protesting at once both ignorance and innocence.

The magnitude and extent of the countryside itself amazed us once we had left the crowded confines of New York. Even the relative compactness of New England, when contrasted with western states unknown to us, seemed inconceivably vast and various to our alien eyes. The bright, sharply defined landscape constantly changed like some kaleidoscope. White villages slipped by, their houses made of wood instead of brick or plaster; white churches with steeples and gilded weather vanes; generous red or white barns, sometimes oddly attached to the houses by other white buildings, sometimes standing by themselves. We looked in vain for thatch.

"Do you think we shall have a barn in Pepperell?" Ansie asked. "I hope it will be red."

"Very likely," my father said. "Everyone here seems to have a barn."

He sat staring out the dirty window, which he had discovered to his discomfiture could not be raised or lowered by a strap. He was like a child who all the year has been looking forward to a rare orange in the toe of his Christmas stocking and, instead, has been overwhelmed by possessions unexpected and innumerable. Occasionally he reluctantly interrupted his gazing to consult a thick paper folder which named the cities and towns through which we were to pass.

"Does this train stop at a place called Concord?" he inquired of the burly, blue-clad conductor, who punched our long tickets.

"Which Concord?" the conductor asked. "There's one in Massachusetts, and there's another in New Hampshire."

"The one nearer Boston," my father said.

"They're neither of them on this run," the conductor said. He was clearly worried over us all. "You haven't made a mistake, have you? You wan't planning to go to Concord?"

"No," my father said. "At least not now. It's only that I have a friend who once lived there."

We went past fields, high fields, low rolling fields, ploughed fields given to garden produce, tall stalks of corn, harvested grain, a thousand fields beneath the blazing early September sun. No familiar hedges separated one from another, but, instead, fences of grey, interlocking logs or walls of piled grey stones. Sometimes brilliant red berries flamed against the stones. Now and then in a thicket a tree or a bush was crimson. The whole land, fields and thickets, valleys and hillsides, even the hollows beside the railroad tracks, were bordered or filled by the brilliant yellow plumes of some plant strange to us. Ansie's curiosity over all this prodigal splendour could not be curbed.

"Could you tell me what the yellow flowers are?" he asked a boy on one of his many trips to the water tank at the end of the car.

"Goldenrod," the boy said. "Ain't you ever seen goldenrod before? It's all over the place, come fall."

"It's goldenrod," Ansie said proudly, returning to his seat. "And the white and purple Michaelmas daisies, they call asters here. What's fall, father?"

"Fall?" asked my father. "Fall? Oh, I remember now. It's autumn. It's the American word for autumn. It means the falling of the year."

More falls of a different sort, falls of tumultuous water sliding over high dams by busy mills and factories. Waterfalls in the wide courses of rivers, which we thundered across on bridges or followed for miles past woods and farmlands. Tiny falls and swirling eddies in countless swift streams.

"American rivers are not much like the Little Ouse or the Stour," Mary said. Or the Lark, I thought, slipping beneath the abbot's ancient bridge, the drooping willows, and the limes at Bury.

"Many of these rivers have beautiful names," my father said. "Remember how we read about them in the encyclopedia? *Piscataqua, Androscoggin, Penobscot,* and *Kennebec?* I wish now I had found out their meanings in the Indian tongues, but I daresay we can learn those presently. Thoreau visited the Penobscot River about fifty years ago. He tells all about it in a book called *The Maine Woods.*"

Pastures with rough outcroppings of ledges and grey boulders, pastures which seemed always to be climbing hills and then losing themselves in the transparent distance of the clear hot sky. Cattle edging their way among the rocks, staring stupidly at the train, or galloping off in panic at our uproar and our billowing smoke.

"There don't seem to be many sheep in New England," my father said.

Forests of dark trees, pines and firs and larches, and others strange to us. At times we hurtled through miles of such forests, thin white birches on their borders, a thick tangle of interlacing green beyond.

"It's easy to see why most houses in this country are made of wood," my mother said.

Numberless lakes and smaller ponds, reflecting the blue of the sky, sparkling beneath the sun. Small boats with fishermen as the day waned, their long poles sharp against the western light, their oars dipping in the cool water.

On the short coastline of New Hampshire, suddenly the sea with low islands far in the distance.

"The Isles of Shoals," the conductor said.

"I can't imagine anything shoal in this country," my mother said, wiping the soot and dust for the hundredth time from her streaming face.

"What's shoal?" Ansie asked.

"Shallow," my mother said.

Again the sea in Maine, waves rolling in to burst in white surf on long sandy beaches, the sails of ships against a far horizon, a white lighthouse on a rocky promontory. Miles of marshes with green and yellow grasses and thick reeds with sharp tops like spikes of brown felt. Tidal inlets making their way over pale, wrinkled mud, which was set with thousands of tiny blue and white shells. Hundreds of sea gulls, swooping in great circles through the air, resting on their wide grey wings, perching on poles rising here and there from the ooze, tracking through the slime and shallow water in search of food.

"The fens in the old days must have been much like these marshes," my father said.

Wider rivers, larger lakes, more white villages, fewer towns and cities, higher, rockier pastures, more small rushing streams, longer stretches of woodland. And always, until the night fell, the illimitable height and width of the sky, blue, cloudless, shimmering, looking even from the grimy windows of our coach as though it were boundless, far beyond the reach of human eyes, so vast that beneath it one felt unprotected and alone.

When in the darkness we changed trains for the last lap of our journey, this immensity of our new sky smote yet more intensely upon us. The sharp circumference, the unimpeded outlines of the moon, the brilliance of the constellations, the infinite number of the stars made us, as we gazed upward through the now cold air, incredulous, stunned. Here no low-hung clouds, no wandering wraiths of mist and fog, brought the moon closer to the earth or set the few visible stars almost on the tops of church towers or glittering among the very branches of the trees.

## 2

No foreigner coming to our shores, provided that his tastes are rural rather than urban, ever forgets or, indeed, quite recovers from his first experience of an American autumn. Especially is this true of the English countryman in whom is bred from infancy a passion for the land, for open air, interminable walks, a close and profound association with meadows and streams, animal life, trees, clouds, mist, rain, and soft sunlight. Autumn in England is lovely, to be sure—the green of summer, less vivid but lingering; the pale yellow of beeches and elms; the bronze of oaks; days likely to be windless; early twilights shadowy and still. Yet there the colouring, for the most part, is subdued and sombre: pale blues and greys of close skies, the fading brown of the hay ricks, the tans of cropped downs, the rusts of ploughed earth, the indifferent hues of the stubble fields. There is no blazonry on English hills; no ranks of trees in massed scarlet, gold, orange, and purple; no long succession of brilliant, diaphanous days; no New Jerusalem on every mean roadside.

Pepperell in September and throughout October overwhelmed us all. Its almost perfect half-moon of a harbour was enclosed by two high points of land, heavily wooded above their red cliffs with fir and spruce; but this growth was so interspersed with birch and beech trees that its darkness was fired by tongues of yellow flame. The rough fields above the rocky shore were tangled with red sumac and dense clusters of goldenrod, which glowed more brightly after the early light frosts. Behind the white houses along the main country road tumbled the pastures, purple, rose, and scarlet from great patches of blueberry, rising northward toward the hills which were clothed in like pageantry. In every marshy hollow the swamp maples were crimson; over every stone wall the red woodbine clambered; vast flocks of golden-winged birds hovered above the clumps of mountain ash, robbing them of their orange berries. The constant sun irradiated all, bathing the land with light, gleaming upon the full tide, heightening colours, lengthening shadows, silvering the wings of the gulls. As October ripened and waned, the sparkling air was filled with drifting leaves which, rustling downward, lay in road-side hollows and upon village lawns like open mines of gold and jewels. In the early evening after their work men raked these into piles for burning; and as the blue smoke curled upward and the piles were turned and scattered, the frail golden threads of ribs and stems glowed for a brief instant before they were consumed.

Autumn here in this new land had its sounds as well as its colours, sounds accentuated by the stillness and thinness of the atmosphere. The resonant trill and hum of millions of unseen insects filled the air by night as well as by day, not plaintive and intermittent like that of the hedge crickets at home, but shrill, high, buoyant, continuous. It was easy when walking among trees to hear the quick snap of leaves severed from boughs and twigs to float downward. Migrating birds in countless thousands flew overhead at dawn, twittering and crying, or, pausing for a brief space on their flight southward, chirped or sang all day as they foraged and scratched among the roadside growths. The calling of the gulls was clamorous; and the crazy laughter of the loons was repeated in high, tremulous echoes. Even the heavy, muffled sounds of labour, the thudding of mallets, the thumping of boards, the rattling of chains became more thin and clear as they resounded shoreward from the piers and slips where men worked at building small fishing or pleasure craft or from the open harbour when the fishing boats dropped their anchors.

3

My father in all this radiance of colour, this harmony of sound, now moved from strength to strength like those high-hearted pilgrims in the Psalm. Whatever unexpressed misgivings may have puzzled and tormented him as we crossed the Atlantic faded into nothingness. Hope rose again within him, strong and unassailable, that larger, all-encompassing hope inclusive of faith. The convictions and affirmations which since early manhood had shaped his thoughts and determined his manner of life became again steadfast and unshaken. Men were at heart again generous and kind, aware of their parts in the drama of existence, able and eager to play them nobly and well. Humanity moved ever onward, out of evil into good, out of ignorance and indifference toward wisdom and desire, sensible, however dimly, of the purposes of God. Without humanity thus created and endowed by Him, God could have no meaning, perhaps even no Being. All these thoughts, flooding his mind like a returning tide, seemed in this new freedom, under this high, limitless sky and among these bright hills, more invulnerable than they had ever been; and my mother, seeing him again both resilient and sure, confident, expectant, and content, looked herself more serene and happy than she had looked since we left Saintsbury, though I felt certain that she was more homesick than any of us for the old ways of England.

The meagre portion of humanity exemplified by the town, or perhaps more accurately the village of Pepperell, Maine, satisfied and reassured my father from the beginning of our sojourn. He felt secure and at home among men who laboured with their hands, believing as he did with the Apocryphal philosopher and poet that they, in truth, upheld "the fabric of the world." His impatient ardour to learn everything at once about his new environment amounted almost to voracity. He even seemed, to my mother's amusement, to be abandoning at least for the time being his Suffolk slowness and deliberation. He spent hours upon the small docks and wharves, asking eager questions about the building of boats, lending a hand at ordinary tasks. The intricate mysteries of weir-setting excited him as did the simpler framing of lobster traps and the constant mending of nets, spread out to dry upon the beach in the sun or on the grassy slopes above. He acquainted himself as well with the upland farming carried on not too prosperously above a rugged coastline given over largely to the various pursuits of seafaring. He sadly missed the presence of sheep and walked miles in order to discover a few on some distant hills. As to a lambing meadow, no one among either farmers or fishermen had ever so much as heard of such a phenomenon, which he took vast pleasure in describing to them.

He was almost equally engrossed in lesser matters: Mary's entrance into the academy, which was a red-brick building with a white-columned porch on a high hill above the harbour; Ansie's and mine into the grammar school, a battered wooden structure far less pretentious than the academy, on the country road a mile beyond the village centre; Ansie's new lore of baseball, and of football scrimmages, kicks, and passes. After tea, which we enjoyed a bit surreptitiously since it did not seem to be the general custom of the country, and before supper, Ansie initiated him into the batting of tosses in the field behind our house, both of them laughing at his good-humoured awkwardness, his almost complete ineptitude. The differences in the uses of words amused and charmed him. We children garnered these from our early days at school and sprang them upon him and my mother at meals.

"A boy at school ate too many crabapples and was terribly sick to his stomach," Ansie said.

My mother looked horrified.

"Ansie!" she said. "Kindly watch your language."

"I am," Ansie said. "They don't say just *sick* here. They say *to your stomach* as well. *Stomach* is a good American word. I wish I could say it to Katie or the vicar, or best of all, to Grandfather Oldroyd."

"They say *bug*, too," Mary contributed with a slight reminiscent shudder. "Bugs here are any insects at all, not just—you know what—as at home."

"Well, why not?" my father said. "Very graphic, I'm sure."

My mother looked unconvinced about the helpful vividness of *stomach* and *bug*, both unmentionable in decent English circles; but she added to our linguistic researches by telling how she had that day almost failed to buy a spool of thread in a village shop because she had asked for a *reel of cotton*.

"Incidentally, my dear," my father said, "you don't say *shop* here. *Shops* are *stores*, just as *cupboards* are *closets*, and *sweets* are *candy*, and *biscuits* are *crackers*, and *taps* are *faucets*."

He looked so pleased with himself that we forbore to tell him that we had discovered all these differences weeks ago.

4

Ansie got his red barn in Pepperell. It was not attached to the house as were several of our neighbours' barns, but instead stood well beyond it to the right behind our driveway and in front of our field. It had a spacious opening between two great doors to receive racks laden with hay in July, and, higher up, a smaller door for the pitching and stacking of the hay in its loft above the lower floor. On this lower floor there was room for three stalls, a grain bin, and an open space for carts and carriages. It was a generous barn, wide and relatively low, with a most agreeable roof slope. It looked snug and hospitable with its fresh red paint in honour of my father's arrival. Ansie loved it at sight, and, indeed, we all felt fortunate in its possession. In material comforts we were clearly far better cared for than the families of most Maine country parsons.

The barn and the parsonage itself had been bequeathed some ten years earlier to the church by a wifeless and child-less Methodist deacon or elder. We were never quite sure of his exact identity, though we were grateful heirs to his bounty. "Whatever do you call these sidesmen, or wardens, or clerks in this odd church of yours?" my mother used to ask my father; but in spite of her frequent irritation over Methodism in general, she shared our pleasure in our new establishment. The parsonage was white with green shutters —or blinds, as we learned to say. Its rooms were large and sunny, and its furnishings, also bequeathed by the deacon or elder, were singularly free from eyesores like the Royal Family and Susannah Wesley. The Wesleys seemed, indeed, not to figure prominently in American Methodism, at least not in nomenclature. My father here in Pepperell was the Methodist minister, never the Wesleyan parson as at home.

Our lands, too, were generous. Behind the house and barn was a large, open field, which extended toward an equally large pasture, which in turn gave place to ample acreage of woodland. The field and the pasture were ours to use as we liked. Within a fortnight my father had bought a cow, an amiable, docile creature apparently of mixed parentage, since her dull-red sides, blotched liberally with white, marked no discernible inheritance. Her name was Lilla. At first we allowed her to roam in the field and feed well on the second growth of grass; but once my father discovered that Maine fields were sacred to hay and that pastures were the scantier portion of Maine cows, he moved her. He was excited daily over this unexpected mingling of small farming with his ministerial duties. His youth was returning, he said; but it would never be wholly with him again until he had a few sheep cropping around the pasture rocks with Lilla.

One of his parishioners, neither a deacon nor an elder, but merely the superintendent of the Sunday school, insisted on the loan of a horse since the nature of our parish in this land of vast distances demanded frequent drives into the outlying countryside. My father, overcome by such benevolence which, he said, exemplified all the Old Testament commands toward strangers together with half the New Testament parables, gladly welcomed an elderly yet adequate white mare named Snow White, complete with harness and a light carriage. With Lilla in one stall of our red barn and Snow White in another, he awaited only his sheep in our pasture for entire contentment.

My mother sorely missed a garden. In Maine there seemed to be no enclosures either behind or at one side of the houses and given to flowers, shrubs, and privacy. Instead, there were only neat lawns, punctuated by a few circular flower beds. A garden here meant a sizable plot of earth devoted to vegetables only and usually cut out from a field at close proximity to a house. Such was ours. We did have an orchard, however, which flanked our barn and nurtured a dozen hardy apple trees well laden with fruit. Ansie and I gathered the apples with great pride and stored them in barrels in our cool, dry cellar, also an innovation to us all.

5

The final bequest of the deacon or elder had been his housekeeper, who had not only cared for him during his declining years but for three Methodist preachers and their families preceding us. Her name was Mrs. Baxter. She was a permanent fixture of the parsonage, as much a part of it as a floor board, or the sitting-room fireplace, or its front door, or the invisible joists and timbers which framed it. She was not so much essential and necessary as she was inherent, intrinsic, and intact.

She was a widow of late middle age, in appearance solid rather than actually stout. She had very red cheeks, firm and smooth like Peggotty's in *David Copperfield*, discerning brown eyes, and steel-grey hair, so tautly drawn back from her forehead and ears into a tight pug at the exact centre of the back of her head that not one errant spear had any hope of escape or even momentary release. Her standards of exactness and perfection seemed almost awful to my mother, after Katie's easy, casual ways. Mrs. Baxter was by both conviction and inclination an enemy to anything casual. She was totally unable to understand those wholesome periods of indifference to mere detail which promise freedom and refreshment. Details were her sacraments. She yielded up her being with complete devotion to her spotless floors, her dustless tables and chairs, her folded, snowy sheets, her loaves of fragrant bread; and only after she and they had experienced full communion was she fully satisfied.

Inured as she had been for a decade to ministerial incumbents and their families, she had grown both sharp and sagacious in her summing up of human personality; and yet I am sure that our collective demands upon her discernment were costly at the beginning of our life together. My father was quite beyond her ken so far as Methodist parsons were known to her. She was puzzled by his courtesy and his quiet, slow ways. His absorbing pleasure and curiosity in his new parish at first startled and then delighted her. She was unused to such enthusiasm, such hourly interest and enlivenment. She was unused also to his apparent freedom from those niggling domestic anxieties which she had thought inescapable in the life of any rural parson. The quality which astonished her most, however, was his utter lack of domination both over his family and toward all church matters. This singular respect for the thoughts of others, even for those of us children and for her own (for he often came to her for information and advice), aroused at times uneasy speculations in her mind, first as to the manner of man he actually was and then as to whether or not he would be valued by his practical, hardheaded congregation. Perhaps these half-formed misgivings hastened her allegiance to him and prepared the way for what finally became her almost fierce protectiveness.

She was understandably chary toward my mother, cautious, perhaps at the start more than a little suspicious. The ministers' wives whom she had known were sobered and burdened by countless cares, borne nobly for the sake of their husbands. They had obviously expected no lives of their own. My mother's cares rested lightly upon her, or at all events gave that impression; she apparently had more life of her own than she could well manage and intended to preserve and enjoy it; and her treatment of my father often included a flippancy outside the range of Mrs. Baxter's imagination or of her former association with loyal Methodist helpmates. Nevertheless, although all her robust principles governing a woman's responsibility to her husband and home were constantly shattered by my mother, the fact that she was willing and eager to entrust Mrs. Baxter with the entire running of the household was not without its compensations. She grew slowly used to my mother's gay disregard of what to her were weighty decisions. Each morning they held a colloquy, revealing to them both, in the kitchen:

"What did you plan for supper, Mrs. Tillyard?"

"I didn't plan a thing. You always know. Do I need to plan?"

"Well, most women do around here. Perhaps they don't in England."

"Oh, I'm sure they do—that is, the really good ones."

"What I mean is, the other preachers' wives always did."

"I'm afraid I'm an utter failure as a preacher's wife, Mrs. Baxter, but possibly I might improve with time."

"I never said you was a failure. I only asked about supper."

"What is there at hand?"

"Well, there's baked beans to warm over, and applesauce, and I'd thought of some red-flannel hash as well."

"Do Maine people exist entirely on beans? Beans have been our 'meat day and night,' as the Psalmist says, ever since we came."

Mrs. Baxter winced perceptibly at this airy reference to the Psalms as well as at my mother's equally airy disposal of beans.

"Well, beans are cheap and filling, and I never want to throw away good nourishing food. Has the minister considered buying a pig? Most families around here keep a pig. There's a natural place under the barn for one, and pigs always pay their way, come time for killing. Reverend Perkins had two, and they kept us going all last winter in hams and pork and bacon, to say nothing of hogshead cheese, and the eating up of all the table scraps."

"Kindly forget a pig, Mrs. Baxter, for the moment. Just now my husband thinks of nothing but sheep."

"Sheep don't flourish in this part of Maine. Leastwise, almost no one keeps them. They get ticks."

"I don't know what ticks are, but tell him they're frightfully dangerous to human beings. Please don't forget."

"Where is he this fine morning?"

"He's fishing in the stream behind the pasture."

"Brook, we say here."

"Brook, then."

"Is he likely to bring home a string of trout in time for me to clean and fry them? They're always tasty and a real treat."

"Not a chance in the world. He took a book with him."

"Don't he ever go anywhere without a book?"

"Never, I'm afraid."

"Oh. Well, if you're sick and tired of beans, there's plenty of stuff for a nice red-flannel hash."

"Whatever do you mean by red-flannel hash? It sounds like a poultice."

"Good beets and potatoes and some leftover bits of meat. We Methodists favour it for church suppers, but the Baptists stick to beans and brown bread."

"I see. Red-flannel hash will do superbly. The children will have something new to write home about."

"You haven't forgot that you entertain the Ladies' League tomorrow afternoon, have you?"

"Alas, no! I wish I could. Whatever do we feed them?"

"I'd planned on cupcakes, plain and chocolate both. With tea, I suppose."

"Admirable! I'll make the tea. At least I know how to do that."

"You English drink a powerful lot of tea. Are you sure it's good for the children? Folks around here always think that too much tea is—well, binding to the bowels."

"It's never bound me. I've drunk it from six months old on, and I don't know anything that's made me feel more free. I hope I have a good cup or two on my deathbed."

Mrs. Baxter winced again at this irreverent mention of a solemn hour.

"The ladies really prefer coffee, but the cream's slack just now. The cow's not giving down too well. I tell your husband she's skittish from being in a new place. She'll calm down."

"I'm skittish, too, and I'm afraid I won't calm down. I'm going for a walk. I ought to stay inside and darn socks and write letters and help you in a dozen ways. But I can't—not with all this amazing colour."

"It *is* nice," Mrs. Baxter said, glancing through her clean and shining windows. "But I've seen it so often that I suppose I just take it for granted."

"Don't take anything for granted!" my mother called back from the open doorway. "It's fatal, and I mean just that. Fatal, Mrs. Baxter!"

Probably our new housekeeper took us children for granted far more easily than she was able to take our parents, who, although neither exerted any mastery over her, were her overseers, not to mention the added fact that my father was the present leader and custodian of her sturdy religious adherence. From the hour of our arrival Mary won her respect because of her tidy ways. Ansie and I, whom she looked upon as an inseparable team since we did most things together except when other boys claimed Ansie's time and interest, clambered more slowly into her good graces through our early dependence upon her in the matter of food. When we hurried home from school in the late afternoon, we always burst in the side door upon her faultless kitchen. For the first few days we hardly knew whether to be pleased or terrified to see her sitting there, by the window, in her red rocker, herself scrubbed like her yellow floor boards, her skirts covered by a starched white apron, her hands always busy at knitting or crochet, her eyes on the clock on the shelf above the sink, her nose carefully assessing her oven or her polished stewing pans, her hair in strict precision. But once she began putting out cookies and milk for us of her own free will without our so much as hinting at hunger, we knew that the game was won.

I understood from the beginning that she favoured Ansie over me just as all women, I was discovering, really preferred boys to girls, just as the faces of mothers were always more brightly illumined at the sight of sons rather than of daughters. Even Mrs. Baxter's firm red cheeks creased with pleasure whenever Ansie asked her for an extra cooky or a bit of twine, or sniffed expectantly around her gleaming stove. She proved a help to him with his arithmetic, which he fell into the habit of doing at her kitchen table in the evenings.

"Sorry, father," he would say, when we had all gathered in the sitting-room after supper, "but I'm afraid Mrs. Baxter is a bit better than you are at these queer problems. Do you mind awfully if I ask her?"

My mother always answered him before my father had gotten around to do so.

"Not in the least," she said. "Delighted, in fact. And don't forget to ask her—most politely, mind you—for our tea tray at nine o'clock. You can bring it in yourself."

Of Mrs. Baxter's further past we knew nothing, since, like all English people, we were shy of personal questions, and she did not evince any eagerness to enlighten us. She seemed to have been eternally involved with Methodist preachers. Reverend Hinckley, Reverend Wilson, Reverend Perkins, our forerunners in the parsonage, were but three among the many whom she had known and without doubt rigorously nurtured even though not under the inherited rooftree. Mr. Baxter had evidently died at a fairly early age. What his life had been like with Mrs. Baxter was, to my mother at least, a subject of amused conjecture.

6

My father's immediate pleasure in Pepperell extended to his church. This stood perhaps a quarter of a mile westward from the parsonage and on the opposite side of the rising country road. It was a dignified, even stately white church of the type often seen in old New England villages. It had four rounded white pillars at the entrance, a graceful steeple, green shutters, and high, clear windows, three on either side, through which the sunlight fell across its high-backed white pews. Behind it woods rose, green and still, and it was flanked by open fields. In every respect it was a church rather than a chapel.

From his researches into the ecclesiastical history of eastern Maine my father learned that the church had originally been of the Congregational denomination like the great majority of those Maine coast churches founded in the late eighteenth and early nineteenth centuries by stout Puritans from Massachusetts, of which Maine itself had been a northern province until 1820, when it became a state. He also gathered that among the various Protestant sects in Maine and, for that matter, throughout New England the Congregationalists from the time of the earliest settlements had held first place in social as well as in religious esteem. The Methodists and Baptists, who had appeared later in most communities and largely by way of itinerant or of lay missionaries, were in a distinctly subordinate position from the start and also of relatively inferior variety in matters of learning and in terms of cultural background.

Just where the descendants of the Congregational founders of our parish now were, whether their zeal had diminished or whether they had left Pepperell for wider and more gracious fields of activity, was never quite clear. If any of them remained among us, they were not voluble concerning their former doctrinal adherence or apparently dissatisfied with their present lot. Community memories, and loyalties as well, are destined, however sadly, to grow dim and uncertain during half a century. All that my father seemed able to discover was that the Methodists had superseded the Congregationalists some fifty years previously and most wisely had taken over their really beautiful church. And this wisdom was more strongly borne in upon him as he grew further acquainted with examples of purely Methodist architecture in neighbouring coast towns and villages.

The only other church in Pepperell besides our own was the Baptist church; and it was always called the Baptist meetinghouse instead of the Baptist church. Since this difference in terms was at first confusing to my father, who was aware of no visible social contrast between the two congregations and in his new freedom would have deplored any such distinction, he tried to discover the source of its widespread usage. There was none, the Baptist minister told him, except that of custom. For some reason, doubtless as unimportant as it was obscure, the Baptists favoured this name for their rather graceless, nondescript brown-shingled building which stood nearer the centre of the village than did ours. In quantity they were much the same as we; in quality, likewise. Indeed, it was difficult to detect any outstanding dissimilarities between our respective congregations except for the practice of immersion of converts in the cold water of the harbour which the Baptists strictly observed whatever the season, and, as my mother somewhat lightly added, their predilection for baked beans instead of red-flannel hash for their frequent church suppers. In general we typified two inconsequential country parishes, strongly Protestant by inheritance rather than by informed intelligence, uninclined to question matters of either doctrine or observance, each devoted by habit and tradition rather than by studied conviction to its own adherence, both struggling to obtain the means for a separate and decent existence, mildly competitive in social affairs and in public performances, covetous of new recruits only once a year. Our counterparts might have been found in a thousand other rural communities, similarly situated and as meagrely endowed.

Mr. Kimball was the Baptist minister, and like all other ministers in our region he was called Reverend Kimball, a title which was never granted any helpful article to lend it grace or dignity. He was an elderly man and had held his charge for years, since the Baptists, unlike the Methodists, tended toward permanence in the tenure of their pastors rather than toward frequent change. The most charitable estimate of him could not accord him more than a modicum of learning or any deep desire for increasing it. His theology was rigid and unyielding; but its terrors did not seem to cause him any personal alarm though he often gave fervent utterances to them from his pulpit. He was kind and cordial. In his hours free from pastoral duties, which he performed diligently and well, he dug clams, picked berries, and fished for flounders on the high tides in order to provide for his own table and, therefore, eke out his slender salary. Not infrequently he brought us some of the fruits of these avocations. His wife was a busy, tired, angular woman, who was famous locally for her unsurpassed cooking, for her good works, and for her cheerless willingness to perform all manner of parish duties unpalatable to others.

My father and Reverend Kimball did not discover many interests in common. Mr. Kimball's theology was so tightly done up and put away that it was difficult of easy access, unlike that of the vicar at home—which was probably, on the whole, fortunate. He did not care much for books in general, and he recognized no past beyond that of Pepperell and his long stay there. There were no discernible antiquities in Maine; my father preferred trout to flounder fishing; and Mr. Kimball, like most of the people in Pepperell, neither rode a bicycle nor was interested in ranging the countryside to observe its natural gifts. Nevertheless, they got on well together, forbearing with one another after the good advice of St. Paul; and if my father was puzzling to his fellow preacher, that in itself was not strange, my mother said, since he was still a puzzle to her after some fourteen years. Moreover, any whims or vagaries on his part which seemed odd and unorthodox to Mr. Kimball could be safely and even generously explained on the ground that he was a foreigner and, of course, as yet unacquainted with the ways of a new religious environment.

We all sadly missed the Church of England, at least in its outward and visible forms. It was difficult to accustom ourselves to the total absence of those square, grey-stone towers rising above clusters of trees and snug green church-yards, never to see in this new land Norman porches or fourteenth-century window tracery, never to smell that damp, musty, clinging smell of many centuries, never to hear peals of bells echoing for Evensong across quiet meadows and over slow streams. My mother unwillingly learned to call Anglican churches Episcopal; but the name itself was all she could possess of her early religious upbringing since only the larger towns and cities in Maine had any Episcopal church.

They were all out of her reach except by a considerable train journey even if, under the circumstances, she had felt it wise upon rare occasions to seek one out.

The Roman Catholics had no existence whatever at that time in rural Maine. They were all safely confined to the few distant industrial centres or to the French settlements well beyond the Canadian border. Needless to say, both their absence and their remoteness were sources of suspicious relief to a community so entirely Protestant as our own.

In short, the Methodist bishop had been quite accurate in what he had told my father. The State of Maine, New England, and the greater part of the United States as a whole were at the turn of the century almost entirely, in the English term, Nonconformist; and since America from the start had determined against an Established Church, from the very idea of which her founders had fled, she had no need in her religious vocabulary for the word *chapel* to designate any of her various sects.

Surely, no costs which my father was to pay for his decision to come to America were levied by his new religious environment. They could not be ascribed either to the Baptists or to his own Methodist congregation. Instead, they lurked, as such costs always lurk, within the fabric of his own nature, in that Fate which as the ancients well knew each man bears inescapably within himself "for good or for ill" and often for a mysterious and unfathomable entanglement of both.

## 7

During our first winter in Pepperell my mother occasionally observed that, in a country dedicated to the principle of nonconformity, we were in actual practice required to conform to more than a few distasteful customs. My father's

cheerful reply to that observation was, first, that any archdeacon's daughter who had been rash enough to marry a
Wesleyan parson should not at this late date be overly distressed by distasteful features in her recklessly chosen life,
and, second, that in all honesty she should use the adjective
to describe her own opinions since he was not aware of any
incurably distasteful custom in his new parish. In general,
he said, he saw as yet no reason to disagree with Alexis de
Tocqueville in his praise of the simplicity which marked
Christianity in America.

It was true that he and Mr. Kimball hardly saw eye to
eye in church manners and methods; but he had met such
divergence elsewhere and had no intention of conforming to
habits not his own. It was even more true that the first week
in January, known as the Week of Prayer and dedicated in
Pepperell, as in many other Maine villages at that time, to
the fervent recruiting by both churches of those who were
outside their folds, did cause him more than a little distress
because such covetous zeal was at variance with his own
convictions, which held that, though all men were erring,
none was irretrievably lost. Still, one week out of fifty-two
meant only an infinitesimal percentage of vexation, especially
since Mr. Kimball was only too happy to take precedence
over my father in its ardent practices. And as it beneficently
happened, a three days' snowfall at the beginning of that
trying period helped immeasurably to tranquillize its annoy-
ances.

None of us, accustomed to the brief and infrequent snow
flurries and squalls of East Anglia, had ever before imagined
such snow, coming in the midst of what was known in
Maine as an "open winter," lying five feet deep in the
valleys, softening the contours of the hills, etching the black
trunks of the trees, enclosing all in profound white silence.

My father, watching the flakes drift downward from an almost windless sky and experiencing for the first time that feeling, old to rural New Englanders but unknown to him, of the snug safety of man and beasts, was so overcome by wonder and satisfaction that my mother forgot for the time being those distasteful customs which had prompted her exasperation—the endless succession of church suppers, missionary meetings, Sunday-school parties, ladies' sewing circles, Youth Leagues, not to mention the Week of Prayer itself, which had tested all her powers of endurance and charity.

There was one custom, however, to which conformity was clearly inevitable: that of family prayers. Even my mother conceded their necessity from the start. What with Mrs. Baxter's Methodist upbringing and the examples of Reverends Hinckley, Wilson, and Perkins together with their respective families, it would have been unthinkable to dispense with them in a parsonage inherited from a Methodist deacon or elder. Mrs. Baxter had upon our arrival granted us a few prayerless days to get settled in; but it was evident that she considered this interim one of real sacrifice on our part, and we all lacked the courage to disillusion her.

Still, when I look back on family prayers in Pepperell, I do not for a moment regret our conformity in this respect. They seemed a part of the newness of everything rather than unreal and awkward as they had seemed in Saintsbury. They had many redeeming, even attractive features. Once my mother had recognized that circumstances made them imperative, she conceived several notions to make us all enjoy them. Among our temporary legacies in the parsonage sitting-room was an old square piano, a bit tuneless and plaintive, but responsive to her fingers in playing hymns. We always began prayers, which were held directly the breakfast table had been cleared, with a hymn, the first verse of which

Ansie was encouraged to sing by himself. Then, as a further innovation, each of us children in turn became responsible for the daily Bible reading, which we might select as we chose, and this honour in itself afforded us no little pride. With the imminence of school in mind, my father's prayer was always brief, quiet, and assured, as though the presence of God among us were certain rather than asked for. If there was time after his Amen, we sang another hymn, which Mrs. Baxter always wanted, clearly because of Ansie; and then a great clatter ensued as we got our books, lunchboxes, and coats together and dashed to school.

Mrs. Baxter herself added impetus and enjoyment to family prayers although I am sure she was quite unconscious of any such contribution. She came in from her kitchen always clad in a clean white apron, having as a mark of respect shed the sombre grey or black one in which she did her work. She looked solid and reliable like some tutelary guardian of stout tradition, or, as my father said, like one of those capable women in the Book of the Acts who had welcomed and cared for the earliest apostles on their missionary journeys. During the first days of our corporate devotions she seemed austere and somewhat solemn, but by perceptible degrees she grew much less severe up to the point of expectancy. She was not used to hearing the Scriptures read by children, yet she was clearly pleased by it. She loved to hear Ansie sing, and, if our choice of hymns seemed odd, since she was more accustomed to the "Throw out the Life Line" variety, she became reconciled to them, especially after my mother in a flash of inspiration confided to her that they were Ansie's favourites. Our form of worship may well have seemed singular in comparison with what the Methodist parsonage had previously housed; but that she could always safely attribute to unfamiliar English ways.

She had a large, sleek tiger cat to whom she was devoted and whose name was Chessy. One late October morning when the last of the bright leaves were floating slowly downward and the early sunlight was streaming across the sitting-room, Chessy crept into prayers. Her entrance went at first unnoticed since we were at that moment on our knees awaiting my father's Amen; but when she began to purr loudly as she entwined herself around his legs, her embarrassed mistress sprang up to extricate and banish her. My father, however, merely scooped her up in his arms and hastily closed his prayer with her draped over his shoulder. From that day on she came regularly to prayers, sitting on Mrs. Baxter's lap while she cleansed her face with delicate sweeps of her paw or entwining herself about any legs she fancied. Unorthodox as her presence seemed, at least to Mrs. Baxter, she really lent an air of delightful informality to our family group. And once my father had insisted that Mrs. Baxter take her turn at reading the lesson while one of us children held Chessy, we all found ourselves quite converted to morning prayers in Pepperell.

8

The village of Pepperell, like most other sizable villages on the long, deeply indented Maine coastline, was in the year 1901 a far different place than it had been a century or even half a century earlier. In those distant days it was a busy seafaring town, given to the building of ships designed for foreign commerce, able to boast of shipowners and merchants, men who knew the world far beyond the confines of narrow harbours. Upon the invasion of steam, which had meant the death of busy trade by sail, and the shifting of population either to the cities or to the free farming lands of the Great West, these more substantial citizens, if they had not died, had departed for more challenging and lucrative pursuits than fishing or than hammering upon small boats in a drowsy village. Perhaps among them, my father thought, had been those superior Congregationalists who had built our church; and in this supposition he was, as a matter of fact, quite correct in spite of the fact that there remained few active memories to bolster his assumption.

The invasion of summer residents which was shortly to recast the entire social and economic aspect of the coastline had not as yet reached eastern Maine or for that matter transformed many of the harbours westward. The prices soon to be offered for land on the sea frontage had not begun to amaze its owners; country roads were still muddy, dusty, frozen into ruts, or packed with snow with the change of seasons; and the rare sight of an automobile making awkward progress over them during the summer months meant not so much a prophetic warning as merely an object of curiosity to surprised onlookers and of complete terror to horses. Pepperell in common with a hundred other coastal communities was during our sojourn there experiencing not too consciously an interim between two civilizations, one decaying and all but dead, the other totally unimaginable.

In such a village the last institutions to undergo decline were probably its schools, both because educational habits are slow to change and because throughout New England, as a result of tradition, there has lingered a tenacious pride in at least the idea of all good learning. When we three children went to school in Pepperell, moving from the grammar school to the academy, we escaped by fully thirty years the relinquishment of Latin on the ground that it was too difficult for the average boy or girl and "useless" as well, just as we escaped the pounding of typewriters, the classes in home economics and "shop," that change in emphasis from the mental toward the manual, from the attainment of knowledge for its own sake to its practical application in daily affairs which for good or for ill was eventually to invade most American public school systems. Country schools in isolated districts still flourished at the turn of the century and for fully fifteen years thereafter, for in a motorless age consolidation was beyond comprehension. History was still history instead of a social science; and it had not yet occurred to anyone in authority that a stiff drilling in English grammar was not as crying a necessity as the dull study of square and cube roots in arithmetic. Even though past prosperity together with its relation to a larger world had vanished in villages such as Pepperell, there still tarried among its more thoughtful citizens an almost curious pride in the stamp which it had once placed upon the community; and nowhere was this pride so nurtured as in its schools.

Without doubt our teachers, many of whom were local products, were largely responsible for its continuance, for they had known Pepperell in its better, more dignified days. They were, for the most part, middle-aged or elderly women, who in a time of little running about had held their posts for years. They could not, I am sure, have been too richly endowed; yet, since we possessed no standards of comparison higher than Miss Caxton and the elementary school in Saintsbury, they seemed not only adequate but excellent to us. And our parents, seeing that we were strictly disciplined and encouraged toward diligence in study and recognizing themselves as strangers in a land of new educational manners, felt no intelligent cause for complaint.

I have often wondered since those days about my father's contentment, even extreme delight, in Pepperell. Not a little of it sprang, I suppose, from his own country upbringing, from those basic, ingrained satisfactions which only the countryman knows: the skies, the seasons, the soil, the weather, the friendly struggles with them all possible only from a long and sympathetic association. And here in this new land these satisfactions were increased by a human intimacy which he had not known in England. There, few if any village parsons cut and gathered in their hay, cared for a horse and cow, shared those common, fraternal experiences not alone with all members of their parishes but with the community at large. Here, although a man was in no sense a farmer in terms of his actual vocation, but instead a boat-builder or a fisherman, or perhaps a storekeeper or a house painter, or even the village doctor or lawyer, he nevertheless had a barn in which he kept his animals and a field or two from which to feed them. These alliances, together with the unsparing hospitality always characteristic of an essentially pioneer people, afforded my father that gift of freedom in social relations, that underlying harmony in human fellowship and mutual dependence which he had all his life desired.

He must surely have missed the nearness to libraries and museums which he had known in Cambridgeshire; Saxon remains and relics; the Devil's Dyke; and Bury St. Edmunds; but for the time being even these seemed to be compensated for. He had his books and, as in Saintsbury, spent long hours within them. All true scholars and thinkers are lonely; yet their loneliness is never that of the egotist, or the thwarted, or the cynical, whose sense of isolation is often embittered by resentment. The solitude which is the lot of the idealist or the visionary knows no anger or resentment, because he lives, or believes that he lives, with the imperishable rather than with the transient. My father's life, in comparison with the lives of most men, was doubtless a dream, never completely fulfilled except in hope and confidence; and yet it was a dream ill exchanged for those half-fulfillments which must incompletely content most of us during our threescore years and ten.

And lastly he could enjoy, at least at the beginning of our stay, that perverse, slightly absurd pleasure which aliens instinctively feel from finding themselves in an unfamiliar land, that sense of individualism tinged perhaps with a certain quite harmless importance. This, as all perceptive travellers and sojourners recognize, often with amusement, is in itself a remedy against the pangs of homesickness, the loss of the familiar and the well known. Strangeness and even sadness resulting from voluntary exile possess a paradoxical way of enlivening themselves. We children felt this odd contradiction in emotions during our first year in Pepperell. We enjoyed our alienism, our difference in speech and habits, the curiosity which we engendered. My father, I am sure, for he was intensely sensitive to all human experience however simple, shared this singular excitement. In his turn he enjoyed the respectful regard of his new parishioners; their pride in a minister "from far away"; their eager interest in his ways and manners. In the end these may have proved a frail support; but in the beginning they were not without their strength and their ingenuous pleasure.

### 9

None of us was ever to forget our first New England spring. Even without the events which it set in motion, it was memorable in itself, perhaps not so overwhelming as the autumn, but startling enough for those, like us, totally unused to its sudden ways, its quick release from the long, close bondage of winter. A few warm days in late April, and everything burst forth at once with none of the laggard reluctance of an English spring. The snow melted as if by magic from hills and meadows to form a thousand tiny streams and grassy pools; the tides, resentful of their narrow boundaries, inundated the lower fields and marshes; in a matter of hours, it seemed, the harbour ice, which for months had distorted the rocky shores in jagged slabs and ungainly chunks, had fled to sea. Everywhere there was the sound of running water. The catkins of the willows quickly clothed their sober grey with flecks of gold; the ferns along the road-side ditches cut the gravelly earth with their tightly rolled fronds; through a warm, soft night or two, buds swelled and burst until the treetops were mists of green in the morning sun. The woods with no warning at all, my father said, began to foam with the white of shadbush and the frail panicles of the wild cherry. The arbutus trailed its pale-pink flowers through the damp undergrowth of the pastures. Birds came back, apparently all at once like everything else. On one morning the familiar rippling of water; on the next the vivacious outpourings of song-sparrows, the whistles and grace notes of whitethroats, the falling, bell-like cadences of thrushes. The gulls came sweeping in, no longer riders of winter winds and prophetic of storms in their slow, dark circlings, but darting and swooping in the sunlight, busy on their own swift errands between sky and sea, or massed in drowsy silence on the new warmth of rocks and piers. One evening at sunset we were excited by a high clear trilling which seemed to be so completely surrounding us that to locate it was impossible.

"Peepers," Mrs. Baxter said. "When they begin all at once to sing like this, there's sure to be no more winter. It's gone for good."

Spring burst almost as suddenly into our red barn and across our pasture. Lilla's calf, expected in mid-May, came a full week earlier and in no time at all was frisking among the hummocks and the blueberry bushes. Snow White's stiff old legs limbered up so quickly that she surprised my father by her speed and litheness when he drove behind her into the hills to see how some upcountry Methodists were faring. And since they were faring well and were unable to resist this prodigal deliverance from snow and cold, these warm winds which melted their tough hearts as well as their stark uplands, they insisted on his bringing home two lambs from out of their scanty flock. Now, one of his more tangible dreams come true, my father felt, he said, like a country squire viewing his acres, appraising his livestock, even though his estates were borrowed and his suddenly multiplied creatures, except for Lilla herself, gifts of good will.

With all this blossoming and burgeoning of what had been so lately a frozen and snow-clad land, this bursting forth of new life in barn and pasture, a similar quickening reanimated the parsonage. Mrs. Baxter sang lustily over her spring house-cleaning, a work of complete redundance, my mother said, since we were almost indecently clean at all times, yet one clearly of sacramental importance to Mrs. Baxter, who, only too eager to perform her rites alone, rejoiced when my mother made herself scarce withindoors to study American birds or to gather boughs of wild crabapple for our fireplaces. My father fished the swollen streams or was initiated with us children into the delightful mysteries of catching smelts, which crammed the brooks on spring tides and which we scooped up by handfuls in the half-light of dawns. In the evenings, while the peepers called, and Mrs. Baxter communed happily in the kitchen over her starched muslin curtains, and we drank our tea, we made beautiful, chimerical plans for summer holidays in this immense country of our adoption.

"I do want us all to see the White Mountains," my father said. "And there's California. We must manage that before too many years."

## 10

On the afternoon of Memorial Day, a new commemoration to us, but one of vast importance to Pepperell and, we quickly gathered, to the whole of America, my father gave the annual oration to the village at large and to much of the surrounding countryside as well. The invitation was doubtless tendered out of courtesy to him as a stranger, or perhaps only because in a district as sparsely settled and relatively unimportant as our own, speakers were difficult to obtain; yet whatever the reason for the distinction, complimentary or merely convenient, he made such a notable address on "Lincoln in the Eyes of an Englishman" that he added many cubits not only to his own but to our combined stature. Mrs. Baxter, sitting in the front pew of the church with us all, was overcome by such astonishment and pride in my father's eloquence and bearing that any misgivings which once had troubled her as to his success as a preacher or as a person were wholly obliterated. She became, indeed, so exuberant and expansive on our triumphal walk homeward that my mother forgave her even the turmoil of spring cleaning and willingly acceded to her determination to bake a fresh cake in honour of the bishop, who would arrive later with my father for tea. For this Methodist dignitary, the selfsame one who had met my father in London, had without any warning travelled miles by train and carriage to see how his alien protégé was making out in his new parish and had fortunately chosen Memorial Day for his pastoral visitation.

The tea party, which we held in the orchard under the blossoming trees, was presumably an unconditional success, although it was not without its anxious moments. Mrs. Baxter confided to Ansie and me, after we had excused ourselves from it to scrape her frosting bowl and finish up the remains of the cake in the kitchen, that she had never in all her years in the parsonage seen its like. In the long run, she said, she saw no point in decent folks eating out-of-doors, what with caterpillars, bugs, bees, and general messiness; but in this instance my mother had without doubt been in the right. The bishop had obviously looked upon the tea party as a delightful novelty which he had enjoyed to the full; and to say that he had been impressed by my father's eloquence in his address expressed, she was convinced, not the smallest common fraction of his actual admiration. I could detect an undertone of sadness in Mrs. Baxter's generous enthusiasm, which Ansie, busy over the frosting bowl, was not so quick to sense, even though he himself was responsible for the major part of it. I knew, with an odd rush of affection for her, that she feared lest the bishop's regard might result in our leaving Pepperell before too long for some richer, more fruitful Methodist vineyard; and I carefully refrained from telling her that the conversation at the tea party had made her fears far from groundless.

I felt sure that my mother, far more acute than my father in the summing up of human personality, was not drawn toward the bishop from the start. Perhaps her hesitancy had its origin only in her early and long experience with ecclesiastical potentates; perhaps the bishop's size, his distinctly pompous language, and his somewhat complacent manner hindered her approval of him. She allowed none of these reservations, however, to alter in the slightest degree her role of hostess, which she executed with such grace and charm that the bishop easily extended his high opinion of my father to include her also. Nor was he in the least aware that her ambitions for my father and her extemely realistic view of Pepperell as a place of more than temporary sojourn for him were most assuredly playing their invisible parts under the apple trees. We children, cautioned by her in advance as to our behaviour, comported ourselves with quite the proper mixture of respect and friendliness.

"Well," said the bishop, when he was once settled in a wicker armchair, which Ansie had brought from the house for his comfort and which creaked beneath his weight, "this *is* a delightful and a rare occasion. An old English custom in a New England setting. Most refreshing to see the former ways still venerated and the latter ways so quickly and easily embraced. I trust, my dear lady, you have not found your displacement too difficult."

My mother's slight wince, caused both by his manner of address and by the notion of tea as an object of veneration, was, I am sure, perceptible only to us.

"Not in the least," she said brightly. "How could anything be difficult with everyone so kind!"

The bishop rubbed his rather fat hands together in satisfaction.

"Capital!" he cried, while the chair creaked ominously. "Balm in Gilead, if I may quote the Scriptures. Precisely what I hoped and prayed for when I saw your husband in London. A man in my position with the future of so many human souls in his keeping has onerous responsibilities, I assure you. Our Conference has never before imported a foreigner to a parish; but I felt impelled to do so in the case of Brother Tillyard. And his really superb performance this afternoon has amply justified my faith, or, I may more truly say, my vision of what he had to offer us."

My father from his seat beside Ansie on a long wooden bench looked uncomfortable. His eyes kept straying across the field to the pasture where his two new lambs were already merrily at home. Ansie broke the somewhat heavy silence.

"We all love America, sir," he said helpfully.

"Fine, my son," the bishop said. "Precisely what I have hoped to hear." He turned again to my mother. "America prides herself on her kindness to the stranger. She has a welcome for all. She throws out the life line, as it were, across the dark wave to all who want better things. She's a refuge for the homeless and the oppressed. She's a land of promise in very truth."

My sister Mary at this moment from her stool beside my mother felt called upon to make with some spirit a not too tactful remark.

"We really weren't homeless or oppressed in England," she said.

The bishop, to do him credit, was amused.

"That's right, my dear," he said. "Keep the home flag flying along with the Stars and Stripes! We're one people in very truth in spite of old differences. I often used to say to myself 'God Save the Queen' after singing our own national anthem. The fact is, I said it this very day in respect for your father as well as for that truly noble sovereign of so many years. How the world misses her venerable presence!"

Mary now felt called upon to atone for her first remark.

"But I love America, too," she said.

"So do I," I echoed from my seat beside Ansie.

My mother kept glancing nervously at her watch pinned on the front of her blue muslin dress. My father still looked at his lambs.

"Mrs. Baxter *would* make a fresh cake for you, sir," my mother said, "but I'm sure she'll be only a moment more. She was icing it just as you arrived."

"A noble woman, Mrs. Baxter," the bishop said, "and what a veritable tower of strength to a long succession of our pastoral brethren. Would that we had a hundred Mrs. Baxters in our communion of saints!"

"She's most awfully good at arithmetic, too," Ansie said. The bishop laughed again.

"Capital!" he said. "That's capital. How old are you, my boy?"

"I'm going on for twelve, sir," Ansie said, though we had really only recently passed our eleventh birthday.

"And what are you planning to do with yourself? Shall you go to Harvard or Yale or perhaps to Bowdoin in this good old State of Maine? I can see that you're cut out to be a most able scholar like your father here."

"I'm thinking of going back to England," Ansie said, "to go to my father's college in Cambridge. But that's after six more years, of course."

He looked at my mother then as though, since she had saved him from York, she could, singlehanded, secure Cambridge for him; and she smiled back at him, her whole face all at once alight, even the bishop in his creaking chair forgotten. In her smile I suddenly saw all the old familiar things: the slow fen streams with their swans and ducks; the church of St. Peter the Apostle; the glory of King's Chapel where Ansie might once have sung had the ghost of John Wesley not intervened; even Bury St. Edmunds which she had once deplored. Perhaps my father saw all these things, too, for he said to the bishop:

"I'd rather like him to go back. I don't want any of them ever to forget England."

"Quite right and proper," the bishop said. "Let young men dream their dreams according to the ancient prophet. But who knows what may happen in the next few years?"

"Who, indeed?" my father said, after the manner of some-one who must say something.

Tea mercifully came then, Mary and I running to help Mrs. Baxter with the tray. The bishop dutifully thanked her for all her faithful service in behalf of Methodism over many years; and she swelled visibly with pride within the ample folds of her best white apron. He made a most excellent tea, as we should have said in England, with three well-sweetened cups, four slices of bread and butter, and two large pieces of Mrs. Baxter's superlative cake. As he ate, he talked more about America and the opportunities it offered to all ambitious men. Methodism, he told us, had spread like a tornado during the past fifty years, and even today it was sweeping phenomenally through certain of the newer western states. Ansie nudged me then, and we both shot sly glances at my mother, all of us with the Plimsolls in mind.

"I take it," he said to my father, "that you've found all the things I told you in London to be very true?"

"Quite," my father answered.

"I always believe in calling a spade a spade," the bishop said. "But with a great country like ours I could hardly mislead you or exaggerate. No Established Church, no foolish social distinctions, no discrimination among our many religious sects. In America, I'm proud to say, all men are free and equal in the sight of God."

My father looked worried, even distressed.

"I believe that all men everywhere are free and equal in the sight of God," he said slowly and quietly. "It's only in the minds of other men that they're sometimes not free and equal."

The bishop moved uneasily in his creaking chair and looked, I thought, more than a little discomfited. We were all conscious of an atmosphere of tension.

"Why don't you take our guest down through the field to see your flocks and herds?" my mother said quickly to my father, meanwhile giving the bishop the most companionable of smiles. "My husband has become quite a farmer," she explained, "thanks to the generosity of our new friends. He's immensely proud of what he calls his stock."

It was remarkable how swiftly the bishop regained his composure.

"The stock I'm interested in just now is what I call my rolling stock," he said to my mother with an almost conspiratorial glance, as though only he and she completely understood each other. "Good Methodist rolling stock, I mean. In other words, if I may be permitted a pun, we like to keep our ministers rolling. And when we find a really outstanding specimen," he continued with a deep and conciliatory bow toward my father, "we find a parish worthy of his gifts. In other words, my dear fellow, our Conference is going to see that your talents are not buried in the earth, so to speak."

"Thank you, sir," my father said, for he could hardly fail to acknowledge the bishop's bow. "Thank you very much, but there's no haste. We're quite contented where we are."

I'm sure my mother at that moment in at least a portion of her mind longed to send the bishop another and more companionable glance, but love and understanding of my father forbade it. Seeing them both sitting there, one contented and secure within the narrow boundaries of his own small sphere of paltry power and dull activity, the other quickened and eager in a measureless world of thought and selfless desire, she felt her ambitions for my father's future perhaps more tawdry than they actually were. Pepperell as a place suddenly seemed to be of no consequence, of little real significance. It might instead have been London, or Rome,

or ancient Athens. She smiled at my father instead of at the
bishop.

"My husband is quite right," she said. "We're not at all
dependent on places. We always find what we most want
wherever we are."

"I'm immensely gratified to hear it," the bishop said,
including us all in broad, pastoral smiles. "All in God's good
time, of course. It would be a pity to snatch you away too
soon from these good people here. But there's sure to be
another call for you, my good man, just as there was a
definite one only a little more than one brief year ago. For
I've never had the slightest doubt that your propitious coming
to our shores was the result of a direct call from God."

We all knew then that we were again on dangerous ground.
I looked fearfully at my mother and she at my father, who,
we both saw, was getting ready to speak, struggling within
himself between his honesty and his courtesy. Mary was the
first to save us. She told me later that she all at once remembered that night in the parsonage at home when my father
had set us straight about calls from God.

"Would you please excuse me, sir?" she said now to the
bishop. "I must do my lessons."

"Certainly, my child," said the bishop, rising from his
chair to take her hand, "though with regret, of course."
He was so tall that a sprig of apple blossom from a bough
above him rested on his smooth, bald crown. "And what
lesson are you bending your pretty head over just now?"

"Latin," Mary said.

"I used to know Latin myself, but I'm afraid most of
it has long since vanished. *Trans Alpes Italia est.* That was
the motto of my school once upon a time. I'll wager that you
can tell me what it means."

"It means 'Across the Alps lies Italy,' doesn't it?" Mary

asked.

"Capital!" cried the bishop with a resounding laugh. "Capital, my dear! There may be many Alps for you to climb before you all reach your Italy. But it's out there somewhere waiting for you, I'll be bound, with Cicero here to give orations to a far larger audience than Pepperell."

By this time my mother's silent appeals to my father had, however unwillingly, told upon him; and the bishop's fulsome comparison to Cicero had clinched the matter. Calls from God were clearly not to be discussed at the moment.

"And now," my mother said, crossing the grass to slip her arm within the bishop's, "before you start back on your long journey, you simply must see our new lambs."

It was then that Ansie and I excused ourselves to carry back to the kitchen the remains of Mrs. Baxter's tea and to scrape her frosting bowl, which, against all her principles concerning the washing up of cooking dishes immediately, we knew she had been saving for Ansie.

## 11

We all felt more than a little depleted by the bishop's visit, and when he had once been loaded into the carriage of the kind parishioner who was to drive him ten miles to the nearest railway station, we proceeded to relax in our various ways during the hour before supper. My father and mother went for a walk in the pasture, telling Ansie that they would be responsible for bringing Lilla homeward; and, since my father was careful to carry his pipe with him, we all realized that they had things of importance to talk about and welcomed no other companionship. Mrs. Baxter managed to salvage a quarter of an hour to sit down on the steps at the side door where she proceeded to admonish Chessy in her lap against her predatory instincts toward a pair of robins nesting in the woodbine overhead. Mary, forsaking her Latin, climbed an apple tree with a tablet and pencil. I suspected that she had a poem in mind. At going on fourteen she was given to outbursts in verse with Longfellow and Whittier as her rather distant models. My mother encouraged these, since they were a safety valve against her far more disturbing outbursts in prose which she not infrequently discharged upon the household. Ansie, freed from his task of fetching Lilla, decided to write Katie a letter about the doings of our momentous day while they were still fresh in his mind. And I, not a little disgruntled because no one, including Ansie, had any desire for my company, took *David Copperfield* into the hayloft where I promptly fell fast asleep over my favourite chapter about David in his little whitewashed room in Peggotty's queer home.

The events of that afternoon were to come sharply back to me many years later when Katie showed me Ansie's letter, which she had kept among her treasures:

My dear Katie,

I think my father is likely to rise higher very quickly now. You will remember that bishop whom he went to London to see on the day when I learned the poem on the Statue of Liberty which at first you did not much like. Well, he, I mean that bishop, has been here to see us and to hear my father make a very fine speech indeed. He made it this afternoon at two o'clock in our church here which as I have said before is not ever called a chapel as at home. I wish you and my grandparents, I mean Tillyard, not Oldroyd, might have heard the speech as you would all have been most awfully proud of my father. His speech was about Abraham Lincoln who was a very great American who freed the slaves or black people who were being opressed by their owners. If you should care to read a book called *Uncle Tom's Cabin*, you could discover just how much they suffered in the fields of cotton in what is called the South. It is a most interesting book.

This day, 30th May, is called Memorial Day or sometimes

Decoration Day. It is a very great day in America like Guy Fawkes Day or a Bank Holiday at home, only much more solem, when people decorate their graves and the graves of soldiers who died to make the slaves free. There is always a speech or an orration made, and this year my father was invited to make it. I wish you all might have heard him. This bishop at tea which we had for him in our orchard which as I have told you is like a garden at home only not so nice said my father's orration was *supperb*. I don't think it is spelled quite right, but you can see what I mean.

I didn't like this bishop very much. He laughs a lot at things which are not very funny and talks a lot in large rolling words, and I don't think my mother liked him much either. But he is the man who moves Methodist ministers or Wesleyan ones to any place he wishes, just as he likes, and I am sure he means to move my father soon to a more important place than Pepperell. He actually said that very thing. He said my father's talents must not be buried in the earth. Please tell my grandparents this because they will like to hear it.

I shall be very sorry to leave Pepperell for I like it very much, but of course we all want my father to rise higher. Even if he doesn't much care whether he rises higher or not, my mother does and so do I.

Please tell my grandfather that we have two lambs now. They are named Primrose and Cowslip. They are a present quite free like Snow White and Mrs. Baxter who is not quite free but mostly, except for what my father calls a pitance. Many things in America are free, but at times I am very homesick for England and for you.

Now I will answer all your questions.

1. No. I do not ever hear from Moses. I am afraid he is not very happy in those Dakotas.

2. Yes. We both do quite well at school, and Mary does even better.

3. Yes. We do have family prayers, but my mother makes them nice. Yes. I sing every morning and sometimes in church, too.

4. No. I don't use too much soap on my hair.

5. No. Boys do not play cricket here. It is all baseball in the spring. Baseball is a most dificult game to explain, but I will try one day when I have a great deal of time and draw you a plan

of it too.

6. No. I never forget that I am coming back to Cambridge to college.

Y's faithfuly forever.
Ansie.

P.S. Now, Katie, it is 9 o'clock and I am just going to bed, but I will add this news of great good luck. At supper this evening a man who is called a Select Man and is very important in Pepperell brought my father 5 new American notes for $5.00 each to thank him for his speech. That means 5 whole pounds in English money. We are all terriably excited as it was a great surprise. My mother knows just how we are to spend it, but she won't tell how until tomorrow. I will tell you later or my father will. He asks me to say that he is writing my grandmother at once.

Ansie did well to add his postscript for we were all dumfounded by the contents of the long white envelope, which Mr. Packard, the First Selectman of Pepperell, delivered into the hands of Mrs. Baxter while we were just finishing our supper. When my father had opened it, read aloud with modest hesitation the few lines which said that the town wished to pay a tribute for a truly noble address, and spread the five fresh notes on the table, we all sat staring alternately at them and at one another as though neither we nor they could possibly possess any actual reality. Yet here we were and there they were, green, crisp, and clean, snapping and crackling in their newness as my father took each up in his fingers and then laid each down again on the white tablecloth. There they were, with on one side an Indian chief in a feathered headdress, with narrowed eyes and a stern face, and on the other so many *fives* amid scrolls of leaves that there could be no doubt whatever about their value. In both upper corners there was the figure 5; in both lower corners there was the very word *FIVE;* and as though to make my father entirely certain that there had been deposited for him in the year 1899 in the Treasury of the United States of America in Washington, D.C., five silver dollars, there was in the centre of each note the Roman numeral V. My father separated them, making each to lie singly, then put them together again, then separated them once more. My mother finally found her voice after she had wiped her eyes with her napkin as my father read the letter.

"And they don't smell in the least!" she said.

"Smell!" cried my father. "Smell! Whatever do you mean, my dear?"

"All the money in this village smells of fish," my mother said. "Or of clams. Or of lobsters. Or has dried scales on it. You don't mean to tell me you haven't noticed it?"

"Like the smell in David Copperfield's room in the Peggotty barge," I explained to my father, once I, too, had found my voice.

"Fetch Mrs. Baxter, Ansie," my father said. "It's just possible that she knows something."

"Mrs. Baxter!" screamed Ansie, forgetting his manners and in the tumult escaping reproof from anyone.

Mrs. Baxter came in hurriedly to stare at the money on the table, but, although her presence added to our excitement, she knew nothing at all. She said, however, that she was vastly proud of Pepperell, which had never before, she could swear, given a speaker anything except the honour of the invitation itself.

"The Selectmen must have called a special meeting," she told my father. "And no wonder at all, sir, for, mark my words, there'll be little else talked about for weeks by Methodists and Baptists alike. As to the bishop, I'm sure he's never heard such an address, no, not even from the Conference."

"Thank you, Mrs. Baxter," my father said. "I must say it's all quite incredible."

Mrs. Baxter still stared at the money.

"I hope I'm not presuming," she said, "but just in terms of plain arithmetic, that's a real tidy sum, ministers' salaries being what they are. As I reckon it, just in my head, of course, it's more than two weeks' pay, that is, if you don't count in the parsonage and me."

"It's overwhelming," my father said. "But we never forget to count the parsonage and you, Mrs. Baxter."

"Whatever shall you do with it, father?" Ansie asked, with the awe which we all felt in his voice.

"I really can't think," my father said. "I'm quite too stunned. I'd rather like to give it to the church for—"

"Never!" my mother cried so vehemently that we all jumped in our chairs and Mrs. Baxter braced herself for support against the table.

My father laughed from sheer surprise.

"Well," he said, "if that's that, and I gather it is, how about putting it in the savings bank? At six per cent compound interest, Ansie, it would take you across the ocean to Cambridge in six or seven years."

"I hope you don't mean steerage," Mary said anxiously. He smiled at her.

"No, I don't mean steerage this time," he said.

"We're not waiting for any six years," my mother said briskly, "to spend that money on Ansie. He can pick blueberries to pay his fare to Cambridge."

We all looked toward her sitting opposite my father in her blue dress with its round white collar. It was quite clear that she was the maker of decisions, the framer of destinies, as she had been for as long as we could remember. She looked young and eager in the low sunlight which streamed through the western windows. Her blue eyes were shining, but she suddenly covered them and all her face with the upright palms of her two hands in a gesture to which we were well accustomed. Sometimes it meant that she was confused or irritated or even angry, or had had in general more than she could stand from all of us; sometimes it meant only that she was thinking. You could always tell from the pressure of her fingers against her forehead just how dangerous it might be. Tonight we knew that it was not dangerous in the least.

"There's always my sheep," my father said a bit nervously, watching her fingers. "This would buy six more lambs at least, eight tiny ones perhaps."

Mrs. Baxter started to speak, as though she, too, might have a suggestion about the disposal of at least a small portion of our new wealth; but before she had gotten a word well out, my mother pulled her hands away from her face and surveyed us all. I thought I had never seen her eyes so blue or her face so resolute and sure.

"No sheep," she said firmly. "Not even one more lamb. And, Mrs. Baxter, you can get rid of that pig right now, for I can see him sitting in your head. No more livestock, no savings bank, no present to the church. I know precisely how that money is going to be spent. I've spent it a hundred times already in my mind, only it's never been here to spend. But now it's here, and you can all just put away any other silly ideas you may have."

"How?" we all cried at once. "Tell us how you mean to spend it."

"In the morning," my mother said. "Not a word until tomorrow morning!"

Ansie ran from his chair to wheedle her by putting his arms around her.

"You're mean!" he cried. "You'll tell father once you get to bed. You know you will!"

My mother was obdurate.

"I won't tell him one word," she said. "I promise I won't. He wouldn't sleep a wink if I did, and he's tired after all his glory and that wretched bishop."

"She won't tell me, Ansie," my father said. "You can rest assured as to that."

"Will you tell us before prayers or after?" Ansie and I asked together.

"We'll omit prayers tomorrow," my mother said, smiling benignly at Mrs. Baxter. "We'll all get together right after breakfast to hear my secret."

Mrs. Baxter seemed entirely acquiescent about the omission of prayers. She merely said as she began to clear the table that she didn't expect to sleep a wink herself. We children helped her with the washing up but, although the kitchen buzzed with speculations and guesses, not one of us proved to be so much as warm in our nearness to my mother's secret.

## 12

"I feel rather like the Hundred Thirty-ninth Psalm," my father said, staring at my mother who had just told us all her secret. " 'Such knowledge is too wonderful for me.' I simply can't get it into my head."

"Well, you really don't need to," my mother said. "All you have to do is just to go on Monday week. I'll pack your bag for you. By that time you'll probably wake up. At least, if you don't, the rest of us will. Mrs. Baxter will drive you over for the train, won't you, Mrs. Baxter? I just can't manage Snow White. She goes to sleep the minute I take the reins."

"Of course, I will," Mrs. Baxter said, although she looked as though the parsonage would either disappear or be utterly demolished without her presence for four short hours. "Of course, I will. I'm ashamed to say it, I really am, but I just don't know about this Walden Pond or this famous man—what's his name again?"

"Thoreau," my father said. "Henry David Thoreau. He's a great hero of mine, Mrs. Baxter."

"Idol, he means," my mother said. "We've all been brought up on Thoreau, Mrs. Baxter."

"Living or dead?" asked Mrs. Baxter.

"Dead years ago," Mary said.

"But immortal," my father said. "He wrote a very great book, Mrs. Baxter, called *Walden*. I read it when I was a young man, and it has shaped my thoughts all my life. I've wanted for many years to see Walden Pond—that's where he lived for a time—but really, my dear, this is quite too much. I just can't take it in."

"Nonsense!" my mother said. "I've set my heart on your seeing that pond, so just don't say another word."

"If you would only come, too! I'm sure that twenty-five whole dollars—"

"I don't want to go, so that's that. I want you to go by yourself on your own pilgrimage. I'd only get uneasy with you mooning about. If you're by yourself, you can go off into all the trances you like."

"I still can't believe it," my father said. "I feel very selfish, I must say."

"You couldn't be selfish, sir, if you put all your mind to it," Mrs. Baxter said. "Could I perhaps read that *Walden* book so I'd know what to say when folks ask me where you've gone to?"

"Certainly," my father said, looking a bit worried. "Ansie, please fetch *Walden* from my study for Mrs. Baxter. I'm sure it's lying right on my desk."

"We weren't even warm, were we, Mrs. Baxter?" Ansie said, starting for the study. "My guess was for another cow, father. Then we could sell the extra milk like the Kimballs."

"No more cows," my mother said sternly.

"Lilla cost thirty dollars," my father said, "and really I only fully paid for her a few months ago."

"It's a great pity her calf wasn't a heifer," Mrs. Baxter said. "Don't let him live too long, sir, else you can't beef him."

My father looked distressed.

"I really couldn't have him killed now," he said. "He loves the pasture. We might sell him at the County Fair in the autumn."

"Few folks around here buy young bulls," Mrs. Baxter said. "And by then it'll be too late to ox him."

"My guess was a new suit for you, father," I said quickly. "You need one awfully."

"Mrs. Baxter and I will get his grey one all pressed up," my mother said. "He won't know what he has on anyway. He'll do nicely."

"And come to think of it," Mrs. Baxter said, "there's two nice white shirts left at the church for the missionary barrel to Africa. If I just put on fresh neckbands, they'll be good as new. Never give the heathen what you can use yourself. That's my motto."

"You'll see Boston, too, father," Ansie said, coming back with *Walden*, which Mrs. Baxter began to page through with deepening anxiety, though she was somewhat comforted by my father's careful markings. "And you'll see where once the embattled farmers stood and fired the shot heard round the world. If there's money enough, I'd like a postcard of the Minute Man to show at school."

"I'll not forget, Ansie," my father promised.

"Frankly," Mary said, "I guessed a new fishing rod and perhaps a bicycle."

"I wouldn't know how to fish here without an alder

pole," my father said, "and my old bicycle is good for years longer."

"This *Walden* looks rather deep for me," Mrs. Baxter said, "but I'll try to read all the marked places, sir."

"That's fine," my father said. He turned to my mother. "You remember Horace, my dear. *Nil est ab omni parte beatum.* Well, for just once he seems not to have hit it."

"Horace who?" Mrs. Baxter asked. "I don't recall any Horaces around here."

"He was a Latin poet," Mary whispered to her. "He's another idol of my father's, like Thoreau."

Mrs. Baxter with slightly heightened colour returned to *Walden*.

"Horace," my father explained kindly, "is just someone my wife and I have in common. He once said, 'Nothing in every respect is happy.' I suppose it holds true in most circumstances; but just now with a dream of my life about to come true, I can't see one thing that isn't perfect."

My mother beamed upon him.

"Why don't you go fishing, darling?" she asked. "Let your old sermon go for once."

"I *am* tempted, I must admit," my father said. "I'm afraid I can't settle down to sermons."

"Well, if I keep this *Walden*," Mrs. Baxter said, "and you don't go taking along that Horace man or someone else, you might get a nice string of trout. It would be a treat for us all and not cost a cent."

"I think I'll just take my thoughts this time," my father said. "I surely have plenty of those with this wonderful thing that's happening to me. I'll dig my worms right now."

Mrs. Baxter looked doubtful about even thoughts on a fishing trip; but she hurried off to work on my father's suit while we reluctantly got ready for school. My mother began singing to herself. She did not then remember that the most innocent of plans are sometimes subject to unexpected accidents, like King Saul's searching for lost asses, which forced a tragic kingship upon him, or like Oedipus unwittingly meeting his unrecognized father, or like foolish young Camilla, who paid dearly for the flame-coloured garment which she coveted.

### 13

My mother kept hoping from his departure on Monday to his return on Friday that my father would not be in the least disappointed in Walden Pond. She need not have worried for a moment, for he came home quite enraptured. Even with the railway running too close to it as, we would recall, Thoreau himself deplored (though he had hoped that the engineers and firemen of his day were better men for the sight of it), and the consequent loss of some of the great trees on its borders, it was still perfect in my father's devoted eyes. It was deep and pale green just as Thoreau had said and so transparent that one could see thirty feet down to its very bottom where the remains of old timbers lay in the yellow sand or pale, swaying reeds grew. Myriads of small fish flecked with gold darted about in the still, clear water precisely as Thoreau had seen them.

"Some form of perch, I think," my father said in the explanatory way of the dedicated fisherman. "Perhaps what they call sunfish here."

"Were you in a boat then?" asked Ansie, as we all sat listening on the evening of his return.

"Yes," my father said. "We rowed out just before sunset and sat there for a full two hours. And—will you believe it? —there were swallows skimming over the water, white-breasted ones just like those he writes about, and two hawks circling high in the sky. We sat there until darkness began to fall. The white-throated sparrows were singing all through the twilight, and the hermit thrushes. The only possible drawback was that I couldn't seem to realize that I was actually there. That consciousness kept escaping me in spite of all that I could do to grasp it."

"Did you see the pond in the morning, too?" Mary asked.

"Yes. It was blue then from a distance, reflecting the sky, just as he says in *Walden;* but in the centre, in the deepest part, the water was pale green again. And very cold when we put our hands in it. You remember he says it was his well already dug for him. We explored the shores, too, which are sandy in some places and rocky in others; and we went to the place where his cabin once stood and where his bean field was. But it was being on the pond itself which made all the difference. I shall never forget it."

He looked around upon us all, but rather as though he were far away in some singularly transfigured world of his own which made further questions about Walden almost an intrusion. Mrs. Baxter, less used to him than we were, may have felt uneasy, for she said abruptly:

"You must have done a good bit of scrambling around, for I see you've torn your pants. Maybe on a blackberry bush."

My father surveyed the damage to the right knee of his trousers.

"That's right," he said. "I hadn't noticed. I'm so sorry."

"It don't matter a mite," Mrs. Baxter said. "I can set a patch. I'm sure we're all glad that you had such a good time. Everybody at the church was real pleased about your going, even if I couldn't find many that knew about this Thoreau."

"That's not strange," my father said. "We all have our special heroes, don't we?"

"I did read the places you'd marked, though, in that

*Walden* book before you took it with you; and I can see he was a man full of good thoughts."

"He was," my father said. "If all men thought as he did, there would be less sorrow and trouble in this world, and far more faith in life itself."

"Perhaps now you will love Walden Pond as much as Bury St. Edmunds," Ansie said with a shade of regret in his voice.

My father smiled at him and with the smile came back a littler closer to us.

"No," he said. "Bury always holds its own place. Someday we shall all go back to Bury. Walden is quite different. I don't know just how to distinguish between them. Perhaps Bury is first in my imagination and Walden is first—shall we say?—in my soul."

"I see," Ansie said politely, although of course he didn't in the least.

"Who's this *we?*" my mother asked, scenting things that my father had not yet told. "This *we* in the boat with you, sitting on that pond for hours?"

"A most remarkable man," my father said, returning now fully to the parsonage sitting-room. "I'm not much given to believing in Fate as you know, but meeting this man, who became my friend almost at once, makes me wonder if things aren't sometimes arranged for one in a peculiar, even mysterious way."

"Well, go on," said my mother. "Just forget Fate and tell us about him."

My father, thus admonished, told us then about his new friend, who, first of all, felt his own devotion to Thoreau. He had boarded the train in Augusta and shared my father's seat; and when he saw that my father was rereading *Walden* in preparation for his visit, what did he do but pull out an almost identical copy from his own pocket.

"What a moment *that* was!" my father said. "You can imagine it didn't take us long then to start talking, and we were in Boston before we knew it."

"Is he a parson, too?" my mother asked.

"No, he's a doctor and, I take it, a very eminent one though he's most modest about himself. He has charge of the big state hospital in Augusta for the insane. He was bound for Boston on some business connected with the hospital, but he couldn't resist going to Walden again, though he's been there several times before. He's been an admirer of Thoreau for years, and he knows all his writings far better than I do. I must say that falling in with him seemed far more than just a coincidence. And on Wednesday and Thursday, when he was free, he joined me in Concord." He hesitated. Then he said to my mother, "I don't think I've had such companionship since those faraway days when you and I were in Cambridge, at least in the realm of books."

"I'm glad," my mother said. You could see that this was one of the moments when she loved everything about him, even his irritating ways. "Perhaps, Mrs. Baxter, you could bear to get us all some tea. And now," she continued once Mrs. Baxter had discreetly closed the door to the kitchen, "let's hear the rest of it. I know there's more than just sitting in that boat. What about this doctor? What does he want from you?"

My father drew his pipe from his pocket, rose from his chair, and stood by the fireplace where some logs were burning. It was so exactly what he had done on the evening in the Saintsbury parsonage upon his return from London that I think we all felt alarmed as well as excited as though all our futures were at stake, as, indeed, they were.

"It's quite extraordinary," he said. "I'm not yet used to the idea. I had meant to tell you alone later on, but the children may as well know at once since it might conceivably affect us all in one way or another. This doctor, whose name is Thomas, Dr. Edward Thomas, wants me to be the visiting chaplain of this great hospital. They've never had a visiting chaplain before, and his Board of Governors has left the choice of one quite up to him. He seems to feel as though I should look upon the people there in much the same way as he does, I mean his patients, some of whom are very ill, and others, he thinks, hardly ill at all, but only lonely for some outside companionship. He wants me to come there every month or so for a few days, talk with some of them, and try to help them. He thinks I could be of great service to them. I confess I was overcome by his request. I told him I couldn't say at once whether or no until I'd discussed it with my wife and family."

Not one of us said anything for what seemed a long time. Even my mother was at a loss for words. Thoreau and Walden with its clear green water faded from our minds. Finally Ansie said:

"Do you mean crazy people? I mean *really* crazy people? Or just queer ones like—well, like poor Smike in *Nicholas Nickleby?*"

"I really don't know, Ansie," my father answered. "I suppose there are all sorts. Only I don't like the word *crazy* for anyone, and Dr. Thomas doesn't either. These people are ill, and many of them are ill because they are lonely and desperate or have suffered sorrows and tragedies which they couldn't weather. I can't believe I'd have much to give them, but it would make me very happy to try. We're all so rich in everything that matters that I'd like to think we were sharing our wealth with those less happy than we are."

My mother suddenly left her chair and stood beside him. She put her arm through his. The love which she had felt for him a few moments ago was still bright and warm within her, giving to her, as such love always gives, a longing to know all his thoughts, in so far as one can know another's thoughts, to enter into his dreams whatever they might be, and to further their fulfillment.

"Then you shall, dear," she said. "We'll all help you to do what you most want to do."

Many times in the years since that evening, more than half a century ago, all its assurances have returned to me, all that singular confidence and faith which love within a family alone can generate and nurture if only it is actuated by freedom and balanced by humour and understanding. As I saw my mother standing there with her arm within my father's, I must have realized, else I had not so often seen them in my memory, what values they had all unconsciously taught us to place upon such illumined moments in human existence, what safety there might be in the very throwing away of safety for the sake of pure desire and hope. Beneath my parents' love for each other there was something unassailable and immovable. On its surface it might willingly find room for irritation and annoyance —what love does not?—and yet in between, where we all really lived, there were respect and ease and gaiety. Such love within a family is seldom the subject for words, perhaps because by nature it is silent; but wherever it exists (and it is rare, indeed) it may well be the source for all other pure and passionate affections.

At this moment, however, I was by no means lost in such abstractions, but rather seized by the most mundane and earthly of anxieties. Mary and I had all at once thought of another question. Perhaps we had seen it stirring around in my mother's mind, in which many divergent and contradictory questions and emotions were always colliding with one another, and asked it in order to save her the embarrassment.

Mary as usual got it out before I did.

"Are you paid for being this chaplain?" she asked my father.

"Or do you have to pay for being it?" I concluded.

My mother looked relieved that we had thus brought it out into the open, for even in the midst of those sorrows and tragedies which were uppermost in my father's mind it was an important item to us all.

"That's another extraordinary thing," my father said, "though in itself I don't think it matters so much. But if we do decide that I shall go every month for a few days—and, of course, the Conference or at least the bishop would have to approve it—I would be paid fifty dollars for each visit together with all my expenses."

"Whew!" Ansie said, whistling through his nose in a distasteful way which he had recently learned from a boy at school. "I guess you *are* beginning to rise higher, father!"

"I don't think of it in terms of rising higher, Ansie," my father said quietly. "But if I could help these ill people to rise a little higher in their minds, it would be wonderful."

Mrs. Baxter at that moment brought in the tea; but, though my mother invited her to share it with us, she declined. I suspected that she might well be wishing just then, in the unpredictable way that most minds change from one point of view to another, that my father were a bit more like other Methodist parsons whom she had more safely known and my mother *much* more like their sensible and practical wives.

## 14

In the late summer my father began his monthly visits to the asylum at Augusta with the full approval of the Conference and of the bishop. These continued throughout the autumn and the winter and into the spring of 1903 without noteworthy incidents except for the fascinating stories which he always brought home about his new friends there among the patients. Quite clearly the doctor had been right in his estimation of his new chaplain. The patients loved and trusted him, for with his genius for entering into the lives of other men and women he could make them feel free to talk with him about their problems and anxieties.

I am sure that Mrs. Baxter disapproved of his sharing his often strange experiences with us children, and perhaps my mother sometimes questioned the wisdom of his confidences; but he looked upon this quite differently and was, as usual, rather obstinate about his thoughts.

"I've never believed that painful things should be kept from children," he said one evening in the midst of an especially exciting narration, for this time Mrs. Baxter had expostulated in a really definite way. "I think they ought to know about the hard, sorrowful things in life as well as about the happier ones. It won't hurt them at all. On the contrary, it ought to make them far more thoughtful and kind. I know I think quite differently from many others about this; but I've never believed in shielding children from a knowledge of things as they are. People are responsible for most of the sadness in this world, and people alone must make things better, as I'm sure they can and eventually will. I don't want my children sheltered from the sad things in life. No one can really experience pleasure unless he knows pain as well. It's Plato who tells us that, you remember," he concluded, turning to my mother.

"Is this Plato another of your heroes?" Mrs. Baxter asked, with a distinct tone of unwilling resignation in her voice.

"Yes," my father said.

"Go on about the lady who makes the flags," Ansie begged, impatient at the interruption.

"It really was funny," my father said, "and quite charming, at least in the way it turned out. We were walking around the grounds yesterday morning, the doctor and I, when we came across this woman sitting on a bench and sewing some strips of red and white cloth together. It seems that at times she believes she is Betsy Ross and that she made the first American flag. She's quite harmless and goes about pretty much as she likes with her bits and pieces of red, white, and blue. She's a great help to him, too, Dr. Thomas tells me, for she's always gay and pleasant, and everyone likes her. The doctor introduced us, and we had a nice chat about her years in Philadelphia before General Washington asked her to design the flag. This all seemed so real to her that I began to believe it myself. And then all at once she seemed to come back from her special world to this one, for she said to me, 'Are you a minister as they say you are around here?' I told her I was, and then she said, 'You wouldn't by any chance be a Methodist one, I suppose?' 'Yes,' I said to her, 'that's just what I am.' 'I don't like them,' she said. 'I've never liked Methodists in general, with good reason, and I hate Methodist ministers. One of them nearly killed me, many years ago when I was young.' I didn't know quite what to say to that, but luckily I didn't have to say a thing. For she suddenly drew a yellow rubber ball from the bag which held her red, white, and blue pieces, and said, 'Well, let bygones be bygones. How about a nice throw or two?' And before I knew it, we were tossing that ball back and forth in an open space on the lawn."

"I hope you were better at catching than you are with me," Ansie said anxiously.

"You won't believe it, Ansie," my father said, "but I didn't miss a throw. I really caught every one, and some of them went quite wild, I assure you. She caught all mine, too.

The ball was one of those big ones that children play with, and we tossed it back and forth for all of ten minutes. You really would have been quite proud of me. I rather felt that all of Methodism was at stake. We got a lot of applause from men working about and even from some patients watching us from the windows. She seemed to forget how she hated Methodist parsons, and we had a wonderful time. She's really a remarkable woman."

"Is she old?" Mary asked.

"Yes, she's even very old," my father answered, "but she seems very young. There's something quite unique about her. I haven't discovered just what it is, but I shall in time. She's been there for years, the doctor told me, but she's quite contented, whether she's Betsy Ross or just herself. She's had a tragic, unbelievable life—he's going to tell me more about it the next time I go—but she's much better, even quite normal most of the time. I gather that she could leave at any time, but she doesn't seem to have any place to go even if she wanted to."

My mother looked uneasy at this piece of information. "What's her name?" she asked my father.

"Mrs. Gowan," he said.

### 15

When my mother on Saturday, the 6th day of June in the year 1903, saw fit to consult Mrs. Baxter about my father's new and startling plan for certain of his friends at the asylum, she took me along to the kitchen with her. I suppose there were a number of reasons actuating her decision to talk over this problem with Mrs. Baxter. First of all, of course, was the purely practical one. Since Mrs. Baxter as the manager of our somewhat unpredictable household would perforce bear the largest share of the responsibility for any changes in it, she must in all fairness be allowed to express her opinions. Yet I am sure my mother was prompted by other considerations. I think she needed to bolster her own misgivings by Mrs. Baxter's down-to-earth realism, her hard-pan common sense, her peculiar, unreflective knowledge of us all. Moreover, behind and shot through our housekeeper's solid, matter-of-fact, honest discernment of mankind and of its diverse ways there was an unmistakable, even imaginative respect for other minds. She might be puzzled by Thoreau and ignorant of Horace; yet she recognized through a curious, perhaps paradoxical intuition that, though there were worlds into which she herself found it difficult, if not impossible to enter, such worlds might be the source of nourishment, even of life, to others. In short, in spite of Mrs. Baxter's rigidity in matters of her hair, her kitchen, and her spring cleaning, she was a flexible, extensible human being; and my mother on that June morning was really in desperate need of pliancy as well as of common sense.

I don't know exactly why she took me into the kitchen with her. Perhaps she needed even my frail support. Perhaps, in the way that most generous people in anxiety want instinctively to be of help or comfort to others, she saw that I had been rudely deserted by Ansie, who was building a raft on the shore with his friends, and scorned by Mary, who was in another poetic frenzy, and that I felt disconsolate and unwanted. Anyhow she said as she went through the sitting-room, "Come along and help me through this tough assignment," which remark banished all my resentment and made me feel of immense importance.

When we reached the kitchen, Mrs. Baxter was about to submerge four squirming dark-green lobsters into a huge kettle of boiling water, thus to end their lives and make them ready for our dinner. The lobsters had been a present from

Reverend Kimball earlier that morning; and Mrs. Baxter as always was deeply satisfied over the thought of a delicious and quite costless meal.

"Just a minute," she said upon our invasion of her domain. "And if you don't relish hearing them hiss as I dump them in, stop up your ears. I can't say I like it much myself, but it must be a sudden death else they wouldn't turn red so quick. And folks claim they don't feel a mortal thing."

She lifted each of her wriggling victims most cautiously by encircling its back with her fingers and popped it into the steaming kettle, which she covered at once with its close lid.

"Twenty minutes to go," she said, glancing carefully at the kitchen clock. "Now what's on your mind?"

"I'm sure it was most generous of Mr. Kimball," my mother said, disregarding Mrs. Baxter's question for the immediate moment.

"Yes, 'twas, but, there, what can he do? Sell them, I suppose, but if he sells them uncooked to the neighbours, that's giving his wife away in kind of a public fashion. You see, she won't boil them."

"Won't she? Whyever not?"

"Oh, some odd nonsense, I take it, about cruelty to animals. She's a good woman, but awful notional. Between you and I, he has his worries, poor man! Why don't you sit down?"

My mother sat down in the red rocker while Mrs. Baxter took a chair by the kitchen table after she had fetched me a cooky from the crock in the pantry. I sat on the kitchen table beside her.

"Yes," she continued. "I often think that life's no bed of roses for Reverend Kimball. He's a good man, too. Not that I'm for a minute comparing him with our own parson. Ours may have his quirks, but after nigh on to two years I think he's about the best man I ever knew. You're a lucky woman."

"I realize that," my mother said, grateful in view of the foreboding future that Mrs. Baxter had thus far almost dangerously committed herself.

"Where's he off to this morning with Snow White?"

"Someone's sick up in the hills," my mother said.

"Wouldn't you know it? And on a sermon morning, too? But, there—never thinking of himself. I sometimes wonder—I really do—what he'll find to do in Heaven."

"At the moment," my mother said, sturdily summoning up her courage, "I'm more concerned with what he wants to do on this earth. That's, in fact, what I've come to talk with you about."

Mrs. Baxter looked surprised, if not alarmed; and I, ignorant of my father's plans, shared her concern and curiosity. The water in the kettle bubbled and steamed above the now-deceased lobsters.

"We'll, whatever it is," Mrs. Baxter said, "it's bound to be good for someone or other. He may be a bit queer in his ideas, but he couldn't be anything but kind, so let's hear the worst. I can see that you're plumb worried. I can make you a nice cup of tea in a minute if you've got a feeling for one."

"No, thank you," my mother said. "I'd rather get this matter off my mind and have the tea later. I just don't know what you'll think, Mrs. Baxter, but he's quite set his heart on inviting some of his friends from that hospital down here. I may as well be quite frank. He means those patients. He's got the idea firmly in his head that certain of them need a change more than anything. He's convinced they are quite all right—I mean harmless—only just lonely and friendless. They'd be allowed to come, that doctor says, if only my husband will be responsible; but as you very well know, that means you and me, too, actually you most of all, for you really run this house. His idea is to ask two or three of them for a few days each, or maybe for longer if things work out all right. Now whatever are you going to say to *that?*"

Mrs. Baxter lifted the lid of the kettle and poked somewhat viciously at the lobsters with a long-handled fork in order to ensure an equal space for all. She was quite clearly trying to hide her consternation and to get used to this formidable information at the same time. I choked on my cooky, and she brought me a glass of water. My mother put her hands over her face in the familiar gesture, only at this moment her fingers were pressed too firmly against her forehead.

"Well," Mrs. Baxter said, "I'm not going to say I'm not some taken aback. I've never had anything to do with crazy folks before."

"Father says they're not really crazy," I said.

"I trust your father in most ways, dear," Mrs. Baxter said. "But when it comes to who's crazy and who's not crazy, I'm not so sure he's entirely dependable."

She looked anxiously at my mother, whose fingers were still tight against her forehead.

"Now don't you go to fretting overmuch," she said. "If that's what he's set his mind on, I suppose we'll have to look at it straight in the face. Maybe we're all a little bit crazy now and again, who knows? Anyhow just stop mulling it over in your head, or throw it all out of yours into mine for a spell. That might help a mite. Who are these folks he wants to entertain?"

"I honestly don't know," my mother said, pulling down her hands to stare helplessly at Mrs. Baxter. "He's told me about so many of them that I get them all mixed up. I'm sure they're not in the least harmful—just—well, let us say, overly imaginative. After all, he wouldn't do anything danger-ous to us. One he's especially interested in believes at times he's a Roman emperor."

"Are there any Roman emperors left?" asked Mrs. Baxter. "I know there's a Pope in Rome, but I didn't think there were any more emperors."

"There aren't, of course. That was centuries ago. It's just in this man's mind. My husband says he's really a very intelligent man. He was a teacher once, it seems."

She started to cover her face again with her hands but hesitated before Mrs. Baxter's gaze.

"Now don't you go getting all het up again. I'm here to help you out, not to make things worse for you. Just you say what *you* think about all this. I'm ready and willing to listen."

"Well," my mother said, "you just have to understand, first, that my husband isn't like most men, or most anybody for that matter. He lives in a different world from ours. He's always longed to help people who are unfortunate or sad or troubled. He's always believed that life is better than it is, or at least can be made better if everyone does his best to make it so. He was just the same when he was young as he is now, always trusting people, always believing that they're just like him and want everything that's—well, noble and good. I suppose you'd call him an idealist, or a romanticist, or—oh, I really don't know! I only know that at times it's terribly trying, Mrs. Baxter."

"It's possible, of course," said Mrs. Baxter in an unusually thoughtful way for her, "that he's just a Christian, which the rest of us aren't."

"Perhaps," my mother said. "I've had hours in my life, though, Mrs. Baxter, when I've wished he were anything but *his* sort of Christian. Still," she continued bravely, "I suppose if you ask me what I honestly think, I'll just have to say that I hate to be always thwarting him, or bringing him down to earth, or disbelieving in him, or putting barriers in his way.

I suppose it's a little like what I feel about Ansie."

She had touched a tender spot in Mrs. Baxter's armour. "What's Ansie got to do with it?" she asked.

"Not a thing," my mother said, "except by comparison. It's just that I think people should be encouraged to do the things they most long to do in this world, even if only in their dreams. Just now Ansie thinks about nothing but being one of those cowboys in that new book we've been reading aloud —you know, *The Virginian*. Of course, he'll be nothing of the sort—it's just a silly fancy—but it's terribly real to him. I was ashamed of myself when I laughed at him the other day, really made fun of him, and he burst out crying. After all, it's his dream, and it's cruel to laugh at dreams, Mrs. Baxter, no matter how wild they are."

Mrs. Baxter gave another, less vicious poke at the lobsters and moved the kettle farther back on the stove.

"I haven't had too much occasion for dreaming dreams in my life," she said, "but I hope I know better than to mock at folks that do. Well, go on with this queer dream of the parson's."

"That's just it," my mother said, her voice trembling. "It *is* a dream, and I know it. It's only another of his lovely ambitions which he's had all his life. But if it's cruel to shatter ambitions and dreams like Ansie's, which belong to the real world, then it must be even more cruel to tear them to pieces when they're in the world of one's faith, in the place where one really lives. I'm saying it very badly, I know, Mrs. Baxter, but my husband is always somewhere in an ideal world which just plain, ordinary people like you and me can't reach. He just doesn't see evil and confusion and selfishness, or if he ever does, he thinks we can all make things perfect or at least less imperfect, if we only believe that we can. It's absurd, of course; but I suppose that's really why we love him as we do."

She hesitated for a moment. Now that Mrs. Baxter was not occupied with the lobsters, but looking straight at my mother, conversation was more difficult.

"There's another thing that perhaps I ought to try to explain," she concluded. "I don't think I'm really being quite fair to him. This isn't all just a dream. It's more than that. It's—it's a conviction that God can't work out His purposes without us—I mean without people who have faith in Him. It's a kind of obligation as well as merely a dream. Maybe it's even a dedication—I don't know, though I've lived with it all these years. So now perhaps you can see, Mrs. Baxter, that if I tell him he can't try to help these people and that he's just as mad as they are with his impossible hopes and longings to make the world better and happier—well, I don't —really—think—I can."

She put her hands again against her face, and to Mrs. Baxter's and my utter distress we saw tears begin to trickle down below their palms. I was at a complete loss as to what to do, but Mrs. Baxter rose at that awful moment to her full stature as a human soul. Though her hair was as tight as ever and her cheeks as firm, I could fairly see her insides softening and crumbling beneath her stout shoulders and her firm calico-covered chest. She said nothing until she had hurriedly filled the teakettle with fresh water and put it on the hottest part of the stove in place of the lobsters. Then she advanced upon my mother with a clean dish towel for a handkerchief, pulled her hands from her face, and put her strong arms around her.

"You poor, forlorn little mite!" she said. "Now don't you go taking on another second. I guess you've had your worrisome moments, and I haven't been too nice about them neither. But I'm not so weak-minded as I sometimes seem.

We'll just bear up together, with all these dreams and fandangoes of your husband's. When's this Roman emperor due?"

"I wouldn't know," my mother said, drying her eyes on the dish towel. "I don't really know anything except what my husband wants. You've been wonderful about it, Mrs. Baxter. I did so hate to tell you."

"What about that Betsy Ross woman?" Mrs. Baxter asked, a trifle curtly perhaps, for she was clearly embarrassed by this unwonted display of genuine emotion in her kitchen. "Is she likely to come in her turn? I can't say I'm exactly eager to see *her*."

"I am," I said feebly from the edge of the table, since I felt distinctly out of the picture at the moment. "She sounds the nicest of them all to me." Neither of them paid any attention, however, to my observation.

"Without doubt she'll show up before we're through with this mess," my mother said. "My husband hasn't named her definitely, but I've learned never to be surprised at anything he gets into his head."

Mrs. Baxter began assembling the tea tray.

"I'm just a dight puzzled as to what to say to folks," she said. "At church, for instance. Suppose folks get nosy as to who these people are?"

"I don't think we need to say anything," my mother said, "except that we have—guests. Won't that do?"

"Maybe," Mrs. Baxter said. "Maybe not. We'll just have to wait and see. Now you take this nice cup of tea to the sitting-room and keep calm in your mind. In the meantime I'll bust up these lobsters. And let's not go looking for more trouble than we've got already."

Once my mother had gone into the sitting-room with her tea, both Mrs. Baxter and I felt easier in our minds. I helped her break up the lobsters or at least pick the meat from them, after she had demolished their shells with a hammer. She was still too agitated to cope with the claws, which for reasons of thrift she usually insisted on splitting, but which she now gave to me to chew. As we worked, she took me into her confidence about a far lesser matter than the one which had so recently engaged our attention.

"When you get a real good chance," she said, "and not before, you might give your mother this sixty-nine cents. It's change from a dollar bill. Your father forgot to pick it up from the counter when he bought some oatmeal yesterday. Mr. Wood from the store gave it to me last night. I really don't think your father is any too capable about the family shopping."

"I'm sure he isn't," I said in my most adult manner.

"Well," Mrs. Baxter said loyally, "you can't expect everything out of anyone. Just let's contrive to keep him away from the grocery store if it's at all possible."

### 16

Mary and I often reminded each other years afterward, when she was married and living in the Berkshire Hills of Massachusetts and we had been telling bedtime stories to her children about our own childhood both in Saintsbury and in Pepperell, that if our father, after Mr. Wheeler's weekend with us, had been like almost anyone else in the world, not only the summer of 1903 but the future in general would doubtless have been different for us all.

"But he just wasn't like anyone else," one of us always said, "and I suppose, all in all, we ought to be glad he wasn't."

"Johnny and Hilda always think we had a much nicer childhood than they're getting," Mary said. "It's lucky that one generation of children can never understand just what an earlier generation was like—I mean what actually happened inside their minds. And still I'm never quite sure that we weren't really the lucky ones."

Usually at some point like this she had to go indoors or to call dire threats to Johnny and Hilda, who were taking their time to go to sleep. When this happened, I sat in the garden and listened to the whippoorwills wheezing away in the nearby thickets.

"Do you like these wretched birds?" I asked once, when she had either reappeared or paused in her warnings to the children.

"No, I hate them, especially now with Bill in France, but he adores them. He even wants to name this place Whippoorwill Hill." She laughed. "You spoke just like mother then. Remember how everything was always *wretched* with her?"

"It still is," I said. "At least it was five years ago, and you can see how it keeps cropping up in her letters."

The whippoorwills continued to sound their sibilant, hissing, querulous notes through the darkness.

"Perhaps I owe Bill to Pepperell," Mary said reflectively. "When we were in college and telling each other about our childhoods, he always said that after those years in Pepperell, I ought to make an extremely adaptable wife."

I don't know that any of us consciously adapted ourselves to Pepperell, or at all events to that extraordinary summer of 1903. Or perhaps I should say "adjusted" in the tiresome, shabby terminology of today. Fifty years ago people were rarely made aware as they now are in a thousand inescapable ways of the necessity for adaptation or adjustment. They just took things as things came along; and, of course, a more stable and quiet world was immeasurably helpful in the process. Children took things, too, partly because their parents were happily ignorant of those dangers with which now they are constantly pelted and dismayed, partly because the best of parents respected their children enough to allow them to learn what life is really like in order that they might assume its obligations with a natural robustness and buoyancy sadly mistrusted in families nowadays.

At all events I have always been grateful for that summer. In spite of its many entanglements none of us was ever so completely enmeshed in them that every vivid detail of it was not stamped indelibly upon our consciousness and our memories. It had its consoling, reassuring features as well as its alarming ones; and, in spite of its seeming unreality, it was real in the sense that it contributed lavishly to the richness and the mystery of human experience.

Perhaps Mr. Henry Adams Wheeler, our first guest from the asylum, was an unfortunate choice, but we were not made aware of that fact until the final morning of his weekend visit. My father brought him down on the train from Augusta, and Mrs. Baxter somewhat reluctantly drove Snow White over on Friday afternoon to meet them at the railway station while we anxiously awaited their arrival. When they had driven into the barn and Mrs. Baxter had left my father and Mr. Wheeler to the unharnessing of Snow White and the other chores, we all made for the kitchen except Ansie, who ran out to offer his services. My mother looked inexpressibly relieved over Mrs. Baxter's serenity.

"Quiet as a mouse," she said. "A very nice man far's I can see. Just like anyone else and real interesting in his talk. Not a thing to get flustered up about. Thanks for setting the table and getting supper ready."

Mr. Wheeler was a tall, thin man of some sixty years with large, dark, and rather troubled eyes. My mother told my father in the few minutes which they had together while Mr. Wheeler was straightening out his belongings upstairs that she thought his eyes looked resentful, but my father said they were merely thoughtful. He was "soft-spoken," in Mrs. Baxter's term, slow and dignified in his speech. He had little to say at supper except about his ancestry; and my mother in her anxiety to make him feel at home and the centre of interest really pressed him into telling us a good deal about his family history. He came from two fine New England families, he said, the Adamses and the Wheelers, with which we must be familiar, especially the first-named, which had contributed so many presidents to the United States and so many foreign ambassadors, statesmen, and authors that he had lost track of them. The Wheelers had not been so spectacular, he added, but they had, all the same, played their parts well on the American scene.

"The famous poetess, Ella Wheeler Wilcox, is a second cousin of mine," he said. "I wrote to her some time ago recalling the relationship, but she has not as yet replied to my letter, though Dr. Thomas thought it courteous and not presuming in any way."

"Poets are awfully busy people, I'm sure," Mary said. Mr. Wheeler smiled kindly at her.

"That's very likely," he replied. "I have not yet despaired of hearing from her. And there are always the Adamses. They are almost a dynasty, in the imperial sense, I mean."

"You've taught a great deal, my husband tells me," my mother said hastily and perhaps not too happily.

"Yes, for many years," Mr. Wheeler said, "in more schools and colleges than I could easily name. My subject was ancient history, with an emphasis on that of the Roman Empire."

"How about a walk after supper?" my father said. "I want you to see my lambs. Mr. Wheeler is very fond of animals," he added in an explanatory note to us all.

"I love animals, plants, all things in a state of nature," Mr. Wheeler said quietly, and largely to himself.

My father told us afterward that Mr. Wheeler's knowledge of Roman history, which they talked about in his study later in the evening, was really quite phenomenal. He was entirely familiar with Caesar's campaigns in Gaul, Hadrian's elaborate building projects not only in Rome but in Britain and the other provinces, and the persecutions of Nero and Domitian.

"He truly knew just what he was talking about," my father said.

To Mr. Wheeler's keen enjoyment they went fishing on Saturday morning, for trout in the morning and for flounders on the full tide in the afternoon; in the evening they talked again about ancient Rome; and on Sunday, after he had gone to church and behaved quite like anyone else, Mrs. Baxter said, he spent the afternoon in the barn. Snow White evidently held a fascination for him. Ansie reported with some excitement at four o'clock when my father was just up from his afternoon nap, with which he indulged himself on Sunday in view of prayer meeting in the evening, that Mr. Wheeler had not only curried and brushed her well, but had completely scrubbed her with soap and water.

"She looks wonderful," Ansie said, "but I think you'd best have a look, father. She's not used to being washed, and she seems uneasy to me."

Snow White was uneasy. Perhaps in those odd perceptions granted to animals she had sensed more about Mr. Wheeler than we had. He had tied her for her scrubbing to both sides of the barn entrance, and she was straining at her ropes and kicking about in protest. Mr. Wheeler suggested that he ride her bareback about the pasture in order to dry her better in the sun and wind, but he desisted willingly from his plan upon my father's disapproval. Instead, they put her back in her stall, where after a few carrots and lumps of sugar she quieted down.

At Mrs. Baxter's sacrificial offer she entertained our guest while we were at prayer meeting, where my mother, who usually heartily disliked that Sunday evening service, was clearly relieved and delighted to have us children under her wing in the front pew. When we reached home, Mrs. Baxter reassured her further. Mr. Wheeler had gone to bed after a short walk in the pasture and an hour's talk with her in the kitchen over raspberry shrub and cake.

"About blueberries," Mrs. Baxter said.

"Blueberries?" questioned my mother. "Whyever blueberries?"

"He's got all sorts of new ideas about them," Mrs. Baxter explained. "The fact is, he's quite a prophet. He claims that in fifty years blueberries will grow as big as grapes and make fortunes for folks here who own these rocky old pastures. 'Twas all blueberries. He never so much as mentioned a Roman emperor."

"I told you all," my father said with a somewhat irritating complacency, "that he was a most intelligent and farseeing man."

Mrs. Baxter looked thoughtful and, to my mother's quick eyes, apprehensive.

"I'm sure you're right, sir," she said. "He's both. And that's just why I can't see how it comes that I've felt squirmy all day about him. I can't put my finger on a thing, and I keep telling myself there's not the least reason, but I'm still squirmy."

"I'll just go up and see if he wants anything," my father said.

He came downstairs a few minutes later to report that all

was well. Our guest was sitting quietly by his open window enjoying the stars and the late June evening. He wanted nothing, he told my father, except his own thoughts.

Mr. Wheeler rose at dawn the next morning. Mrs. Baxter, aroused by the sound of his bare feet stealthily descending the back stairs and now overcome by her squirminess, dressed quickly. By the time she had reached the side door, however, on her way to the barn, she decided to call my father. Mr. Wheeler had again tied Snow White on either side of the entrance to the barn, where she was trying her best to free herself by rearings and stampings. He was on her back and with a pitchfork, which he had evidently mistaken for a lance or a spear, raised high in his right hand was proclaiming loudly that he was one of the Caesars making ready for his triumph through the streets of Rome. He had no clothes on whatever except for Snow White's tattered blanket which he had draped across his shoulders, apparently in the illusion that it was a Roman toga.

My father never discovered which of the Caesars poor Mr. Wheeler was impersonating. He sent Mrs. Baxter hurrying down the road for the village doctor, fortunately both a Methodist and a friend; and together he and the doctor persuaded Mr. Wheeler to dismount and to dress himself in the clothing procured by Mrs. Baxter from his room. He was not at all violent or even rebellious. He was, instead, like a child who at the last moment has been forbidden to put on a carefully prepared show, or like a playwright who has seen his cherished drama fold up after the first night because of lack of popular understanding and acclaim. When he realized that my father and the doctor were planning to take him back at once to the asylum, he neither questioned their decision nor showed any signs of regret. Perhaps in the confused world of his mind such a decision meant more clarity and order than he was capable of achieving by himself and was, therefore, not unwelcome to him.

While these proceedings were taking place in the barn, my mother and we children were gathered in the sitting-room watching from the windows or just staring at one another in disbelief. Or, more accurately, Mary, Ansie, and I were watching and reporting from time to time to my mother, who was actually far beyond any of these activities. She looked so indifferent and abstracted, so quiet and sad, that I felt worried about her even in the midst of such unparalleled goings-on. A long time afterward, when in the process of growing up I had discovered more clearly certain things for myself, she tried to tell me—in England it was—just how far removed she had been that morning from things that were happening and how, just because she had been far removed, many other things happened later on.

For she had suddenly found herself in that rare, salutary, and lonely state of mind when one accepts the imperfect just because there is nothing that human desire or human pity can do to make it any different from what it is. Of course, in lesser ways most thoughtful people accept the imperfect— the imperfections and faults of some treasured house or piece of country, the frailties and defects in ourselves as well as in those we most love, the imperfections of language in which one's thoughts are formed, but can never be entirely conveyed. Yet to accept the imperfect in the nature of life itself, to come face to face with injustice and tragedy, accident, irony, and pathos, and to know by some ruthless, quickening understanding, mingled with a wise, restrained fury toward things as they are, that one is forever caught among them and helpless against them—this acceptance and knowledge are quite another matter. If my mother had been merely indignant and angry at my father as she had been in times past and was often to be in the future, I doubt if we should ever have known any other of his friends at the asylum. But, since such superficial emotions were for the time being lost in this dark, yet clear vision of life itself which was inundating her as my father with the doctor's help made ready to take Mr. Wheeler away, most of her quite practical and rational defenses against his ideas and hopes had suffered a shattering blow.

## 17

Although, with that inconsistency which, in the course of mediocre events, makes havoc of all our revelations, my mother was to forget, or at least to set aside, that flash of understanding granted her on the morning of Mr. Wheeler's departure, I have always felt sure it was responsible for her willingness a month afterward to assent to Mrs. Nesbit's visit. At all events she came in August after the hay had been cut and gathered in and the goldenrod had begun to fill the thickets and to border the roadsides. My mother and Mrs. Baxter accepted her with wary resignation; we children with curiosity; my father as always with fresh hope. I don't think that any of us experienced a shift in these emotions during the week except that the resignation lost its wariness, the curiosity was never satisfied, and the hope, since it found no tangible cause for diminishment, at least slightly increased.

Nevertheless, though Mrs. Nesbit gave us no ground whatever either for alarm or for acute embarrassment, she exacted a heavy toll simply by her imposition of an atmosphere which so surrounded us all that it became an enclosure, an encirclement, all but a blockade. This atmosphere was silence, not the silence of contemplation or of meditation, of reverie or reflection, but merely an almost complete absence of human utterance. Until the last night of her stay with us Mrs. Nesbit literally never spoke except in occasional single words, which ranged from pleased comments to equally pleasant and sometimes startling ejaculations.

All of us, I am sure, revised our opinions concerning the value of silence during Mrs. Nesbit's visit, each, of course, according to age and experience. From a solacing, reanimating gift, not only extolled by poets and philosophers, but welcomed by all quite ordinary human beings, it became during that week a harrowing, nerve-racking, even peculiarly sinister environment. Although there was nothing tangibly threatening about it, it assumed the nature of a lowering, unpredictable cloud or of a heavy, clinging mist. It harboured secrets, was fraught with problems which baffled solution, was frustrating beyond description. Yet in its essence, that is, in so far as Mrs. Nesbit herself generated its character, it was calm, harmless, quite free from any esoteric translation. We were clearly its misinterpreters, and still we were its unwilling, thwarted, perplexed prisoners.

Whether Mrs. Nesbit was at all conscious of her silence we never knew, for she gave no sign. Nor did she seem in the least aware that it was causing any uneasiness or distress. She was like some small boat floating on a flat, unruffled sea, in the vast depths of which currents swirl and undertows surge, but which on its surface betrays none of these agitations. It had been in the hope of discovering those disturbances, which at some time in the past had wrecked the frail craft of Mrs. Nesbit's life, that her sojourn with us had been encouraged; but no such discoveries were made. She never evaded questions; she simply disregarded them. Whether or not she so much as heard them, we never knew.

She was a tiny, middle-aged woman, so small-boned and fragile that she seemed shadowy. She crept about like a shadow, too, suddenly appearing in a doorway or on the stairs and startling one quite unreasonably, for like any other shadow she gave the impression of lacking all corporeal substance. So far as one could gather, she was completely self-sufficient. In whatever world she dwelt it was apparently peaceful and untroubled. She had a vague, kind, benevolent face which never changed its expression of silent pleasure. She had delicate manners, too, as though she had once been well brought up, and a marked fastidiousness about her clothing and general appearance. She acquiesced wordlessly in all that we asked or expected of her. If one of us proposed a walk, she went happily, flitting about the fields or pastures like some small butterfly in the sun; if she helped Mrs. Baxter shell peas or remove the strings from beans in the kitchen, she worked quickly and skillfully in silent composure, looking all the while as though such co-operation were the most charming of occupations; if my father took her on a drive, as he frequently did to ease the growing tension in the house, she sat beside him, impassive, smiling, speechless.

On the first of these hushed excursions we children went along in the back seat, since my mother said that my father was himself becoming nervous and uncertain and that we could lend him support.

"Talk," she said as we started for the carriage in which Mrs. Nesbit was already quietly sitting. "Don't forget to talk. Just talk as you always do. Never mind if she doesn't say a word."

This was without doubt simple and wise advice, and we did our utmost to carry out her wishes; but we were vanquished before we had gone a quarter of a mile. I called attention to some early autumn colouring; Mary reminded us all that school was but four weeks away; Ansie saw and communicated briefly the presence of a squirrel. That was all. Some elusive, indefinable power clamped our lips, snatched all efforts from our minds, settled down over us like some heavy, invisible blanket. My father, too, became swathed in its folds although he did his utmost now and again to emerge from them.

"Were you born in New England, Mrs. Nesbit?" he asked, as we began slowly to ascend a hill.

A wood thrush answered him from a nearby thicket.

"It's late for a thrush," my father said. "Too early for migrating, too late for song."

He turned sharply around to stare at us all, disapproval together with a plea for help in his eyes.

"Yes," we said in unison, avoiding his gaze, ashamed of our absurd inability to help him.

Snow White's iron shoes clanged against the stones of the road. One of the wheel axles, wanting oil, whined. We rumbled slowly across a corduroy bridge above a swift stream.

"Brook!" cried Mrs. Nesbit in delight.

My heart gave a huge leap from surprise; Mary's mouth flew open; Ansie looked white.

"Yes," my father said in almost equal delight. "A brook to fish in. Did you ever fish for trout, Mrs. Nesbit, when you were a little girl?"

We went on up the hill. Then we went down another hill. We stopped at a roadside spring to give Snow White a drink. The afternoon sun flecked the water with gleams of light.

"Let's sing something, Ansie," my father said. "We often sing on drives," he explained to Mrs. Nesbit, whose face did not alter from its empty, rather winning smile.

"I don't feel like singing," Ansie said. He looked whiter.

"Nonsense!" said my father sternly. "Let's sing 'Annie Laurie.' "

He began with the first words, "Maxwelton's braes are bonnie." When he realized that Ansie was not joining him, he turned quickly around, ready with reproof, which was, however, not uttered, for he saw that Ansie was being quietly sick over the wheel. After that episode Mrs. Baxter only accompanied my father on any drives taken for Mrs. Nesbit's entertainment.

Mrs. Baxter was, in point of fact, a veritable anchor to windward throughout that long, memorable week. Her hold on things never slackened. Nor was her stout moral sense outraged when we discovered that any respect for the possessions of others had left Mrs. Nesbit, perhaps at that undiscoverable time when so many other qualities had taken their leave of her. By observation or intuition she had ascertained the drawer in the kitchen chest where Mrs. Baxter kept her starched white aprons. These apparently fascinated her, for she began removing them one by one to her room and stowing them away in the canvas case in which she had brought her belongings. When my mother, bent on redeeming them, inspected her room while she was with my father, or sitting silently in the orchard, or placidly wandering about the field and pasture, she discovered several other unrelated objects, a cooky cutter in the shape of a star, a ball of Ansie's, one of my hair ribbons, a spool of bright thread. We had no means of knowing whether Mrs. Nesbit resented or even noticed this reclamation. She continued to gather in, my mother to retrieve.

The weather held fair throughout her stay, in itself a blessing since silence without was less oppressive than silence within. We even went on several picnics, which Mrs. Baxter not only tolerated but proposed in spite of her considered opinion that they were untidy indulgences. Mrs. Nesbit accepted them all with mute equanimity. Infrequently, but always to my father's waning encouragement, she said "Sea gull!" or "Sailboat!" and invariably with the appearance of mild surprise and happiness. One day when we were fishing from an abandoned pier she hooked a flounder, which Ansie, seeing her line taut and trembling, drew in for her; but she remained imperturbable in the midst of our lavish and vicarious congratulation.

During her last evening with us we all sat in the orchard for an hour after supper. My mother had for some days previously suggested various other occupations for us children, and Mrs. Baxter was constantly inventing excuses for our absence; but either from a sense of loyalty to my father or from mere curiosity we usually managed to remain within the family circle. Perhaps because of the assurance of freedom on the morrow we found ourselves more able to talk with some degree of naturalness. My father and Mrs. Baxter reviewed seriously the best candidates for a Methodist conference in Bangor; my mother, Mary, and I made plans for Mary's birthday, which would fall in late September; Ansie in his turn rehearsed a recent letter from Katie descriptive of two swans which unexpectedly had taken up their residence on my grandfather's small stream. Mrs. Nesbit in the gathering darkness smiled on.

Suddenly the orchard grass and the air above it became punctuated with intermittent glints of light.

"Fireflies!" cried Mrs. Nesbit.

There was more than pleasure in her voice; there was rapture, as though the glimmering, darting flashes were illuminating some more obscure darkness, or some perpetual twilight in which she dwelt. She slipped from the bench where she was sitting between my father and Mrs. Baxter and began stealing about in the grass and reaching into the air for the fireflies. She was like some child who wakens in the night and gropes toward the thread of light beneath his door which promises safety and companionship outside. She was laughing in odd little ripples of sound as she ran hither and thither under the trees. Now we were the silent ones as we collided with one another, snatching after the elusive flickerings; but we all helped her to catch the fireflies which even in our hands still flashed and glowed. Ansie ran to the house to fetch a box for them. When we had caught a good number, Mrs. Baxter said:

"Let's take them to the kitchen and put them under a bit of glass. I think they light up just the same, inside as out."

"Let's," Mrs. Nesbit said, with genuine excitement.

They did light up just the same. When we had put them under a little glass saucedish and Mrs. Baxter had blown out the kitchen lamp, we all stood about the table and watched them glowing in the darkness so brightly that all our faces bending above them were brought now and again into sharp, fleeting relief. The fireflies had succeeded whereas we had failed; for as Mrs. Nesbit watched them, entranced, she continued to laugh and to look happily at each of us in the fitful gleams of light. She was transfigured, radiant, a new creature. I felt all at once as though I were going to cry. Ansie was the practical one among us.

"You can take them back with you tomorrow, Mrs. Nesbit," he said. "I'll put some grass in their box so they'll feel more at home. I'm sure they'll keep on sparkling in the night."

"Thank you, Ansie," Mrs. Nesbit said. "Thank you very much."

She looked smaller and more fragile than ever in the evanescent gleams, her narrow thin shoulders incapable of holding her upright, the tiny bones in her clasped fingers, which she had raised to her face, twitching like little sticks.

Yet she did not seem shadowy any longer even in the half-darkness. The vagueness had left her eyes, and her empty, ceaseless smile had been vanquished by her laughter.

"Thank you, all," she said.

The next night when Mrs. Baxter was getting supper, she reached for the glass saucedish in the kitchen cupboard in order to put some preserves in it. It was not there. We never saw it again.

### 18

I think that the most memorable thing about Mrs. Gowan among many memorable things was the way she widened her eyes as though she had never seen before just what she was looking at, as though she were continually in a state of primeval, boundless surprise. She always did this upon greeting a person whether familiar or unfamiliar to her, and it had the effect of making one feel of importance. She did it, too, again and again, while she was listening to a story or upon her first sight of anything at all unusual, an odd seashell, a bird's nest, a scurrying sandpiper.

Perhaps her eyes themselves lent significance to this distinctive trait or mannerism. They were long rather than round eyes and of a rather pale, yet clear blue. They had a shining, innocent quality like those of a happy child. Whenever she widened them in this singular way her eyebrows, which were high and quite beautifully shaped, rose, too, and gave puckers to her forehead, or, more accurately, deepened those already there.

This way of looking at people and things lent her an air of almost constant astonishment; and yet together with it and seemingly at complete variance to it she emanated an atmosphere of tranquillity and assurance—an atmosphere usually characteristic only of those few persons who have managed somehow to know satisfaction in its most basic, substantial forms or else who by some rare power or gift denied to most of us have been able to reach some mysterious mental and emotional citadel where fears no longer exist. Nor was this composure vacant or negative, as one might expect, given her environment over many years. It was instead positive and vibrant, as though she had spent her mature life grappling with the pros and the cons of abstract ideas and theories and had at last come to an honest or at least workable conclusion about them. My father once said to me, some years afterward when he and my mother had returned to England, that he never saw a shorn, harvested Suffolk wheat field, lying quiet beneath an autumn twilight, without being reminded in an odd way of Mrs. Gowan.

There were no discernible aspects about Mrs. Gowan's earlier life as we learned about it from her in the late summer of 1903 which could account either for her serenity or for her attitude of gay, quickening surprise. Serenity had been entirely absent from it; and, although it had richly furnished her with violent surprises, its rudeness and turbulence could hardly have produced that sense of artless wonder with which she viewed the world in her old age. It was as impossible to discover the source of these traits which made her so distinctly what she was as it was impossible to forget them.

I think, in fact, that they were in large measure responsible for my mother's surprising invitation to Mrs. Gowan to visit us which she extended once she had met Mrs. Gowan in Augusta. Such an invitation was surely absent from her mind, indeed anathema to it, at the close of Mrs. Nesbit's sojourn. Like most other reasonable persons in a similar situation she had decided that we had had quite enough of my father's experiments in hope and faith; yet I cannot honestly say that reasonableness in any form characterized her behaviour during a most complicated and embarrassing week at the end of August. Whimsical and volatile by nature, she was given to swinging capriciously from one mood to another, and now she swung with no discretion whatever to the outer limits of vexation and resentment. She forgot or pushed aside the sorrowful burden of human knowledge which Mr. Wheeler had afforded her and the fitful light of the fireflies beneath the saucedish on the kitchen table which had seemed to free Mrs. Nesbit from her particular captivity, just as she forgot or chose to disregard her earlier resolution to co-operate with my father. For fully seven days she was captious, indignant, and irritable, to use but the kindest of adjectives. My father, looking like a child who is bewildered by the illogical and quibbling censures of upbraiding parents, took daily to trout fishing; we children sought for diversion anywhere but at home; Mrs. Baxter was puzzled and anxious.

"I wouldn't wonder a mite but what she's close on to hy-sterics," she said to Mary and me one evening at the close of this harrowing week while we were helping her with the dishes, all of us uncomfortably aware of ominous silence throughout the house. Ansie had long since disappeared.

"No, she isn't," Mary said. "She never has—those." I knew she was politely refraining from the correct pronunciation of Mrs. Baxter's noun. "You should have seen her on that horrible steamship, Mrs. Baxter. She was wonderful, every single minute. And you must admit that father can be— well, difficult."

"Your father," Mrs. Baxter said, pausing to rinse the dishes with more boiling water than was necessary, "is the best man I've ever known in my whole life."

"I know that, of course," Mary said. She stood with a cup in her left hand and the dish towel in her right. She was looking at neither Mrs. Baxter nor me, but staring dreamily at nothing. Then she said slowly, "I often hope I'll not marry someone just like father."

I have never forgotten the shock which my sister's words gave me. I suddenly felt lonely and lost as though she had travelled to a strange country, leaving me in the worn, familiar one, with some dark, impassable gulf between them. I dropped my dish towel in my confusion. Mrs. Baxter hurriedly gave me a clean one from the rack above the sink. Then she looked quizzically at Mary.

"Aren't you a bit young to be thinking of getting married?" she asked.

"I don't think so," Mary said calmly, still staring at invisible wonders in her new world. "Eventually, girls do get married, Mrs. Baxter."

At just that moment when I thought I couldn't go on with the dish-drying and when even Mrs. Baxter was at a stupefied loss for speech, my mother burst into the kitchen. She was as merry as she was excited.

"Where's your father?" she asked Mary and me.

Mrs. Baxter answered her.

"I have a notion he's in the pasture," she said. "I saw him setting out for a walk. It appears to me he's got a lot on his mind."

"I'm sure he has," my mother said lightly, as she started for the side door. "So have I. I've just now decided that I'm going with him next week on his September visit to that asylum. He's asked me times enough, and now I mean to see things for myself. I'll go find him and break the news."

It must have taken some time to apprise my father of her quixotic decision, for darkness had fallen long before they returned, their feet drenched with dew, their faces calm and shining. Everybody but me had a most welcome reunion over our evening tea; and I pretended to, difficult as it was. Ansie couldn't believe his eyes and ears when he saw and heard us all laughing and talking and knew that he could now describe the huge kite he had been making in readiness for the next high northwest winds after the August dog days.

I didn't stay in the same bed with Mary that night. Once I was sure that she was sound asleep, I stole up the steep stairs to the attic where there was a tiny, unfinished room with a cot in it. What with my mother's petulance and my father's distress, with Mr. Wheeler's thwarted triumph and Mrs. Nesbit's silence, with Ansie's not asking me to help him with his kite, and, far beyond all these, yet heaviest in my aching heart, my sister's new, idiotic, and perilous dreams which made us strangers to each other, I felt so tempest-tossed and desolate that, I told myself, I required complete solitude even at the cost of rough dark rafters and probable spiders.

I felt bitterly disappointed when I awoke in the morning not only to find my griefs less painful but to realize that I had fallen asleep before I had had time for appropriate misery.

### 19

I suppose Mrs. Baxter's treatment of us during our parents' five days' absence in Augusta might well be described as *therapeutic* in the modern term. I have often since wished I could have been inside her mind when she planned it, for I am sure it was the result of deep and secretive design arising from her conviction that we had recently seen quite too much of the darker side of life. It was certainly restorative in every particular as well as healing and curative in its complete freedom from any sort of mental or emotional anxiety. It was daring, too, for she threw all cautions, both physical and economic, to the brisk, clear September winds and gave us, as the first of her remedial ministrations, so much to eat that we were in a perpetual state of overstuffing.

Our five days, by common and tacit consent, were prayerless. Instead, at a late and leisurely breakfast we consumed mounds of hot pancakes drenched in maple syrup. For dinner we had succulent clams fried in egg batter or pot roast thick with gravy; for supper, prodigious slabs of hot blueberry cake yellow with fresh butter. There were all manner of pies, apple, blueberry, lemon, pumpkin, custard, for every meal, steamed puddings at noon and at night, and in the interims sizzling doughnuts dipped from a kettle of boiling lard. Mrs. Baxter was skeptical about the doughnuts, perhaps even guilty, since she knew my mother was given to questioning them. She warned us as she ladled them from the fat that they had been known to cause "fits" in children who ate them too hastily and in too great number. We gobbled them just the same and had no fits.

Much as we loved our parents, it was really a wonderful span of relaxation, with the opening of school just around the corner. Along with her riotous indulgence in food Mrs. Baxter entered into our doings with an abandon which amazed us all. We dug our clams together at low tide, going out so far on the shaky flats to get the big ones that we sank our feet into the mud and slime without a word of disapproval from her; indeed, since she was far heavier, she sank far deeper and always with great good humour. We fished for flounders from an actual dory which she borrowed and rowed a good distance out in the harbour like a seasoned mariner; and once we had brought our bountiful catch home and she had dexterously filleted them, she dotted them with cloves before frying them, after a secret recipe of her own hitherto untried in the parsonage. She harnessed Snow White and took us on long drives. We flew Ansie's kite from the field with an utter disregard of the second growth of grass and sang all manner of songs as we watched it sailing carelessly high overhead. Mary forgot her silly fancies, and Ansie forsook all the boys of the neighbourhood, if not for me personally, at least for our combined and unexpected camaraderie. This became in fact so dependent and hilarious that we fetched Lilla as a foursome in the late afternoon and, while Mrs. Baxter expertly milked her, we three stood about watching. When she skillfully squirted some streams of warm milk into Ansie's mouth, we thought it the most amusing thing we had ever seen and rocked with laughter.

In the evenings we all played parchesi at the kitchen table until long past our usual bedtime. In the place of the counters Mrs. Baxter surprised us yet again by substituting coloured lozenges, a silly innovation which afforded us immense delight, especially since the winner was given all the lozenges as stakes while fresh ones miraculously appeared for the following games. When the clock startled us all by striking nine, the leader of our revels made quarts of rich cocoa which she complemented with delectable, fruity confections called "hermits." As we reluctantly departed for bed on the final night of this boisterous and unbridled holiday, we all, prompted by Ansie, threw our arms around her and kissed her good night. She looked startled and perhaps a trifle culpable, but I think she was pleased.

"It's a relief to think just about yourself for a time at least, isn't it?" Mary said to me as we undressed. "I mean, not even to *want* to do good to anyone at all."

I was too full of cocoa, hermits, and grateful astonishment over our incomparable five days to answer her.

20

My mother made it abundantly clear from the moment of their return home that Mrs. Gowan's visit was at her own suggestion, without any urging whatsoever from my father; in fact, she had previously conveyed this information in a letter to Mrs. Baxter which had not been shared with us doubtless because Mrs. Baxter had determined that no shadow should be allowed to fall upon her program of events for our entertainment while she was in sole charge of us. As it turned out, she need not have had the least misgiving. There was nothing in any way shadowy about Mrs. Gowan.

She was, on the contrary, substantial, tangible, real. She was neither fragile like Mrs. Nesbit nor broodingly reflective after the manner of Mr. Wheeler. Although she was not far from eighty years old, she gave every impression of being twenty years younger. She was of average size and height, quick and eager in all her motions. She carried her head high and slightly inclined toward the left, a position which lent a certain archness to her appearance. She was genial, outgoing, gracious. And yet she possessed in her almost unlined, mobile face an expression of grave serenity, suffused, as I have said, by a kind of perpetual surprise and excitement like the sunlight of Indian summer streaming across some quiet, contained landscape ready and waiting for winter under the autumn sky.

She had an innate, measureless capacity for acute enjoyment as well as the power to convey that pleasure to others; yet unlike many prodigal persons she was never irksome or exhausting. She was rarely averse to talking, which she did exceedingly well; but she was quite contented to sit quiet for hours in the sitting-room or the kitchen busy with her American flags or willingly setting them aside to help my mother or Mrs. Baxter with the family mending. Warned by my father about her Betsy Ross world, we expected her to retreat there often. As a matter of fact, such excursions were rare and could usually be circumvented if one of us thought of an interesting story or proposed a fresh activity. When they did occur and she told us about General Washington's request to her to design the national standard, she made everything seem so normal and actual that we easily found ourselves, too, in Philadelphia in the year 1777.

I have always cherished my own perhaps perverse ideas about Mrs. Gowan's retirements from what is known as the real world. I have no doubt that such hallucinations, self-deceptions, and delusions some thirty years before we knew her had been serious, even violent enough to make necessary her commitment to the hospital. There had, indeed, been every reason for her desperate invention of another sphere in which to live. And yet I am inclined to think that her translations of herself into Betsy Ross and her hurried journeys to Philadelphia and brief stays there were in large measure, at least during her visits to us, excitements and indulgences, especially since with us she had no real desire for escape; nor have I ever been convinced that the purely histrionic offerings of such behaviour did not possess their appeal to her.

She had many of the qualities usually attributed to an actress. She was a genius at storytelling, throwing herself with gestures and even mimicry into her recitals. She had a quick, true sense of dramatic moments and effects. She loved to dance in games with us children and took unquenchable delight in the country rhymes which my father remembered from his Suffolk boyhood and repeated to her, or in the songs which Ansie sang and in which she loved to join, her thin, quavering voice often failing on the higher notes and causing her gay, even quite riotous laughter.

I think I remember her best during our afternoons in the orchard, for in the fine September weather we had our tea there, once we had discovered how she rejoiced in it, how she threw her whole being into every feature of it: Ansie's hungry eyes staring at Mrs. Baxter's frosted cupcakes; my father's relaxation in a long canvas chair recently given him by his friend, the doctor; my mother's assembling of the cups and saucers and her cordial voice saying, "I know you like it good and strong, Mrs. Gowan, just like me." She had a passion for gathering flowers to make wreaths for us all, her fingers as nimble at this occupation as with her needle; and when we were all there during the bright late afternoons she would crown each of us with her handiwork—some garlands of autumn berries for us children, bunchberries or Solomon's-seal or baneberries; a rakish coronet of goldenrod for Mrs. Baxter's severe head; some lacy white asters for my mother; and always for my father a circlet of red leaves, which above his quiet, serious face afforded her a delighted sense of contrast.

There are rare times and occasions in the experience of everyone when things for the moment seem entirely good and right, when life halts on its burdened, inexorable way, when anxieties fade and fears are not. Such, I have always thought, were the hours with Mrs. Gowan in our orchard. Her joy at being among us was so simple, primitive, and uncluttered that we all responded as though we were dwelling in the earliest ages of some ingenuous, single-minded, undesigning world. My father seemed almost transfigured during these hours as though, after countless disappointments and disillusionments, he were at long last realizing the truths upon which he had staked his all. Yet he was never so far away in his shining realms of renewed faith and confidence that he did not readily contribute his share to our parties.

One day, early in Mrs. Gowan's initial visit, when he looked particularly wanton and indecorous with the red maple leaves of her wreath fluttering above his eyebrows, he unearthed an old English poem or ballad, which he said he had not recalled for years but which he thought particularly suited to us all at the moment. It was one, he told us, that the children in his country school at home used to say in unison, clapping their hands as they did so. It might be even centuries old, he said, and never written down at all, just recited from one generation of children to another. My mother, I could see, had some misgivings as he began to repeat it; but once she saw Mrs. Gowan's unrestrained delight in it, she smiled, too, beneath her own wreath of asters.

There was a mad man and he had a mad wife,
    And they lived in Ding Dong Dell.
They had three children, all at one birth,
    And they were mad as well.

The father was mad, the mother was mad,
    And the children were mad beside;
And they all got on a mad white horse,
    And madly they did ride.

They rode by night, they rode by day,
    Yet nary a one of them fell;
And they rode madly all the way
    Till they came to the Gates of Hell.

The Devil was glad to see them all mad
    And gladly let them in.
But he soon grew sorry to see them so merry
    And let them out again.

Then God came down and said to them all,
    "Now come along with Me,
For My House is the maddest House
    That you will ever see.

"It's so full of madness there's no room for sadness,
   It's lasted for endless years.
It's built of gladness, and Grace, and joy.
   There's no room in it for tears."

My father had to recite it fully half a dozen times for Mrs. Gowan, who began to finish each line like a child memorizing nursery rhymes by completing them as they are read aloud to him.

"Why don't I copy it out for you, Mrs. Gowan?" Mary said. "Then you'll have it for keeps just in case you forget it."

"And I could copy out father's other verses," I said. "We could make a real copybook of them for you, Mrs. Gowan. And we could even sew and bind it in some coloured pasteboard so it would be just like a book."

A slightly wary, almost frightened look crept into Mrs. Gowan's eyes at this mention of a book.

"Thank you," she said, "but I like better to have things in my mind. I don't care much for reading books."

My mother looked surprised.

"You speak so well that I would have thought you had read a great deal," she said.

"Oh, I have," Mrs. Gowan said. "A very great deal. When I was young, I lived to read, perhaps partly because I wasn't allowed to. But not so much now. Books bother me, even copybooks."

"Why is that?" my father asked kindly.

"I don't just know," Mrs. Gowan said. "Perhaps all the many words marching across all the many pages. I keep thinking of all the tiredness there was for someone writing down all those words until I get quite tired myself and maybe confused, too. And when I remember all that the words carry —I mean about people and all their thoughts and doings— well, I guess that's why I prefer space-takers. I love space-takers. I can think about those for hours and hours. They never tire me in the least."

We all looked confused in our turn.

"Just what is a space-taker?" Mrs. Baxter asked.

She was knitting a sweater for Ansie under her generous wreath of goldenrod. I knew that she felt awkward and ill at ease with the yellow plumes so absurdly on her head, and I felt especially grateful for her.

Mrs. Gowan looked around at us all, her blue eyes widened in pleased surprise that she could tell us something which we did not know.

"Doesn't anyone here know what a space-taker is?" she asked importantly.

"I'm afraid not," my father said. "We should all be grateful if you could explain one, Mrs. Gowan."

"Certainly," Mrs. Gowan said with marked gravity. "A space-taker is what takes up a bit of space when newspaper editors are done with all the news. You see, when they have said all they have to say about fires, or murders, or parties, or folks going places, or celebrations for this and that great event, they often need to fill the little spaces that are left empty at the end of their long columns. So they just open one of their desk drawers and find a space-taker for the bare places in their newspapers.

"I'll tell you how I know so much about them. Quite a time ago an editor of a newspaper in Lewiston, Maine, came to stay with us for a spell. His thoughts had gone higgly-piggly with all his hard work, and he had other troubling things in his life besides. He was a very nice young man, named Charley Bright. I used to talk with him a lot when we held our parties for the patients on Saturday nights, and sometimes we used to meet about the grounds. He told me all about space-takers. He had thousands and thousands of them all filed away; and when he had empty spaces to fill in his newspaper he just drew several out and fitted them in. Of course, they are very different. Some just deal in facts, like 'Samuel de Champlain sailed along the Maine coast in September, 1604, and named Mount Desert Island' or 'Last year tornadoes killed 146 people in the United States and rattlesnakes with their deadly fangs were responsible for the death of 34.' No one of course would care much for those space-takers, but often there are wonderful ones like—well, like Socrates saying, 'I am not an Athenian or even a Greek, but I am a citizen of the whole wide world,' or like Shakespeare, 'There's a divinity that shapes our ends, rough-hew them how we will.' Space-takers like those give hours of thought. Sometimes they just glow quietly in your mind, or at other times they are like those Roman candles that send out stars in all directions and make you think of a hundred things. A while ago there was a beautiful one. It said, 'The Spirit of the Lord God is upon me; because the Lord hath sent me to bind up the brokenhearted, to proclaim liberty to the captives, and the opening of the prison to them that are bound.' That's from the prophet Isaiah, though I shouldn't be telling that to a real parson, now, should I?"

"Of course, you should," my father said. "Parsons need space-takers, too, and that one is my very favourite passage from the whole Bible."

Mrs. Gowan was illumined by happiness, by importance and new companionship. Instead of a wreath for her own thin white hair (for she had been too busy with framing ours to think much of herself) she had tucked two scarlet geraniums from my mother's front-yard flower bed, one behind either ear where they glowed now against her flushed cheeks. She rose from the orchard bench and stood among us with her arms outspread as though she were garnering unnumbered blessings.

"So that's what a space-taker is, you see," she said. "I learn my favourite ones every week and stow them away in my mind just as Charley Bright put them away in his drawer. And when I have empty spaces to fill, in my days, as I often do when I'm done with the unimportant things in the hospital, I just draw them out and say one or two over to myself and fill up my own spaces with their thoughts. And, will you believe it, that nice young man, that Charley Bright, sends me his paper every week—just for me with my name on it, Mrs. James Gowan, Maine State Hospital, Augusta—and what is more he puts a blue line around his space-takers so I won't have to read the news at all. He even says," she concluded with a shy, half-coy look around our circle, "that he chooses them now with me in his mind."

"I'm sure he does," my mother said, smiling first at Mrs. Gowan and then at my father in his long chair.

"He's such a nice young man," Mrs. Gowan said, "and very handsome, too, tall and straight. I hope he stays well in his head. He said in a letter which he wrote just to me that *he* uses space-takers now the way I do, to fill spaces in his thoughts when all of a sudden they grow empty or muddled. And always on the folder around his newspaper addressed just to me he writes *hospital*. He never writes *asylum*. There's such a difference in words and what they suggest to one, now, isn't there?"

"Yes, there is," my father said quietly.

"What's one space-taker that Charley Bright chose just for you, Mrs. Gowan?" Mary asked.

"A lovely one, Mary," Mrs. Gowan said, her eyes wide and shining. "And only in his paper just last week. It was as though he knew that I was coming to visit you. When I woke up this morning and remembered I was really here among my new friends, and saw the sun, I said it over to myself. It's from Shakespeare. It says:

> Night's candles are burnt out, and jocund day
> Stands tiptoe on the misty mountain tops."

"Well, if you'll excuse me," Mrs. Baxter said, her solid cheeks trembling a little beneath her goldenrod, "I'll go in and tackle supper."

## 21

Since it was Mary's turn to set the table for supper, I could stay in the orchard with the others. Mrs. Baxter seldom allowed more than one of us to help her; and I am sure she consented to that much assistance only because she thought it might be good for us, not in any way for her. The September sun was low in the sky and the shadows were long upon the orchard grass. Mrs. Gowan returned to my father's poem, which he repeated yet again for her.

"I've got it pretty well in my head now," she said. "It's rather long for a space-taker, but it has lots of good thoughts, especially at the close where it talks about the house of God. I like that name much better than Heaven myself. Or is that wrong of me?"

"Not in the least," my father said. "I've never much fancied Heaven. No one knows anything really about Heaven, but most people at times know a little about the house of God."

"I understand about gladness and joy," Mrs. Gowan said. "I feel them both this very minute. But I'm not sure about this *grace*. I've a special reason for asking you, too. Just what it this *grace*?"

My father looked thoughtful. Perhaps just for the moment he forgot Mrs. Gowan in the recollection of his seminary days and their hot theological disputations.

"Grace?" he said. "Grace? Well, that's very difficult to ex-plain, Mrs. Gowan. Many learned men have thought about grace for many centuries. Most of them think it has to do with forgiveness and mercy, but I'm inclined to disagree with them. I rather think grace means just the constant presence of God."

A puzzled, slightly bewildered look crept into Mrs. Gowan's eyes.

"I'm glad you don't think it means forgiveness," she said. "I heard too much about forgiveness when I was young. 'God will forgive you if you pray hard enough,' I heard, or 'God will never forgive you.' I heard that, too. Forgive, forgive, forgive. I got so I hated forgiveness! And even now I don't like it one little bit!"

"I'm sure you don't need to worry at all about forgiveness," my father said, coming back from the seminary and looking suddenly at my mother as though he needed her help.

"Of course, you don't," my mother said quickly, and as carelessly as though forgiveness were not worth an instant's consideration. "Who cares a whit about silly old forgiveness? And isn't it nice, Mrs. Gowan, to think of God's house being mad? You see, madness means being merry just as the poem says—so merry that there's not a bit of room for tears. That's just what it means, isn't it?" she asked my father abruptly with, I thought, more than a trace of accusation in her tone.

"Precisely," my father said, and hurriedly for him. "Pre-cisely. All the people in the poem were so merry, that is, so full of grace that God had to have them, for they belonged there with Him. My wife always explains things better than I can, Mrs. Gowan, as you see. And the house of God, or at least a good-sized room in it, is here, right here in this very orchard, and we are all in it. Only, Ansie, I'm afraid you'll have to slip out for a few minutes to fetch Lilla for her milking."

Mrs. Gowan became radiant again.

"I'm glad to get it all straight in my mind," she said. "And not only for myself, but for Mrs. McCarthy. She's really why I asked you about the meaning of that word *grace*."

"Who's Mrs. McCarthy?" Ansie asked. "I'll go in a minute, father, once I know about Mrs. McCarthy."

"Mrs. McCarthy," Mrs. Gowan said, with the dignity she always assumed when she was asked a direct question, "is a lady in the hospital who usually has the room next to mine off the ward. She was born in Ireland where fuchsias grow like trees and where the mountains are bluer than the many lakes and where people really believe in ghosts and fairies and elves. She's a very special friend of mine. She's almost always clear in her mind, quite like me, but there are times when she gets muddled up and thinks she's back in County Kerry where sad things happened to her on account of her husband and her three sons all going out in their boats to sea. They were fishermen. Sometimes, when these spells overtake her, the doctors carry her away for a few days to do healing things to her; and when she comes back, she always says to me, 'There's not a thing left to me, Mary Gowan, but the Grace of God.' So now I can tell her just what *grace* means."

"Let's all go after Lilla," I said, for I saw the idea stirring in my mother's mind. "Ansie and you and me, Mrs. Gowan."

"I'd love to," Mrs. Gowan said, Mrs. McCarthy and the Grace of God growing dim in her new anticipation.

"And I've a plan for you all," my mother said. "You children put your wreaths on Lilla's horns and lead her home in a triumphal procession. I can hear her now 'lowing at the skies.' "

"We'll do that very thing," Mrs. Gowan cried. " 'Lowing at

the skies.' That sounds just like poetry."

"It is," my mother said. "It's a space-taker of mine, Mrs. Gowan."

## 22

Mrs. Gowan did not tell the story of her life in the orchard, but in the sitting-room and on one evening toward the close of her visit when she had come to feel very much at home. I am sure our parents planned it that way in the thought that we children might well not hear it. At all events after supper that night my mother sent us upstairs to do our lessons for school the next day; and since Mary was in one of her faraway moods and wanted, she said, to read *The Lady of Shalott* aloud in order to memorize at least part of it more easily, I went into Ansie's room to work with him on our arithmetic problems which had to do with wallpaper. We felt unreasonably annoyed with Mrs. Baxter, who might well have been of help to us, but who had gone, laden with soothing custards, to visit Mrs. Kimball, in bed with what in Pepperell was known as "the quincy."

The invitation to Mrs. Gowan to tell her story was given not entirely for her sake. My father, my mother told us later when she shared with us certain carefully chosen incidents from Mrs. Gowan's past, was prompted by what one might call, I suppose, a professional reason. He already knew about her life from Dr. Thomas and the records at the hospital; but both he and the doctor were anxious to see whether her own recital of it tallied exactly with the records or varied from them in any particular. It tallied exactly, my mother said.

Ansie and I, from his room at the right of the stairs leading from the sitting-room, could hear the fire crackling in the fireplace there, for it was a chilly evening. Although my mother had discreetly closed Ansie's door earlier, he had just as discreetly opened it, lowering his lamp as he did so. We both felt it quite impossible to settle down at his table with the hateful rolls of wallpaper, measured by a Mr. A. and ready to be put on walls by a Mr. B., who was relying upon us to determine just how many rolls he would need in view of the many windows cutting up the space. We could hear also my father's quiet voice beginning to encourage Mrs. Gowan.

"There's so much about your girlhood that we just don't know, Mrs. Gowan," he was saying. "You've learned so much about us during your visit that we'd like to know more about you, that is, if you'd care to tell us."

"Of course, I would," Mrs. Gowan said, perhaps a trifle hesitantly. I am sure Ansie felt as I did that she was disappointed in the size of her audience.

My mother was quick to read her thoughts.

"I'm sorry the children can't hear it, too," she said, "but they simply must do their lessons. We'll all have our tea together later, at nine o'clock."

"Maybe it's just as well after all," Mrs. Gowan said. "I wouldn't say my life was especially fashioned for children."

When Ansie and I heard her say that, we were consumed by a single purpose which needed no expression. We slipped out of our shoes at the selfsame moment, closed Ansie's door noiselessly after raising the wick of his lamp so that the thread of light could be clearly seen through the crack just in case someone peered up from below, and crept out on the floor near the head of the stairs. There was no light in the hall; the stair well itself was dark; and we were careful to sit with our backs against the protecting wall just outside his room. We could hear every word clearly and distinctly; and now and again by careful bendings forward and peering around the angle of the wall we could even see the group in the sitting-room below. I don't think we once worried over the ethics of our behaviour. Perhaps we were unconsciously accepting the fact that ethics often grow dim in the light of human drama and tragedy.

Many times since that evening so long ago when Ansie and I huddled against the wall, and Mary's voice murmured from her room down the hall, and the light from the open fire gleamed and glowed across the three faces in the sitting-room, I have reconstructed both the scene and Mrs. Gowan's story in my mind, without doubt distorting some of her words, but remembering the essence of them. My father was in his chair at one side of the fireplace and my mother in hers on the other side, busy with some sewing. Mrs. Gowan sat between them on a fat hassock which she fancied; but every now and then as she talked she began to walk about the room. She was much given to using her hands whenever she told us anything at all; and now we could see from our furtive glances down the dark stair well that she was extending them in a wide half circle, or clasping them together, or sometimes throwing them upward to rest uneasily upon her shoulders.

"I suppose it's usual to begin one's life with being born, isn't it?" she asked.

"I daresay it is," my father said, taking his pipe from his pocket and beginning to fill it. "I think you once told me you were born up in Aroostook County, Maine."

"That's true," Mrs. Gowan said. "And when I was born way up there all those many years ago, Aroostook County wasn't so much as a county, only just the Aroostook. It was a great tract of land with wide-open plains and dark forest regions and, whenever one climbed a hill, chains of lakes at a long distance. They say today there are fields of potatoes up there, potatoes enough for all the world, and huge farms and big, bustling towns. I wouldn't know about that, for I've never seen Aroostook County since I was seventeen years old.

My mother used to say over and over again that I'd burn someday in Hell. I used to think then, and I've thought ever since, that the burnings in Hell couldn't be so bad as the burnings inside me when I was young in that wild Aroostook region."

Ansie and I could hear Mrs. Gowan walking about then. We could almost hear the silence, too, in the sitting-room; but after a few minutes she sat down again on the hassock, and her voice grew more even and quiet.

"When I was young, it was a lonely land enough. There weren't any towns to speak of, only tiny settlements of French and Canadians and us Americans all mixed together, for then no one even knew who owned the Aroostook. There weren't any railroads then. There was just this land going on and on with the wind sweeping over it and great shadows racing under the heavy clouds. I used to think it went on forever and forever without any end. Or sometimes I'd think that God had forgotten it and never finished it. Or perhaps that it was just dead and could never come alive. When you saw a man as you often did putting up a fence to shut in some of the land to make it his, you wanted to go and hang on to the fence because it was a sign that someday there would be a safe, enclosed field, or perhaps because it was just something to hang on to."

"I can see all the land and the fences," my mother said quietly, "but not your father and mother, Mrs. Gowan."

"I can't make you see my father," Mrs. Gowan said. "I don't remember him at all. He went up there to fence in land, too, but he got frozen to death the very first winter when I was only three."

I could hear Ansie draw in his breath beside me. I knew he was wishing for more about Mrs. Gowan's father and was hopeful when my father said:

"How did that happen? That must have been hard on your mother, Mrs. Gowan."

"Nothing was hard on my mother," Mrs. Gowan said. "She was so hard herself that nothing could have made her harder. How did it happen that my father got frozen to death? Why, he went out one winter day to hunt for deer which often bounded across the land from one forest to another. He went on snowshoes as men did then in untamed country, and I guess he just got lost in a blizzard or smitten by the awful cold way up there in the north. Anyhow he never came back, and they found him frozen to death some days later when some men went out to look for him. My father was the lucky one. He just froze to death, but my mother stayed frozen all her life."

"Perhaps you'd like to mend these socks of Ansie's while you talk," my mother said.

"No, I wouldn't like to mend them," Mrs. Gowan said. "I need my hands free, to talk."

"What made your mother frozen all her life?" my father asked.

"God," Mrs. Gowan said sharply.

Ansie and I snuggled more closely together in our dark corner next the wall.

"Too much God, or what she thought was God. Even when I was a child, I never believed God could have any use for my mother. But *she* did. She said that God was right there in our kitchen watching me while I dried the dishes or made our bed in a sort of lean-to we had. And when I was too frightened and shaky to dry them right or to spread the sheets smooth and tight, she said He was watching me and storing up punishments just for me. And what she didn't tell me, the Methodist preachers did. That's why I've always hated Methodist preachers—until now."

"I see," my father said, his voice slow and kind. "Where did the Methodist preachers come from?"

"I don't quite know," Mrs. Gowan said, "but one was always there. 'Twas just a little settlement where we lived, just a huddle of a few houses with a store and a schoolhouse. The Methodist preacher was usually our schoolteacher, too, and after he had scared us all the weekdays, he scared us worse on Sundays in the same place, for the schoolhouse was the church as well."

"Was everyone else who lived there as religious as your mother?" my mother asked.

"No," Mrs. Gowan said. "That's what made a lot of trouble. The Methodist preacher, whoever he was, for they were much the same, told my mother that she had been called upon to save all the other women, who were mostly not saved, only discouraged and tired with too many children to care for while their husbands cleared the distant woodland or set fences around the land they wanted. She helped the preachers on Sunday in the meetings that took up most of the day and half the night. She sang and talked and screamed; and when I was twelve or thirteen she made me get converted so I wouldn't be a disgrace to her, she said.

"But, of course, I never was converted really. She'd write out stories for me to learn, about how God had saved me at a certain hour and how happy I was with a clean heart, and she made me get up in the meetings and recite them. About then I got to roaming about the land, running out even at night whenever I could steal away while she was asleep or holding some meeting somewhere else. I was scared enough outside with the wind and the great, blazing stars, and sometimes with the Northern Lights which way up there burst open the heavens with streamers of fire, but never so scared as inside, in the bed beside my mother or sitting at the kitchen table learning those stories she had written out for me. That's when I found the fences a great help to cling to."

"Perhaps you'd rather tell us the rest some other time, Mrs. Gowan," we heard my father say. "You don't need to tell it all tonight. Perhaps you'd like to play a game of checkers with me."

"No, thank you," Mrs. Gowan said. "I'd rather tell it all. It will make my mind clear and empty so that I can put a space-taker in it when I go to bed. Besides, you haven't heard the most exciting part. You haven't heard how at last I got away from my mother."

We could hear her now beginning again to walk about the sitting-room. I leaned forward across Ansie, for I was in the angle of the wall. I felt better about her when I saw her face, for she didn't look really sad or too much troubled, only excited and eager. Her hands were restless, but her eyes were much the same as when she listened to our stories in the orchard or to my father's rhymes and songs.

"There's quite a bit to tell before that, though," she said. "It isn't exactly pleasant or even good, but it's true. I began to hate my mother. The worst times of hatred were when I was in bed with her at night after she had prayed aloud with us both on our knees shivering in the cold. Sometimes it seemed hours that she prayed. I used to lie against the wall, on the inside of the bed; and after she had gone to sleep, I used to imagine how I could kill her, with my father's hunting knife, I thought, for the men had brought that home when they had found him frozen. Then I'd ask God to forgive me, though I never felt He really did. For that matter, why should He?

"And whenever I'd fall asleep I'd have these awful dreams. I'd dream either about the knife sticking out of my mother's throat, or else I'd dream that she was chasing *me* with the knife in her hand. We were often running around fences in my dreams. I'd often be clinging to a fence post, for help I suppose, and she'd be running along the tops of the logs that framed the fences and getting nearer and nearer with the knife to the post I was clinging to. Then I'd wake up with a start and find myself soaked in sweat whatever the weather, and lie there waiting for the light to come."

"Didn't you ever have any good times at all?" my mother said. "Weren't there any other children or young people for good times in that wretched settlement?"

Mrs. Gowan came back to her hassock.

"Yes, there were," she said, "but most of them thought I was queer enough, and all of them were scared of my mother. There was one boy I really liked when I was around fifteen, and he really liked me. When my mother was out ranting around with the preacher, for on some days they took trips together to hold these meetings in other huddles of houses, he used to come to see me unless they made me go along with them to tell my falsehoods in their meetings. I wasn't bad-looking as a young girl. I had yellow hair which curled nicely, though my mother made me braid it tightly around my head; and I was light on my feet and might have danced well if I had ever been allowed to. And after I got to ranging around outside whenever I could escape or my mother was off some-where, this boy, this John King, would meet me and we'd talk. He hated the Aroostook, too, though his folks were nice and kind. He'd lend me books, and I'd hide them in the deep pockets of my skirt and read them whenever I got the chance. Sometimes I'd read them with my back against one of the fence posts quite a long way from home; and when the wind fluttered the leaves so that I could hardly keep them flat, they made me think how my heart fluttered at night, in bed, be-yond my mother.

"There was one book, *Treasure Island* it was, which I loved. I've never finished it through all these many years, even though it's right there in the library at the hospital and I could read it any time, only I can't because whenever I see it I begin to get muddled and forget who I really am. My mother discovered me reading it at just the place where a boy named Jim Hawkins was hiding in an apple barrel on board a ship and listening to pirates or mutineers. I've never known what happened afterwards or how the boy escaped, for she snatched it away from me at just that very place and threw it on the fire in the kitchen stove."

"Ansie can tell you," my father said. "Or, better still, I'll read it aloud to us all in the orchard. You won't feel in the least muddled when we read it together, Mrs. Gowan."

"Thank you," Mrs. Gowan said. "Well, I'd better get on with my story, for the really exciting place is now close at hand. This boy, this John King, went away to study in some academy farther south. I'd have loved to study more, too, but my mother wouldn't hear to that. She had discovered about his coming to see me and about our meetings far afield. She gave me terrible warnings about what she called 'fleshly temptations of the Devil,' and forbade me to see him any more even when he came home from school now and then to see his folks. So, until I was seventeen, we went on with me hating her and with her really hating me, though she claimed she was helping God to save my immortal soul."

Mrs. Gowan paused in her story then. We thought she had begun to walk about some more, but she hadn't, for we could hear no sound in the sitting-room except the murmur of the fire. Then she said slowly and thoughtfully:

"There's a place in the Bible where it tells about people who walked in darkness. Well, that was where I walked. As I remember that place in the Bible, a great light at last shone upon those people, but none ever shone around me up there in Aroostook, Maine. John King was a bit of a light as I recall him, but he went out just as a match goes out when it has burned away its slender stick. He hoped to be a doctor; he told me a lot about it. That was his dream, but I've never known whether it ever came true for him.

"One day the strangest thing happened to me. If you should read it in some book, you would never believe it, yet it's true all the same. And what's even more strange, it saved my soul, perhaps in a queer way, but saved it no matter what it may have done to me later on. Up there in those great, wide, mostly unfenced fields things were always blowing about before the high winds—sometimes careening brown masses of what they call tumbleweed, sometimes pieces of clothing that had slatted from lines in distant settlements, sometimes even hats and caps, or letters dropped by people perhaps miles away. Newspapers were the most common. When you were walking in a high, strong wind, you were likely to see newspapers, whole or in single sheets, billowing along toward you, end over end, now in the air, now scurrying next to the ground. And whenever you saw one, or at least whenever *I* did, I'd seize it and read whatever I could just in order to take my thoughts away from my mother if only for a few minutes.

"On this day that I'm telling you about I saw a newspaper blowing toward me across the open land. I ran toward it, for I had the sudden, queer notion that there might be something in it just for me. I was feeling more desperate than ever, for the new Methodist preacher we had at that time was a single man who hung about my mother. He said she had been seized by the Holy Ghost and was the holiest woman he had ever seen. He was a big man with a black beard and cruel black eyes. I knew he was up to no good, and I hated and feared him. The only thing he ever did for me was to make it easier for me to get out of the house, for when he was there in the kitchen with my mother and talking in his crazy way, they neither of them wanted me around."

Mrs. Gowan was evidently getting up to walk about again, for we heard my mother say:

"I think you'd best sit down to tell the rest, don't you, Mrs. Gowan? If you'll just sit on your hassock right between us where you'll feel safe and at home with friends, I'm sure you can tell the rest of your story even better."

"Perhaps," Mrs. Gowan said. "I don't want to make you uneasy by my walking about when you're so kind as to listen to me like this."

"It's not that at all," my mother said. "It's only that I can hear better when you're nearer me. I really think I don't hear so clearly as I used to do, and I wouldn't want to miss a word about that newspaper and what you found in it just for you."

We knew then that she was on her hassock again. Now she raised her voice higher, perhaps because of my mother, perhaps because of her mounting excitement.

"That newspaper," she said. "That newspaper all brown with rain and dew and soil. When I had once caught it, I lay flat down on that big, empty space of land and began to read it through. It was better than most straying newspapers to read, for it had once been folded carefully—it even trailed a piece of string—and it wasn't yet blown to pieces. It came from Boston—it said Boston on it—and it was dated only five days earlier. This queer notion kept stabbing at me, this notion that it had something in it just for me, and at last I found it on the very back page. There, on that very back page among the advertisements, was a notice signed with the letters J.G. It was a notice from a man—I swear it's true—who said he wanted a wife. He said she ought to be about eighteen and ready to lead an interesting, adventuresome life. He said he could promise her kind treatment always, and if she would write to him at an address he gave, he'd tell her more about himself. I read it again and again, lying there beneath swirling thunderheads in the sky, for there seemed, if I remember rightly, to be a storm already close at hand; and the address stayed in my mind and ran about there for hours like some old hymn tune.

"When I went back home in the rain and wind and thunder, night was falling and my mother was gone, somewhere with the preacher, I supposed, only I just saw that she was gone, and I looked upon her being gone as just another part of the plan just for me. I decided then and there that I wouldn't wait to write this J.G. It took weeks up there in the Aroostook to get a letter from any place at all. I'd never had a letter all my life from anyone or ever written one that I could remember. I knew if I waited that long, all my courage would leave me, even if I could put down words in a letter or even if my mother didn't ferret things out. I just decided I'd go, and if he wasn't there at that address, or if he'd already found a wife, I'd go out to service. I'd do anything just to get away. I don't think I thought then that I'd really find him, or perhaps even look for him, though the address kept nagging at me. It's hard to know exactly what I thought so many years ago; but I think now it was the address—18 Milk Street, it was—that made me determine to go. It was something to hang on to—18 Milk Street—like those few fences across all that great, barren land.

"Once I'd made up my mind to go, I went into the lean-to, which was the bedroom as I said, and began to get a few things together with the thunder bursting overhead. There was a straw basket with a cover on it on a shelf there, and I put my things in that. Then I suddenly thought I'd have to have some money. I didn't have a cent of my own or any purse either. But it wasn't as though I didn't know where there was money. My mother was treasurer of the church, and she kept the Sunday collections and the prayer-meeting ones in a tin box under her side of the bed. She kept the key to the tin box in the lining of an old hat in the closet. There was $64.13 in the tin box, and I took every penny of it. Then in the midst of all the thunder and the lightning which I knew would be keeping her wherever she and the preacher were, I lighted the stub of a candle and wrote her a letter telling her how I hated her for what she had done to me and how I'd gone, past finding out. When I'd finished the letter and blown out the candle and opened the door to the rain and the wind, I had the strangest feeling—not that I was saying good-bye to my mother or to what she called my home, but to all the fences in Aroostook, Maine.—I guess now I'll have to walk about a bit, but I won't say anything until I can sit down again."

"That's right," my father said. "You walk about all you like, Mrs. Gowan."

It was terribly still in the sitting-room while Mrs. Gowan walked to and fro. The fire sighed and sizzled, but there was no other sound except for her feet when they left the big square rug for the boards of the floor. My legs ached painfully from being folded under me, but I didn't dare stir. Mary's voice had stopped murmuring, and I was prickled all over by needles of dread lest she might come out and find us there. Ansie was so motionless I thought he might be asleep or perhaps even dead from fright. I put out my hand to touch him. He seized it and kept on holding it, which was extraordinary behaviour from him. By and by we heard Mrs. Gowan begin again with her story and knew she had returned to the hassock.

"It was a long way to Boston. First, I had to run four or five

miles in the storm to a larger settlement where I knew the
stagecoach to Bangor, Maine, stopped. I knew that because
that John King boy had told me how he got on it late at night
in order to go south to his school. I kept thanking God for the
storm, though probably He didn't send it just for me. But in
the thick darkness and the awful rain no one was out and no
one could see me on my way. When I wasn't thanking God,
I kept saying 18 Milk Street, 18 Milk Street, over and over,
like a prayer, too.

"I don't recall all the journey now, but I know it took several days in different stagecoaches or wagons and with stops
at inns or boardinghouses where people were kind to me.
When they asked me my name, I said I was Dora Smith and
that I was a servant girl in Boston. They didn't ask me much,
and I didn't say much either. I know it's wrong to say it, but
as I got farther and farther away I felt free and happy, with
the money tied up safely in my handkerchief. I got this fluttering feeling inside me, but light like the sun, not dark like
the flutterings of fear. At first I thought it might mean I was
sick in some odd way, and then I suddenly knew it was just
happiness which I'd mistaken because I had never felt it before. Once, on one of the stagecoaches, a blue butterfly flew
in the open window, and I laughed aloud to see him as free
and happy as I was. I've never forgotten that blue butterfly.
I've remembered it all my life.

"It was on a morning when we got to Boston. I'd heard or
read somewhere about Boston Common, so I found my way
there and sat still in the sunshine. There were pigeons flying
and hopping about, free like the butterfly and me. I don't
think even then that I really meant to hunt up this man, this
J.G., but 18 Milk Street kept running in my mind over and
over; and at last, because I didn't know what else to do and in
all my new happiness was worried because I didn't know any

way of getting any more money or finding any work, I asked my way there. The place turned out to be a butchershop with legs and sides of meat in the window and a fat man inside in a dirty apron using a long knife like my father's hunting knife at home. I went in after a time and asked this man if someone called J.G. lived there. He looked surprised enough to see me there, just a slip of a thing I was then and likely mussed and untidy. 'You must mean Jim Gowan,' he said to me. 'He don't live here, but he comes in every noontime to see if any letters have come for him. Take a chair,' he said. 'It's about time for him right now. You know him? You a relative?' 'Sort of a relative,' I said, 'and I'll wait outside, if you please.' 'Suit yourself,' he said, slicing at some meat with his big knife and still looking surprised.

"I went down to the corner of the street where I could see anyone coming in all directions. I knew him the minute I saw him coming toward me. It was just as though I was told who he was. He wasn't much more than a boy, small and almost puny-like, and he slipped along among all the many people almost like an eel or a snake. He was there, and then he wasn't, in and out. When he got next me, I touched his arm in a corduroy jacket, and he started as though he was scared to death and stared at me. I've forgotten now just what I said, but I think it was, 'Are you J.G. and are you still looking for a wife?' He just stared more at me, standing there with my straw basket. 'By God!' he said. 'Let's get out of here, and damn quick, too!'

"We went back to the Common again and found a place to sit, on an empty bench in a cluster of trees. 'Twas funny about the pigeons. They kept coming to rest on his shoulders, though they fluttered away from me. He could take them right in his hands. We talked there. He had a low, quiet voice, which sounded to me as if he'd come from some unbeknownst place, and he was nice and kind. He said he'd had several answers to his advertisement in the paper, but most of them that wrote were far older than me and rather set in their ways, though how he knew that I couldn't say. He was very honest with me after I'd told him about my mother and how I'd come that long way. 'By God!' he kept saying. 'You won't be well off most likely, with me, but a wharf rat like me is better to live with than that devil.'

"Well, the rest of it won't take long to tell because I've forgotten so much since then. Anyway some days later we went to a priest and got married because he was a Catholic and I didn't care."

"Just what is a wharf rat?" my mother asked. Her voice trembled a little, and we could hear her blowing her nose.

"A wharf rat," Mrs. Gowan said with her customary dignity in explanation, "a wharf rat is a thief. He's able to slink around wharves and piers where cargoes are coming in or going out. In those days there was a vast amount of shipping from many ports, Boston and New York and Philadelphia and Baltimore and New Orleans. We just moved from one to another where things were busiest or when my husband had reason to think there was danger in his staying too long in any one of them. I never quite understood just why he needed a wife, but he said a wife made him more respectable and covered up scents and clues."

"Was this man good to you, Mrs. Gowan?" my father asked. His voice sounded puzzled as well as concerned, as though he couldn't realize the mutually exclusive facts of Mrs. Gowan sitting on her hassock and Mrs. Gowan helping to evade the police in some seaport town.

"Yes, he was," Mrs. Gowan said. "I know he would be called a bad man, but he was always good to me. When he was at home, he helped me with my work always, and when he'd done well in his business, he often brought me gifts, and he never forgot to thank me and to say I was a good wife to him. And just as he'd said in that newspaper, he gave me a very adventuresome life. Where didn't we go? I've been to the southern states and even to Mexico, and once—that was after the railroads came—we went to San Francisco on all its many hills and above its great bay. Sometimes we had plenty of money, and at other times we didn't, but in better days or worse ones he was always good to me. We lived in all manner of houses, in dark, upper rooms sometimes and at other times in real houses with roses blossoming on their back fences. He had many friends or at least companions. They'd come often at night after I'd gone to bed and shift lots of boxes and bags about. Some of them were prosperous-looking men, whenever I'd catch a glimpse of them, with gold watch chains and fine clothes. Others were different, with names like Peg Leg, and One Eye, and Black Bill. Often I'd be alone for a good many months, and then I'd work. I've always been good with my needle—I have my mother to thank for that, I suppose. Once, while my husband was in prison for a spell, I worked in a big factory that made flags, in Philadelphia, that was, and I got so good and quick at making flags that I was made the manager of a whole room of sewing women and girls."

"What became of your husband?" my mother asked. "How long were you married to him?"

"I wish I could tell you both things," Mrs. Gowan said, "but I truly can't. I don't know whatever became of my husband, and I don't know how long I was married to him. It was many years, I'm sure, most of my life perhaps, but I don't know. I think it was while I was making flags in that factory that I got bewildered in my mind and forgot who I really was. There's a long space empty that I can't fill. Anyway, when things got clear again, I was in the hospital, quite safe

and well. Then I realized that I knew all about the Aroostook
and all about my childhood and a lot about my marriage, but
that the rest was sort of a jungle where I had got lost. I love
the hospital. It's been a home to me and, though I sometimes
even now forget exactly who I am, I mostly know quite well.
Wouldn't you say so, sir?"

"I surely would," my father said, pride and confidence in
his words. "We're all glad you're well again, Mrs. Gowan,
and just like one of us."

Ansie and I heard him put another log on the fire, which
began to crackle and blaze.

"There's one thing I didn't tell you," Mrs. Gowan said. "I
had a baby once, but it died before we could get a priest to
baptize it, and that troubled my husband. He said he could
have baptized it himself if only he'd been home at the time.
He said it could never go to Heaven because it had never been
baptized. Is that right? Do you believe that?"

"No!" my father and mother said, both together and very
sharply.

"I'm glad," Mrs. Gowan said. "But when I think of Heaven,
I don't believe I want to go there if it means seeing people I
once knew on earth. I'd be very frightened of that. I'd rather
think the house of God is in the orchard as you said or wherever folks are merry. You don't think I'll ever have to see my
mother again, do you, or even the baby, or my husband?"

"I'm sure you won't," my father said. "You mustn't let
yourself worry about that, Mrs. Gowan."

"Thank you," Mrs. Gowan said in her grave, polite way.
"That's a great comfort to me. When I think of dying, which
can't be far away, I wonder if perhaps I can't sometime come
right back to this earth, maybe as someone else quite different
from me now, but anyway come back. That's one of the
things Charley Bright believes very strongly. I'd like to see

all those places you've told me about in England or in Ireland where Mrs. McCarthy was born. What would you say to that?"

"We don't know anything about the Next World," my father said, "only that it can't be cruel or unjust or even sad since it belongs to God. I often think just as you do, Mrs. Gowan, that there's a lot for us to do right here. Maybe we'll all come back in some strange way. Who knows? If I were you, I'd keep right on dreaming about coming back."

"And who cares?" cried my mother. "We're all right here and happy together, and we all love you, Mrs. Gowan."

At that moment, by the luckiest sort of chance, Mrs. Baxter came in the side door with so much noise and cheerful bustle that Ansie and I could get back into his room without any danger of being discovered.

### 23

I think our evening tea was something of a strain upon us all except at its beginning for Mary, who, still unaware of what had been taking place in the sitting-room, was thinking of the Lady of Shalott floating down the river on her barge at sunset and singing her last song. Mrs. Baxter, bringing in the tray at nine o'clock, was clearly puzzled. My mother, bending over her sewing basket by the table beneath the lamp, was silent; Mrs. Gowan on her hassock with her hands clasped tightly in her lap seemed thoughtful and subdued, though she was evidently not in Philadelphia; my father was even more abstracted than usual; and Ansie and I, hugging our aching knees on the floor before the fire, might well have looked guilty to so practiced an eye as Mrs. Baxter's.

When she had cleared a space on the table for the tea tray, she looked about quizzically upon us all.

"The night's clear as a bell," she said. "Shouldn't wonder a mite if there'll not be a frost by morning. Well, what's my family been doing to keep out of mischief?"

It seemed a long time before anyone answered her. Then my father roused himself.

"The children have all been hard at their lessons," he said. "And Mrs. Gowan has been telling my wife and me a most interesting story."

Mrs. Gowan sent him an anxious look, and he reassured her by a smile.

"That's nice," Mrs. Baxter said. "Nothing like a good story on a cold night like this. What was this particular story about?"

"Why," my father said a bit hesitantly after another awkward silence, "why—it was about a blue butterfly in a stage-coach many years ago."

Mrs. Baxter stared at him in some alarm. Mrs. Gowan looked safe and happy.

"The tea's in, my dear," my father said. "Will you pour out?"

My mother set aside her mending then and began, rather slowly for her, to arrange the cups and saucers.

"Sit down, Mrs. Baxter," my father said. "You'll fancy a good hot cup, I daresay, after your long cold walk. Was it Mrs. Kimball you went to see? How is she?"

Mrs. Baxter drew up a chair and joined our circle, looking slightly suspicious or at least questioning as she did so. Until my father's odd description of Mrs. Gowan's story, she had obviously singled out my mother as well as Ansie and me, flushed and silent by the fire, for the chief objects of her speculation. Now she was concerned for us all.

"She's more than a little melancholy, I must say," she told my father. "Lots of other folks have had the quincy, and as everyone knows it's not pleasant. But, there! Most people take things as they come without so much to-do. Only not Mrs. Kimball. She just wilts."

"I'm sure she liked the custards," Mary said, breaking yet another pause.

"Maybe so. I wouldn't know. She wouldn't try one while I was there though they do slip down nice and smooth. She just kept on feeling sorry for herself."

"Was Mr. Kimball there?" my father asked, taking his cup of tea from my mother.

"Yes, just setting, poor man. Probably plain out of his wits with her takings-on."

"I daresay," my father said, slowly stirring his tea.

"What have you twins been up to?" Mrs. Baxter asked, carefully surveying Ansie and me.

I waited for Ansie to speak.

"Doing stinking problems about wallpaper," Ansie said. Since his forbidden adjective evoked no reproof, he repeated it. "Just stinking," he said, "and I mean plain *stinking*."

"Ansie!" Mary cried. "Mother, you know he's not supposed to use such words!"

My mother finished pouring out the tea, passing a cup to each of us. I sprang to Ansie's defense.

"Well, they *are* horrid," I said. "Just these silly men papering stupid walls. We missed you frightfully, Mrs. Baxter."

"You don't mean to say you didn't finish them?" Mrs. Baxter asked with real anxiety.

"Not entirely, I'm afraid," I said.

"Miss Miller won't take kindly to that, I'm telling you," warned Mrs. Baxter.

"She's stinking, too," Ansie said, growing bolder. "She's the worst old teacher in the whole school. I'll bet she can't do those problems herself. Everyone hates her."

"I think that will do, Ansie," my father said.

Ansie subsided.

"She *is* something of a tartar, sir," Mrs. Baxter said, springing as always to Ansie's assistance. "I understand on good authority that the school board—"

"Mere pupils are not supposed to know about school boards, Mrs. Baxter," my father said, sharply for him.

He put another log on the fire. Mrs. Baxter, after some moments of embarrassment, scrutinized Ansie and me again.

"Well, if you care to get up an hour earlier," she said, "before I start breakfast, I suppose I *could* help you out. Windows, I suppose? Square feet to be subtracted? Those men, Mr. A. and Mr. B.?"

"That's right," Ansie said. "Those silly old paperhangers. Thank you, Mrs. Baxter."

"What have you been doing, Mary?" Mrs. Baxter asked in the somewhat suffocating stillness.

"Just memorizing potty old poetry," Ansie said revengefully. "All they do in that academy is memorize potty old poetry."

"Keep still, Ansie," Mary said, looking about helplessly for support which seemed to be nonexistent. "Frankly, you make me sick and tired."

"What poetry?" Mrs. Baxter asked kindly.

"A beautiful poem," Mary said, "called *The Lady of Shalott*. I'd be glad to say the first verse, that is, if anyone in this dull old tea party wants to hear it."

My father made an heroic effort to pull himself back from Aroostook County, One Eye, Peg Leg, and Black Bill.

"I'm sure we'd all like to hear it," he said to Mary.

"Yes," Mrs. Gowan said, speaking for the first time. "I love to hear poetry. Please say it, Mary."

Mary looked hopefully at my mother for further encouragement, but she looked in vain. My mother's head was bent again over her mending. She did not so much as glance at Mary.

"Stand by me, dear," Mrs. Baxter said. "It's always nicer when one stands to recite."

Mary moved toward Mrs. Baxter's chair. Mrs. Gowan turned on the hassock to face her. A note of sadness crept into my sister's voice:

"The poem's about a lady who loves a knight of King Arthur's Round Table," she said. "Only she's heartbroken because he doesn't love her. So—well, she just dies."

"Coo!" said Ansie with utmost disdain.

My father seemed not to notice him, but Mrs. Baxter actually sent him a dire frown, which threatened no help with wallpaper on the morrow. He reached for another cooky and turned his face toward the fire. Mary's voice filled the quiet room:

> "On either side the river lie
> Long fields of barley and of rye,
> That clothe the wold and meet the sky;
> And through the field the road runs by
>     To many-towered Camelot . . ."

She recited several of the following stanzas about reapers in the barley and piles of sheaves in the moonlight. Perhaps the sadness of the poem itself, coupled with the bewilderment of so strange and unusual an atmosphere in the sitting-room, lent a special eloquence to her voice, for she gave an extremely good recitation.

"Very well done, Mary," my father said.

"Lovely," said Mrs. Baxter. "Just lovely!"

Ansie and I said nothing, but Mrs. Gowan on her hassock sprang suddenly into new life. Her eyes widened with pleasure.

"It must be harvest-time along that river," she said, "when they gather in the grain and the hay. That's my most favourite time of the whole year—when the hay is gathered in. Where I lived when I was young there weren't many fields fenced in and given to grass and hay; but once, when I was about your age, Ansie, a farmer let me tread down the hay in his rack and ride right on the top of it while he drove his oxen into his barn. It was the happiest of times for me. I'll never forget it."

"That's what we do here, Mrs. Gowan," Ansie said, glad of the chance to reinstate himself in the family circle. "When the hay is all dried and raked into cocks, my father pitches it into a hayrack, and we tread it down for him, don't we, father?"

"Yes," my father said. "That's right."

"And we sing the harvest songs he sang when he was a boy," I said, eager now like Ansie to do my bit toward furthering this lightened atmosphere. "We sing them from the top of the rack while we are going toward the barn."

"Oh!" Mrs. Gowan cried, with a sharp intake of her breath. "That must be wonderful. I'd love that."

"Mrs. Baxter's awfully good at treading," Ansie said. "She's helped to make the loads for us for two summers now, haven't you, Mrs. Baxter?"

Mrs. Baxter smiled at him.

"He means I'm good because I weigh nigh on to one hundred and eighty pounds," she said to Mrs. Gowan. "That weight treads down a heap of hay."

Mrs. Gowan laughed with Mrs. Baxter. Then Mary laughed halfheartedly. Finally Ansie and I contributed a few chuckles to the somewhat listless mirth.

At this point my mother folded her mending, picked some stray threads from her skirt, and rose quickly to her feet.

"Next summer when you come, Mrs. Gowan, it must be at haying time," she said.

Mrs. Gowan stared at my mother from her hassock, incredulous, surprised by joy.

"You mean I'm to be invited again," she managed to say, interlacing her fingers in excitement.

"Of course, you are," my mother said lightly. As she passed Mrs. Gowan, she put her arms around the old woman's shoulders, drawing her white head closely against her for a moment. Then from the door to the kitchen she turned to look back upon us all.

"And now, every last one of you, get to bed," she said, more than firmly. "You children, Mrs. Baxter, Mrs. Gowan, and the head of this house. I want a fresh cup of tea and a half hour quite to myself. Mrs. Baxter, take up Mrs. Gowan's lamp for her. John, put up the fireguard. Mary, no more memorizing tonight. And, you twins, don't forget to say your prayers. Now, every last one of you, get out of my way, and don't take any time about it either."

## 24

When Mrs. Gowan came for her second visit in the early summer of 1904 she found many changes among us, all of which delighted her. She could not get over, she said, the added inches which we three children had attained during the year. Mary had shot up unbelievably. At nearly sixteen she was tall and as pretty as she was slender and graceful. She wrote more and more poetry and was much given to roaming off by herself, a habit which annoyed me excessively, although my mother said we must all be resigned to it, and Mrs. Baxter informed me knowingly that it was "all part of the picture." Just what picture she did not describe. Ansie and I at thirteen had grown taller, too. Ansie was threatening daily to overtop my mother; and he had suddenly become so strong that he could pick her up and carry her across the room.

"Elevated, like all the Oldroyds," my mother said to my father. "Let's hope the resemblance stops right there."

Perhaps the most exciting thing we had to tell Mrs. Gowan was that Ansie would go away to school in the autumn, to Phillips Academy in Exeter, New Hampshire. Through Dr. Thomas, who had himself gone to Exeter as a boy, my father had been assured of a scholarship for Ansie. He was to wait on tables in return for his fees, like hundreds of other American boys, my father said proudly. I was to enter the academy in Pepperell where Mary, already dreaming of college though no one knew quite how it was to be managed, had but one more year. Mrs. Gowan's eyes shone when she saw the name-tapes marked *Anselm Bentley Tillyard* in red printed letters; and she happily laid aside her flags to sew them with fine, close stitches on Ansie's new shirts and socks. Ansie inspected these a dozen times a day. I tried in vain to discover the least regret in his heart at leaving me.

Mrs. Gowan herself had changed, and all for the best, my father said with vast pride and confidence. Although she was a year older, she looked many years younger. Her Betsy Ross world had seemingly faded quite out of sight. She did not travel to Philadelphia even once during her second visit with us. She still sewed upon her flags, to be sure, but with a new and absorbing purpose. Through the hospital, which supplied her generously with the bunting, she had been asked to match and stitch the long red and white stripes, cut and set the white stars on the blue background, for some schools and public buildings in return for a payment which she considered phenomenal. To be earning money on her own was an unprecedented joy, more than sufficient to oust even General Washington from her mind. Mrs. Baxter explained to her the somewhat temperamental intricacies of the parsonage sewing machine, which she learned to use with skill and excitement. She was free, radiant, ecstatic, and at the same time, if one could judge from her face, serene and unperturbed. Only her new riches weighed now and again upon her conscience.

One afternoon when my father spread out on the orchard grass her most recent achievement, a really large flag for a school in a thriving Maine town, when we all stood about admiring her delicate handwork on the stars and her even stitching on the long stripes, when Mrs. Baxter had declared that never in all her born days had she seen such a wonderful accomplishment, Mrs. Gowan's clear eyes grew troubled.

"Now that I'm really earning money," she said hesitantly, scanning my father's satisfied, assured face, "now that I *could* pay back that $64.13—perhaps you may remember—those Methodists, I mean, up in that Aroostook—those preachers —my mother—that tin box— I could pay it back, I mean, to any Methodist church at all."

Mrs. Baxter looked puzzled and more than a little disturbed. Ansie and I exchanged surreptitious glances.

"Whatever is she talking about?" Mary whispered to me.

"I wouldn't know," I whispered back, waiting for my father to reassure our guest, relieved when my mother as usual forestalled him, but now with extra vehemence.

"Not a penny, Mrs. Gowan!" she cried. "Not one wretched penny! Forget it all. Promise me you'll never pay back so much as a penny!"

"My wife is quite right, Mrs. Gowan," my father said at last. "That debt has been cancelled a thousand times with quite too heavy interest on it, too. Don't ever think about it again."

"You haven't promised me yet, Mrs. Gowan," my mother persisted, still to Mary's and Mrs. Baxter's bewilderment. "Unless you promise me straightaway, you can't sew one more name-tape on Ansie's things."

Mrs. Gowan in her turn looked distressed, but, with all her misgivings, immensely relieved.

"I promise," she said. "And now what would you say to daisies and buttercups for our wreaths? There's really no flowers quite like buttercups and daisies."

Mrs. Gowan's favourite flowers fortunately bloomed in abundance along the edges of the field so that the gathering of them made no serious inroads upon the grass, tall and ripening now in late June in readiness for haying. She made us all wreaths of them, plaiting them adroitly by braiding and weaving their long stems in and out. Once we were crowned and Mrs. Baxter had brought out the tea, my father told stories of Harvest Home festivals in Suffolk: how the reapers and binders and thatchers gathered together at long tables under the trees or sometimes in the old barns for suppers of mirth and song, for hams and bacon, roast beef and plum puddings, and flagons of home-brewed ale, all furnished by the farmer for his workers after their long hours of stripping the fields with scythes and sickles; how, tired as they were from swinging and pitching and stacking, they continued to smoke their clay pipes, drink their ale and beer, and sing their songs until the stars came out above the new yellow ricks and the bare, cropped fields.

"The suppers were called Largesse Suppers or sometimes Frolic Suppers, Mrs. Gowan," he said.

"There were red poppies then all through the grain, weren't there, father?" Ansie said. "I can remember the red poppies in the fields, Mrs. Gowan."

"So can I," I said.

"Yes," my father said. "I miss the poppies here. People used to say that they weren't too good for the grain; but, even so, they made it beautiful. The best man among the harvesters, Mrs. Gowan, was always called 'King of the Mowers.' He told the men where to swing their scythes in the swaths or work their sickles in the tangled growths next the hedges. He always wore a wreath of poppies around his hat as he stalked about the fields giving his orders to the labourers. Sometimes, when I was a boy, women and girls did the sickling. This 'King of the Mowers' called a halt now and then, a 'breather' he called it, and then everyone had a swallow or two of cold ale from a stone jar which was kept under the hedge."

"I've never seen a real hedge," Mrs. Gowan said. "I mean one that separates fields. I only know fences. Perhaps one day I'll see a real hedge—in England."

"I'm sure you will," my mother said. "Sing the Harvest Home Song, Ansie, for Mrs. Gowan. You'll all sing it on the top of the loads when the hay is cut next week."

"Yes, Ansie, sing it for us," Mrs. Baxter said.

Ansie sang the song, his wreath of buttercups askew upon his yellow hair. His eyes, I thought enviously, seemed to grow far bluer than mine as we got older.

"It's very easy," he said. "You can sing it most any way, Mrs. Gowan. It's really a shout almost as much as it's a song. It goes:

Harvest Home! Harvest Home!
Merry, merry, merry, merry
Harvest Home!"

"When I was a boy," my father said, "we used to sing that song all along the lanes and drifts on August nights, once the harvest was gathered in. After the suppers were over, all the young men and women, even the small boys and girls, went through the villages in long lines and out through the country-side, singing and shouting that old song, especially if it had been a fair, dry harvest. Once in a while some fellow would have a mouth organ or even a raspy old fiddle, but mostly it was just the singing. When we came to a new, freshly stacked rick, standing all yellow in a field or rickyard, we'd sing that song. It was almost more a hymn than a song, a thanksgiving for a fine harvest and for the promise of a safe winter with wheat and barley for our bread, and hay for the animals, and money, too, at market-time. That song always takes me back home again—to Suffolk and its fields."

"And to Bury St. Edmunds, too, father," I said.

"Yes," my father said, smiling at me. "Always back to Bury —the market and the abbey."

Mrs. Gowan's face grew suddenly grave and thoughtful.

"There's really nothing like a lovely memory to live by, now, is there?" she said.

## 25

Just before it was time for haying a soft rain fell which kept us all indoors for a day. No one minded much. My father said that rain of that gentle nature would only help the hay, make its roots pliable for cutting. He seized upon the afternoon to make some distant parish calls behind Snow White. Mary retreated to our room, which she clearly wanted to herself for her own pursuits; and Ansie, in his, studied the catalogue from Exeter which described his new life, although to his regret it gave more space to studies than to sports and games. Mrs. Baxter transformed the kitchen into a veritable jam and pickle factory, my mother said, where she moved happily from a table piled high with the first fruits of the garden and fields, cucumbers, green tomatoes, onions, and strawberries, to a blistering stove where every manner of container boiled and bubbled and sent forth delectable, spicy fragrances which penetrated to the sitting-room through a tightly closed door. My mother and Mrs. Gowan sewed and talked there; and I moved from one room to the other, now hulling strawberries or wielding a paring knife for Mrs. Baxter, who, skeptical of my talents, pestered me with advice and caution, now holding skeins of wool for my mother, who was planning to knit yet another jersey for Ansie.

It was during one of my sojourns in the sitting-room as the lesser of two boredoms that I heard Mrs. Gowan telling my mother about her life in the hospital. She seemed relaxed and very much at ease as she talked; and when she got to Charley Bright and the camels and to Mrs. McCarthy with her feather, I became so interested that I dreaded a summons from Mrs. Baxter, who might at any moment (for my own good, of course) discover that she could make use of me in her jam and pickle factory.

"Folks get all sorts of mistaken ideas about people in hospitals like ours," Mrs. Gowan said. "They think we're all strange and queer in our minds and perhaps even dangerous; but that's not really true. Of course, we've had odd notions and sometimes terrible fears and troubles enough, else we wouldn't be there at all; and often the notions and the fears can't be removed from our minds. There are some of us that talk far too much and others that don't talk at all, just sit, silent for hours on end—I don't mean in thin silences like Mrs. Nesbit's, but in thick, heavy, dark silences that can't be lifted. And, of course, there are others who are very ill indeed, so that they have to be kept shut away by themselves. But even with all these things that are true, there are many of us who are safe and happy with all manner of things to do and people to be kind and understanding to us." She paused for a few moments to look out the window at the softly falling rain. "Sometimes I think," she continued, "that people in the world outside have far greater burdens than we inside have to carry."

"Why would you think that, Mrs. Gowan?" my mother asked with a quick, encouraging smile.

"Well, I'll tell you," Mrs. Gowan said. "Not that I've often seen hundreds of people together as those do who travel on trains, or walk about city streets, or attend churches and other public gatherings, or cross the ocean as you did once. But a few years ago I really did see a vast number of people together which gave me a chance to look carefully at them, or to study their faces, as you might say. It was when that nice young man, Charley Bright, was with us. Dr. and Mrs. Thomas took the two of us to a big country fair so that we could see the farm animals, and the merry-go-round, and all the exhibits of flowers and vegetables. It was a rare treat for us. Charley Bright and I rode on the merry-go-round, on two camels side by side, just like the youngsters, only a lot of older people were riding, too. All the animals rocked as we went round and round, in tune with the music. Then we walked up and down the main thoroughfare, seeing all the people, the side shows and the shooting at wooden ducks, and all the games of chance and luck. They were all new to me after so many years in the hospital; but I think it was the people that interested me most and that made me rather sad when I lived the day over in my mind. I kept watching their faces and wondering what their worlds were like and what they were having to carry about with them, without any help, sickness, perhaps, and loneliness, and not enough money, and failure at their especial jobs, and the fear of death.

"I got thinking of all those secret sorrows and cares, shut up inside of each, and how each had to carry his own sorrow around with him right in this world with small chance of framing any other world to live in. I found myself saying to myself about this one and that: 'What's resting heavily inside *you?* What's gnawing at *your* heart?' You see, people like us in the hospital have other worlds to live in. They may sound crazy to those who don't understand them, but they're worlds all the same, and often they're far easier and happier ones to live in than the real world outside." She paused to scan my mother's face. "Does all this sound queer and strange to you?" she asked.

"Not at all," my mother said calmly. "I've thought the same, too, when I've been in great mobs of people as we were on the steamship coming over here. All their secret troubles and fears weighed upon my mind, too."

"I'm glad," Mrs. Gowan said. "I wouldn't wish to be just alone with this kind of thoughts, but if you have them, too, I can't be so far wrong."

"Was Charley Bright's real world outside a hard one for him to live in?" I asked Mrs. Gowan.

My mother looked startled then, as though she thought I might well be helping Mrs. Baxter; but she relented when she saw how much I wanted to hear about Charley Bright's real world.

"Yes, it was," Mrs. Gowan said. "His only little boy died, and I don't think he was very happy with his wife, though he was careful never to say that. I'm sure that his real world was one reason why he selected specially helpful space-takers in his newspaper so they might give courage to all sorts of people in their real worlds with all their private sorrows.

"Mrs. McCarthy's a good example of just what I mean about other worlds to live in. One day, when I was walking about the hospital grounds, I found a tiny white feather clinging to a bush. It was fluffy as though it had once belonged to a baby bird. I took it indoors and gave it to her, and ever since then it's given her great comfort. She sits for hours in her room changing that feather from one finger to another by means of just a few smears of glue. It looks odd enough to people who don't understand, but it's very real to her. It's a means of moving her about among her nicer memories and thoughts. Sometimes it takes her back to Ireland in her happier days there, and at other times, she says, it carries her far farther away than Ireland. That white feather has provided her with any number of different worlds to live in."

"I wish I knew Mrs. McCarthy," my mother said impulsively.

"Well, you shall," Mrs. Gowan promised, "the very next time you come with your husband. He's a great comfort to Mrs. McCarthy. She likes him much better than she likes a rather sober old priest who visits her and leaves her holy pictures and what she calls medals. Perhaps you could tell her things about Queen Victoria that she doesn't know. Queen Victoria and Mrs. McCarthy were girls together; and even though the Irish, she says, aren't disposed to like the English overmuch on account of what she calls 'the troubles' that happened long ago, she just loves the old Queen. Some days she's a waiting woman in one of the Queen's palaces or castles, lifting the Queen's feet up on a hassock or bringing her a nice cup of tea. That's one of her most cherished worlds, and that little white feather can take her there in no time at all."

"I could tell Mrs. Gowan about the pennies at the Golden Jubilee," I said to my mother. "Mrs. McCarthy might like to know about the pennies."

"Do," my mother said. "It's a nice story, Mrs. Gowan, and meanwhile I'll see whether there's anything to eat in this house except preserves and piccalilli."

The sun burst through the clouds and mist as I proudly told Mrs. Gowan about the offering of the pennies by all the women in England. Its light suffused her face in her chair by the window and lent added glow to her eyes as she listened intently.

"Every woman in England gave a penny to the Queen, Mrs. Gowan," I said. "Even the very poorest, and in all the country places as well as in the cities. If they couldn't get new and shining ones, they polished up the old with scouring powder. Each one wrapped her penny in a bit of tissue paper, and each one took it to the vicar in every parish on a certain day. That was in 1887 for Queen Victoria's Golden Jubilee after fifty years. Ansie and I weren't born then, but we've heard about it so many times that it seems as though we were."

Mrs. Gowan intertwined her fingers in delight.

"How Mrs. McCarthy will love that!" she cried. "She'll spend hours counting all those pennies with the Queen. It will be still another world for her to travel to!"

## 26

The two days of haying were filled with matchless pleasure for us all. Mrs. Gowan glowed and sparkled with such delight that Mrs. Baxter feared the results of such animation in one of so many years. She ardently prescribed some camomile tea for Mrs. Gowan as an early twentieth-century tranquillizer, but her suggestion was received with such summary disposal that she felt presumptuous as well as deflated.

"She's the beatingest creature I ever laid my eyes on," she declared to Mary and me as we dried the breakfast dishes for her on the morning of the mowing. "If anyone had told me three brief years aback that I'd be hobnobbing with an old woman from an insane asylum who's got more brains than I've got and twice the get-up-and-get, I swear I couldn't have countenanced it. I'm giving you my solemn word when I say I've learned a heap in three brief years in this parsonage."

"About us, too?" I asked with real curiosity. "Or just about

Mrs. Gowan?"

"Truthfully, Mrs. Baxter," Mary said, "weren't you a little worried about us all, just at the beginning?"

Mrs. Baxter somewhat furiously dashed the wire soap shaker about in her pan of hot dishwater.

"Well," she said, "I'm compelled to say I did have my doubts—that is, after Reverend Perkins. I wasn't used to foreigners, as you might say, and I didn't know how I'd take to them, or for that matter how they'd take to me."

"Frankly, Mrs. Baxter," Mary said, "you were more than a little overpowering just at first, or perhaps overwhelming is a better word."

"You seem to be taking a fancy to long words at present," Mrs. Baxter said, still swishing the soap shaker.

"Yes, I am," Mary said. "We're studying vocabulary now in English, and we're supposed to familiarize ourselves with a great many exceptional words and use them, too, in our everyday speech."

"I see," said Mrs. Baxter.

"What was Reverend Perkins like?" I asked hastily.

"That's a most for-*mid*able question to answer," Mrs. Baxter said, glowering slightly at Mary. "A real tough one in just ordinary talk. He was a good man enough, but sort of peak-ed in all his ways as though he'd given up the battle from the start. Perhaps it's easier just to say that he wasn't one jot or tittle like your father. And as to his wife, she wasn't any more like your mother than a worm is like a humming-bird."

"What about the children?" I persisted.

"Pale," Mrs. Baxter said. "Puny. Always underfoot. Whiny, too. Where's Ansie?"

"He's out waiting for Mr. Johnson to come with the oxen," I said. "And Mrs. Gowan is out gathering flowers to put on their horns."

Mrs. Baxter received this latter information with marked forbearance.

"Trust her," she said, "for any number of outlandish notions. Still, if I know the Johnsons, they'll enjoy it all, and it'll be a change from the humdrum. I had a chance to set them straight about Mrs. Gowan on Sunday after church. And they aren't like some folks, shut up tight in their minds and nosy about anything a bit queer or out of the common. Leastways, Caleb Johnson isn't, and I can tackle her."

Mary suddenly looked belligerent. I remembered Susan Pratt and the battle in the schoolyard.

"You don't mean that people would *dare* to criticize father, do you?" she asked. "About Mrs. Gowan or anything else?"

"Not with me around," Mrs. Baxter said stoutly. "Once I'm through with them, they're ready to say with everyone else that he's the best man this church has ever seen. It's just that some are a mite slow to take in a new idea. They're like all Maine coast folks, and especially the Methodist variety. But don't you worry. I'll take care of them." She paused. "I've been set upon by a brand-new idea myself the past few days. What would you say to having a real Harvest Home Supper in the barn tomorrow evening after the hay's in and all fragrant-like, up in the haymow? I thought as how it might please your father, like them old days in England that he sets such store by. And Mrs. Gowan, too. She'd probably go into a regular tizzy over it. I thought as how we'd get those trestle tables from the church. Ansie and Mr. Johnson could fetch them in the hayrack, and we'd have it as a surprise for your father. We'd have some of my good spruce beer in place of ale, and I'm planning on a prime roast of beef, costly as 'tis, with Yorkshire puddings, and some sausages thrown in. It'll mean a heap more work, but with you two girls and

Mrs. Johnson to help me out, I think it's worth it. Come haying time, I can see that your father gets homesick for the old ways of England."

"Does mother know?" I asked Mrs. Baxter.

"No, she don't, but she'll be for anything that pleases your father. She may get a mite frisky now and again, but trust her when it comes to him. I saw *that* from the minute you all got here on September the 10th in the year 1901."

"So that was the date," Mary said reflectively.

"Yes, 'twas," Mrs. Baxter said.

"I only remember how strange it all seemed," Mary said. "You must be awfully good at dates, Mrs. Baxter."

"Not exceptionally," Mrs. Baxter said, carefully rounding her unusual adverb. "But I'm not likely to forget that one."

Mary and I were ecstatic over Mrs. Baxter's surprise for my father and would have thrown our arms around her at that very moment had we not seen that she was getting confused and uneasy over her rare wealth of confidence. Instead we joined Ansie at the entrance to the driveway and watched for the Johnsons to appear with the oxen and with the mowing machine in tow. They were the upcountry Methodists who had given us Primrose and Cowslip and, their own haying completed, were coming for two days to help us out with ours.

The July sunshine was strong and dazzling in its brightness. There was no sign of mist or even of cloud. Mrs. Gowan, plaiting her flowers on the orchard bench, waved to us in ecstasy. She had been astir since daybreak. My father walked about the barn excitedly, clad in his blue shirt and blue-and-white checked overalls, seeing that all was in readiness for the stowing of the hay. Through the open chamber windows we heard my mother singing as she made a room ready for the Johnsons. The song-sparrows and the whitethroats trilled and whistled from the pasture and the woods beyond.

We could hear the clatter and rattle of the mower along the stony country road even before it came into sight over the brow of the hill. Mrs. Johnson sat in the wagon driving their horse and towing the machine; and behind her piled on the back seat rose a sharp, shining conglomeration of pitch-forks, scythes, and hayrakes. Her best black hat with its ostrich plume over the crown, for after all she *was* going visiting, looked somewhat out of place backed by so many rude and dangerous implements. Mr. Johnson followed with the hayrack and the oxen, walking beside them with his long goad-stick over their broad backs. They plodded along heavily on their short, gnarled legs, their red muscular shoulders heaving, their huge, patient heads moving rhythmically from left to right, from right to left, under their branching, copper-tipped horns. They were the finest yoke throughout a wide countryside, as everyone knew; and Mr. Johnson, in a worn linen duster over his shirt and overalls, guided them with great pride. Unlike most oxen, who seemed inevitably to bear the names Star and Bright, they were called John and Charles after the Wesley brothers. Mr. Johnson was a man of humour and imagination, who from the first had delighted my father. He, too, had a feeling for tradition and the long past. His grandfather had been an early itinerant Methodist preacher, and the naming of the oxen was an artless, perhaps even sly tribute to his own inheritance. Ansie tore away up the road to greet our guests and helpers and to beg Mr. Johnson to let him wield the goad, while Mrs. Gowan, her floral decorations for John and Charles completed, came running to join Mary and me, her blue eyes filled with joy and expectation.

What a wonderful two days it was! First, the mowing itself,

the rustle of the tall grass falling before the interlacing, clicking knives of the machine, the swish and heavy hiss of the scythes in the corners of the field and around the few trees, the drone and hum of the hones on the scythe blades as my father and Mr. Johnson paused in the hot sunshine to sharpen them after the mower had completed its task and John and Charles rested from their work. They were acquiescent and complacent under Mrs. Gowan's garlands. Perhaps they even enjoyed this bit of gaiety in the light of their early sacrifice of love to mere labour. At all events they chewed their fresh hay under the trees with placid acceptance of their past and present fates.

In the afternoon while the July sun blazed down upon the shorn field we all helped in spreading, turning over the swaths with our forks so that every blade and spear of fallen grass could dry under the heat and light. Mrs. Baxter mixed gallons of cold molasses and ginger water, which she called "swipes" and which we all drank gratefully in intervals from our work. The fragrance of the field grew sharper and more sweet as the bright day moved on slowly toward its close.

"There's nothing like the smell of new-mown hay," Mr. Johnson said, wiping his mouth with his hairy brown hand after a draught of swipes. "I reckon that's what's kept me an uphill farmer all my life."

My brother Ansie on that first day of haying seemed suddenly to burst out of boyhood. He wore a pair of overalls like my father and Mr. Johnson; and with his shirt open at the neck and his yellow hair blowing in the light wind, he strode importantly about the field, taller than either of them, wielding his pitchfork like one possessed, tireless, skillful, scornful of mere girls who were framed to carry refreshment to men rather than to spread hay. To his vast delight Mr. Johnson had allowed him to wield a scythe for the first time, and he did it with such strength and care that even my father looked upon him with new respect. I caught my mother watching him from the orchard. She had tears in her eyes and a look almost of fear in her face.

After a warm, dewless night the hay was turned over and spread once again before it was ready to be shaped into cocks. John and Charles lumbered about the pasture with Lilla, Snow White, the sheep, and the Johnson mare, Jenny Lind, by their very size completing the manorial aspect of our domain, my father said; for since Mr. Johnson had been unable to bring both the mower and the raking machine, the raking was done by hand. Mrs. Gowan in an old pink sunbonnet of Mrs. Baxter's insisted on making a few cocks. She seemed indestructible, my mother said, and so happy in the sun that she added to its light. In the kitchen Mrs. Johnson lent her capable hands to Mrs. Baxter, who, warned hourly by Ansie, knew that she could not forsake the treading of the loads.

At two o'clock John and Charles took their places on either side of the great wooden shaft that drew the hayrack (the "thung-pole," in Mrs. Baxter's speech), and the haymaking reached its joyous climax. Four of us made the loads, Mrs. Baxter, Mrs. Gowan, Mary, and I, stumbling from back to front of the long grey rack, falling, laughing, pressing down the forkfuls as they were thrown over the high sides, colliding with one another, burying ourselves in hay. Ansie pitched this year with the other men, though when the load was heaped and ready, he bounded up on top and rode to the barn, through the field, skirting the orchard, on the way to the great open doors below the loft. Up there with us all he suddenly became a little boy again.

"Sing, Mrs. Gowan!" he cried each time the great load started. "Now's the time for Harvest Home!"

Mrs. Gowan's joy was complete. She disdained to lie down on the hay as the others of us were doing when once the straining oxen went on their way toward the barn. Instead she stood beside Ansie, like him clinging to the handle of his pitchfork plunged deep in the load. Her voice, broken by laughter, rang out with his through the warm air:

"Merry, merry, merry, merry
Harvest Home!"

As I watched her there, with Ansie's arm holding her steady against the joltings of the rack, bits of hay clinging to her white hair, her cheeks flushed, her eyes wide and shining, I thought of her long ago, a girl like Mary and me, riding on top of the Aroostook farmer's load, living her rare bright hour in the midst of her dark, terrifying years. Now, at least for the time being, no trace of those dark years remained. That one bright hour of her childhood had flowed over them like some clear stream to join with these hours of the present. Mr. Johnson drove his oxen; my father, singing lustily, stalked proudly beside his laden racks; my mother trailed behind, singing, too, as with her wooden rake she gathered up the few remnants of hay drifting down from the loads while we made our triumphal processions toward our waiting red barn.

I don't know whether my father or Mrs. Gowan enjoyed more Mrs. Baxter's Harvest Home Supper under our closely packed mows in the long summer twilight. She sat beside him, insatiable for songs and stories. He insisted that Mrs. Baxter take the foot of the long table in my mother's usual place; and Mrs. Baxter, crimson from treading hay and from putting the finishing touches to her feast, was too flustered and happy to remonstrate. Mrs. Gowan had crowned us all with circlets of ripened redtop and timothy as befitted the occasion; and Mrs. Baxter for once was too pleased with herself to feel embarrassed by her Bacchanalian appearance in the presence of the Johnsons. They, though clearly unaccustomed to such festivity, glowed with new pleasure like those who, late in life, have discovered something rich and strange and ardently regret that they had not known it before. Mrs. Johnson from her seat next Mrs. Baxter kept staring at Mrs. Gowan, who obviously was far beyond her ken; but since Mrs. Baxter, whom she had known all her life, was in this new role beyond her ken likewise, she was consumed by two poles of slightly suspicious interest. There were speeches, toasts to Old England and to New, one to Katie, proposed by Ansie, and another to our Tillyard grandparents. Ansie sent his plate up for so many helpings that my mother despaired of his free fees at Exeter ever covering his appetite!

Mrs. Gowan alone seemed to have no desire to eat. From her place beside my father she kept gazing at us all. She was blissful, enraptured. When the sunlight, streaming through the western windows of the barn, had faded, and the hermit thrushes began to sound from the pasture, and my father remembered with reluctance the nightly chores, he invited her as our guest of honour to make the final speech.

She rose to her feet then in a silence not untinged, I fear, by apprehension on the part of us all. We need not have worried. She moved behind my father with her hands outspread as though she might have been bestowing a blessing. Her voice was clear and strong, and her white head, tilted toward the left, was high.

"I've never made a speech before," she said, "or what you call a toast; but here's to long life and gladness to us all in this house of God that's merry and full of grace. Here's to Mrs. McCarthy and Charley Bright, and the good doctors in the hospital, and the oxen John and Charles, and our neighbours who have come to help us, and my new family, one and all. All I can think of is my space-taker which I've thought of since the day broke and which was put in the newspaper just for me:

> Night's candles are burnt out, and jocund day
> Stands tiptoe on the misty mountain tops."

"Whatever was that poor crazy soul from that insane asylum talking about?" I heard Mrs. Johnson say to Mrs. Baxter as Mary and I were helping to carry the remains of the feast into the kitchen, while my mother and Mrs. Gowan were having the far more pleasant task of taking some rewarding lumps of sugar to John and Charles in the pasture.

Mrs. Baxter's face grew stern under her redtop and timothy.

"She's not poor and she's not the least bit crazy," she said to Mrs. Johnson, who cowered perceptibly beneath her onslaught. "And in this house we don't say *asylum*. We say *hospital*. And we never—and I mean *never*, mind you— use the words *insane* or *crazy*. She was talking about things we all know and folks we think highly of. So don't go wasting your pity on her, for she don't need a mite of it."

"But she recited a poem that didn't mean a thing to me," Mrs. Johnson managed to say weakly as she began to scrape the plates in her confusion.

"Well, why not?" Mrs. Baxter asked almost savagely. "We say lots of poetry in this parsonage. That special rhyme was written by William Shakespeare. If you—and I," she conceded unwillingly, "don't know much about him, that's just our own bad luck."

## 27

The autumn and winter that followed Mrs. Gowan's second sojourn with us in the summer of 1904 were filled with utmost satisfaction for us all. In spite of the early cold which took the fishing boats from the water to be propped and

canvased high on the beach or hauled into the more com-
modious fish-houses against the winter, in spite of the ice
which closed the harbour and halted the building of vessels,
and the snow brought by mighty northeast gales, we lived
in a state of almost perpetual excitement and pleasure.

First, there was Ansie at his school in Exeter. He was
very good about writing home, having been warned by my
father that full and frequent news of his doings and well-
being would especially delight my mother. Whenever a letter
reached Pepperell, brought by the mail-stage in the late
afternoon, my father was waiting to claim it at the post office;
and once he had reached the parsonage with it, we all
gathered in the sitting-room to hear it read. Mrs. Baxter even
left her preparations for supper, coming in rosy from the
kitchen in her white apron. She usually brought Chessy with
her, whose sedate behaviour during the reading was sure proof,
Mrs. Baxter said, that she took in far more about Ansie than
any of us could possibly surmise.

Supper was always late on the days of Ansie's letters since
we were given to commenting on practically every statement in each of them. His roommate was named Thomas
Jefferson Ferris. This name elicited remarks from my father
on his own devotion to that remarkable Virginian, who, in
some way of course, had determined Tom's name, although
Ansie had seemingly not yet discovered it. Ansie had joined
the school choir, which encouraged singing in spite of squeaks
and quavers as boys' voices changed. He was more than a
little heartsick at not having been chosen for the football
squad. He thought it was because he was too thin and was
therefore eating prodigiously.

"Thank God!" my mother said. "At least we don't have
to worry this autumn about that wretched, dangerous game."

The food at Exeter was excellent, on the whole, although

baked beans figured rather heavily; and whenever these were mentioned, Mrs. Baxter conceived the notion of sending yet another box of really good and nourishing food.

"Beans are prime for church suppers and Saturday nights," she said, "but not in too great quantities for a growing boy."

"Now, Mrs. Baxter," my father expostulated, "you know what the special circular to parents said about too many boxes from home."

Mrs. Baxter was clearly not only unconvinced, but quietly recalcitrant.

We would all be surprised at Christmas, one November letter said, by Ansie's new school jacket of the proper Exeter cut and colour. He had almost asked my father for it; but when he found that it cost six whole dollars, he and Tom, who also had hesitancy over the matter of money, had bought something called "a popcorn concession," and they had sold so much popcorn at the football game with Andover that they had proudly bought their own jackets.

My father glowed with pride and enthusiasm over this announcement.

"What a country this is!" he said. "Now that's one thing he couldn't have done at an English public school."

"Why not?" Mrs. Baxter asked.

"It's quite too complicated to explain now, Mrs. Baxter," my father said. "I'll try sometime later."

"I do wonder if he's growing any taller," my mother said. "I surely hope not. He's nearly six feet already. I do wish he'd say."

"Well, he won't, my dear," my father said, "unless we put it specifically on our list of questions. It just wouldn't occur to him that we care how he looks."

"It will by and by," Mary said with annoying wisdom. "In just about a year or two more he'll be thinking about girls, and *then* will he care!"

"Don't be so stupid!" I said hotly. "Ansie's got more sense than you think."

Mary looked loftily at me.

"It's not a matter of sense," she said calmly. "It's just—well, it's just plain biology."

"Biology!" said Mrs. Baxter with reproachful contempt. "It seems to me some folks around here are getting too big for their boots!"

"Stop talking, all of you," my mother said, "and let father read on. What about the list of questions we sent? Has he forgotten to answer those?"

Ansie was often brief in his answers to the prepared questions which my mother sent him each week, including carefully those of deepest interest to my father. Yes, he was doing quite decently in his Greek, and his teacher was really a good sort even if, because of his protruding ears, he was known throughout the school as "the Grecian urn." No, he was not neglecting to brush his teeth twice each day. Yes, he had copped an excellent mark from his English teacher for an essay on "Harvest Customs in Suffolk" (suggested by my father) though it was no end of a bore to have to read it aloud in class with the fellows tittering audibly over his accent. He was more detailed in his answer to an earlier question of my father's about migrating birds in southern New Hampshire.

"I really can't say much about the birds," he had written. "Exeter boys don't go about gazing into trees and bushes. One rather queer fellow did just after school opened, and he's been called 'Tweet, tweet' ever since. I'm sure father wouldn't want me called 'Tweet, tweet.' It's quite all right to look at birds at home, but *not at school*."

Aside from Ansie's letters there were other exciting events.

Mrs. Bridget McCarthy sent me a really beautiful round white collar crocheted in Irish lace by her own hands, together with a letter thanking me for my story about the Queen's Jubilee pennies. It had given her great delight, she said, and now she and Queen Victoria often counted the pennies together, making tall, shining piles of them in Buckingham Palace where two footmen in bright red coats arranged the piles on a long table. At their last count they had made 120,-000 pennies. She would be most deeply obliged, she said, if my father at his entire convenience would tell her the value of 120,000 British pennies in dollars and cents since for some odd reason her girlhood arithmetic in Ireland had slipped from her mind. After my father and I had worked it out for her and I had written that the sum would be in the near neighbourhood of $2,500, she wrote again to thank us. Now she could better advise Queen Victoria, she said, just how to spend such a tremendous gift.

Mrs. Gowan, between my father's visits to the hospital, which were veritable springs in the Valley of Baca to her, was a steady correspondent. When she did not write of hospital doings, or review the joys of her visits to us, or anticipate those to come, she sent us copies of Charley Bright's space-takers. And in late January, when my mother longed for mist and rain and even for a wind from Russia in the place of continued bright and bitter cold, when Ansie had returned to school after the most wonderful of Christmas holidays, we were all overcome by a letter from Charley Bright himself to Mary, suggesting that she not only select some space-takers for his columns, but, since he had heard from Mrs. Gowan that she composed poetry, send him some samples of her work, which it was just possible, though in no sense sure, he might wish to print in his newspaper. Mary was in such a state of rapture that my mother likened the parsonage sitting-room to the Poets' Corner in Westminster Abbey, which metaphor, once it had been explained to Mrs. Baxter, gave even her a new respect for my sister. After hours of corporate and critical study of Mary's effusions, three were chosen, copied by Mary's impressed English teacher on the academy typewriter, and posted to Charley Bright. Whereupon there ensued a period of such anxiety, expectation, and dread that Mrs. Baxter declared we were all headed for a state of complete decline.

Charley Bright actually kept us in frightful suspense for only a week. A long envelope, ominous in its very shape and size, came from him one February evening when the mercury was still below zero. When my father brought it in and wordlessly laid it on the sitting-room table, his face was a study in fear and compassion lest disappointment and discouragement for his first-born were concealed within it. I have always remembered him standing there, tiny beads of water gradually replacing the frost on his eyebrows, his eyes imploring my mother for understanding and probable comfort, his face worn with concern for everyone except himself.

In a paralyzed group we stared at the envelope until Mrs. Baxter said the time had come to stop our nonsense and take the bull by the horns whatever the cost. Then Mary, with trembling fingers, opened it to find three one-dollar bills in payment for her three poems and the promise of early publication. And just how, asked Charley Bright, did the youthful poet wish her really excellent verses signed?

## 28

My mother, with the streak of realism always marked within her, kept saying throughout the winter that we really couldn't expect everything to militate in our favour. That was not the way life worked, she said. We couldn't always expect beer and skittles, forever live on top of the world. We must fortify ourselves for a change in our emotional climate.

I am sure the change came with the early spring though, since it chiefly concerned my father, we children were not for some time too cognizant of it or deeply affected by it. In late April or early May, when the peepers had begun to sound in the twilight and the pair of robins had returned to the woodbine over the side door, my parents fell into the habit of taking long walks after supper quite by themselves. Nor did I need Mrs. Baxter's anxious information to be aware that they stole down to her kitchen frequently in the dead of night to brew some cups of tea.

"Mark my words, something's eating away at both of them," she said to Mary and me, "and it's my guess it stems from that Conference in March, on Fast Day, when your father went to Bangor."

Mrs. Baxter as usual was right, although, whatever her apprehensions, she did not know how closely her own future might be concerned with the consequences of several interviews in Bangor. She was quite aware, however, that serious deliberations were taking place between my parents; and she was wise enough to conclude that my mother was more deeply engrossed in these and perturbed by them than was my father. In this conclusion she was also right.

My father was simply not framed to be overly troubled for himself over what certain Methodist district superintendents in Bangor had had to say about a larger parish, a wider and needier field for his obvious talents. Time and place were important to him only in so far as specific human beings might be closely involved in them. In themselves they were relatively incidental, being only the sphere in which one moved and to which one gave one's all. A man might, of course, prefer one sort of environment to another as he had preferred the idea of America to the actuality of England, or as the country possessed a language for him which a city could never speak; yet no merely physical locality loomed large in his thoughts except as a glowing symbol, like Bury St. Edmunds or Walden Pond. The dwelling place of a man's mind was everything, but not the whereabouts of his body.

Nor was he deeply disturbed by the awkward and halting advice of these same superiors in Bangor upon his unusual and perhaps unwise activities in behalf of certain unfortunate persons who, in God's inscrutable scheme of things, seemed destined for tragedy and sorrow. I am sure he did not hesitate to state his own differing and somewhat heretical views concerning the source of tragedy and sorrow and perhaps in so doing increased their anxiety as to the wisdom of their bishop's eager importation of him four years earlier. American Methodism at the turn of the century was committed to sound doctrine and to solid practice, to thriving Sunday schools, weekly prayer meetings, missionary labours abroad, and yearly revival seasons at home. It was not accustomed to odd parsons who held peculiar and upsetting convictions about man's intimate obligations to his fellow man under whatever sort of circumstances, not to mention quite unorthodox opinions about the redemption of the human soul in its ageless and turbulent history.

My mother may, indeed, have felt some measure of sympathy with the puzzled district superintendents. After all, she had lived with my father for nearly twenty years. Yet, although her practical and far more literal mind could not entirely fathom the reflections and affirmations of his own, she was as committed to him with all his vagaries as he was committed to his lovely, if unworldly ambitions. The burden of their frequent discussions on their walks or over their cups of tea in the small hours, as we were to learn later when we were let into their secret, was the effects which a change in pastorates might have not only upon us children and Mrs. Baxter, but even more especially upon my father's hopes and desires, most of which at the moment concerned his friends at the hospital, and mainly Mrs. Gowan.

Once Ansie had returned in June from school, not any taller to my mother's intense relief, but unquestionably older in his ways and thoughts, and Mary had graduated from the academy with so many honours and awards that we were all quite dizzy with pride, we held a family council in the orchard where the last of the apple blossoms had given place to tiny and fuzzy pale-green apples and the grass in the field beyond was already ripening under the warm sun. The clatter of tins and china in the kitchen and the occasional energetic hurlings of pails of grey soapsuds on the shrubs and bushes at the side door proved that Mrs. Baxter was happily scrubbing the kitchen shelves and cupboards as the final rite of her spring cleaning.

Our gathering was not actually planned as a council to ponder over my father's future, but rather to take careful stock of our financial assets in view of Mary's. In spite of my mother's painfully compiled list of figures, which had engaged her attention for weeks and which failed utterly to reach the $600 necessary for mere tuition and board for Mary, my father had determined that she was to enter in the autumn the Massachusetts college of her dreams.

"I just don't see how it's going to be managed," my mother said, a little petulantly since she was by nature averse to figures and dead-sick of adding and subtracting them.

"Nor do I," my father said, "but curiously enough I'm sure it will be. I've always believed that if a thing is unquestionably right to do, one just goes ahead and does it, no matter how impossible or even mad it seems at the moment."

"You don't have to tell me that," my mother said, in a tone of more than faint exasperation.

My father looked distressed.

"How short are we?" Ansie asked, bending over my mother's papers on the orchard table.

"Two hundred dollars at the very least," my mother said, "and we're not even thinking of books and clothes and railway tickets."

Mary looked aggrieved and even angry.

"We wouldn't be adding up and worrying at all, father," she said, "if you hadn't been so stubborn about that hotel in Bar Harbor. I could have earned at least one hundred dollars and probably a lot more."

"I'm sorry," my father said, "but I don't like summer hotels, and I like less our not being together for as long as we can."

"And you're not to blame just your father for that decision," my mother said loyally. "I didn't like it either, as you know very well."

Mary, seeing that she was vanquished, let the subject rest, though not too pleasantly.

"Well, you don't any of you need to worry about me," Ansie said. "I haven't told you yet, but I've got a job in the Exeter library for two hours a day. That's nearly five dollars a week besides my scholarship. I won't need so much as a penny from home all next year."

"Good!" my father said. "That's fine, Ansie. I *am* proud."

My mother smiled at Ansie with the special illumined smile always reserved only for him.

"I've got fifteen dollars in my bank," I said, "from picking blueberries and my prize at school. Add that on, mother."

"No, don't, mother!" Mary said. She was still sulky, but I knew that underneath it all she was grateful, though she glared at me. "I'm not taking any of my sister's money."

"Don't be silly!" Ansie said. "She wants you to take it, like Tom's sister. His sister sent him twenty dollars that she'd earned tutoring at college. He was quite in a rage at first and vowed he wouldn't touch it—with a ten-foot pole, he said—but after we'd talked it over, he realized that it would be mean and unkind not to take it."

"Tom must be a nice boy," my mother said. "When is he coming to visit us? Did you say at haying time?"

"He's tops," Ansie said. He looked troubled at my mother's question. "I don't know just when he's coming. When's Mrs. Gowan coming? Would it be all right if he came *after* Mrs. Gowan?"

"Why, of course," my mother said, sensing his anxiety. "He can come any time at all."

My father was studying Ansie's face and so seriously that Ansie did not wait for his question.

"Tom doesn't quite understand about Mrs. Gowan," he said. "He thinks it's fine that we have her visit us and all that, but all the same he doesn't quite see just *why* we do those things. I'm afraid I wasn't too good at explaining. I'm afraid I rather put it all on you, father. I'm sorry."

"Well, that's just where it belongs, I daresay, Ansie," my father said cheerfully, but with an apparent effort.

"No, it doesn't," my mother said quickly. "*I* invited Mrs. Gowan. I won't have your father held responsible for all that we do here which may seem a bit out of the common. He has to bear enough of it, as it is, but at least I'll take my share when it comes to Mrs. Gowan. Her coming was *my* idea, so will you all please remember that. And I haven't regretted it for one moment either."

My father looked gratefully at her, his face alight with love and admiration. At fourteen I was on the threshold at least of the new world which Mary had entered two years earlier; and I could see in his look all the years which they had known together, their student days in Cambridge long ago, the costs they had willingly paid, each for the other. I am sure that Mary and Ansie saw these things, too, for Mary's peevishness left her and Ansie became flushed and ill at ease.

"I couldn't bear for Mrs. Gowan not to come," he said.

I realized from the way he was crossing and recrossing his long legs on the bench beside my father and wriggling his hands about in his trousers pockets that he was trying to say more and finding it difficult enough. Finally he managed to get it out of his mouth.

"It's funny about saying things at school," he said, "even to Tom. All the fellows are sort of shy about coming right out with what they really think, that is, except about games and studies. They just don't want to be thought—well, different or in the least *good*, if you know what I mean. I'm sure I could have explained better to Tom about the hospital and about how hard Mrs. Gowan's life has been, and about—well, about what we've all been taught at home to think about things. I suppose I just didn't dare. I suppose I was plain cowardly, father. It's awfully difficult to be really brave at school."

My father put his arm around Ansie's shoulders.

"I don't suppose being a parson's son helps much either," he said.

"No, I'm afraid it doesn't," Ansie said. "All the boys with preachers for fathers are sort of expected to be what the others call *holy*. I just couldn't bear to be called *holy*."

"I should hope not!" cried my mother. "Heaven forbid!"

"You see," Ansie said, "God—and all that, you know—isn't a very popular subject around school, except, of course, in chapel."

"I don't think you were really cowardly, Ansie," my father said thoughtfully. "It's never easy to talk about the things one believes in most deeply, especially when one is young. And I don't think it's at all necessary. God doesn't need to be talked about much by schoolboys. I remember how we used to shy away from mentioning Him at my old school in Bury. All that really matters is to know what one believes about Him in one's own mind. I'd care terribly if you didn't know in your own mind what we all believe and value, and if you didn't guard it there; but I don't care in the least that you find it difficult or impossible to explain to others. If the thoughts that really matter just stay always in one's mind, they don't need to be explained."

Ansie looked relieved.

"Let's get on about the money," he said. "After the hay's in I might find a job right here in Pepperell and help some."

"Well, now we've got this far," my mother said, dropping her knitting in her lap and looking very straight at my father, "we may as well go the rest of the way. There's just one chance to make up this two hundred dollars, and we'd better face it. So go ahead and tell them what these Methodist tyrants in Bangor have in their minds about you."

"You tell them, my dear," my father said. "You're much better at telling things than I am."

"I know it's about leaving Pepperell," I said. "I've known it all along."

"Well, it might mean rising higher for you, father," Ansie said, "and I'd be all for that."

"I can't bear to leave Pepperell for good," Mary said, "I hate changes! I positively loathe changes."

"Where's your adverb?" Ansie asked meanly. "You always used to put it first. Why don't you say, 'Positively, I hate changes!' "

"That was simply a childish indulgence," Mary said, with a scathing glance at Ansie. "I've outgrown that now. But just the same I do hate changes."

"I don't welcome them myself," my father said, "but I suppose they're all a part of life."

"If I'm going to tell about this," my mother said, "will you all stop your chattering and let me talk."

Thus admonished we kept silent, though Mary still frowned at Ansie.

"These men," my mother said, "though there's not one who knows a tenth as much as your father does, these district superintendents or whatever they choose to call themselves, want him to take a church in Augusta or one in the neighbourhood of Portland, either in the autumn or at the longest a year from now. They're far bigger churches, of course, with much bigger salaries. I don't want to go a bit either, but Methodists in this country at least seem destined to be forever on the move. And with the larger salary we could manage to pay for you, Mary."

"I don't want father to leave Pepperell, where he's happy, just for me," Mary said.

"It isn't just for you, Mary," my father said. "There are other—considerations, too. I may just have to leave."

"You'd take Augusta, wouldn't you, father?" Ansie asked. "I mean on account of the hospital and Mrs. Gowan?"

"Without a doubt," my father said.

He got up then from the bench and walked about the orchard as though he were deep in thought. Then he came and stood by my mother's chair.

"I realize quite well," he said, "that most people would say we were foolish to let Mrs. Gowan weigh so heavily in all this, but your mother and I both think she ought. She's become a large part of the fabric of our lives. You children don't know as much as we do about her life. Sometime we'll tell you more about it. But Dr. Thomas and I know it's nothing short of miraculous the way she's been healed and set right in her mind just by being here now and again." He sat down beside Ansie. "I often think," he continued, "that if every man felt responsible for the happiness and safety of just one other man or woman, we could make the world happier and safer for us all. We just can't fail Mrs. Gowan. She's old, and there have been times this year when she's been ill, not in her mind, thank God, but in other ways. And there are the others at the hospital, Mr. Wheeler, and Mrs. Nesbit, and Mrs. McCarthy, and those whom you don't know so well. They need me, and I need them even more. So, if we must go, I'm sure it will be Augusta where I can be close at hand."

"I'm afraid there won't be haying in Augusta," Ansie said.

Just at that moment the side door burst open and another pail of soapsuds was flung violently upon the knotted roots of the woodbine. Mrs. Baxter waved happily at us all.

"Whatever shall we do without Mrs. Baxter?" Mary said.

"You mean she couldn't go, too?" Ansie cried, dismay in his voice. "We can't manage anywhere at all without Mrs. Baxter!"

"I'm afraid she's part of the parsonage," my father said. "I really can't bear to tell her."

"Which clearly means I shall have to," my mother said. She gathered up her knitting and rose from her chair. "You girls think twice before you marry Wesleyan parsons," she said, smiling at my father. "Just now I'm tired of my wonderful husband and all my wonderful children. I'm going in to write Mrs. Gowan. If she isn't assured that she's expected for the haying, she'll be off to Philadelphia or else to Ireland with Mrs. McCarthy. Mary, you get tea ready, and don't expect me for I'm having mine with Mrs. Baxter."

"You don't mean to tell her today, do you?" my father asked in real alarm.

"I'm not quite mad," my mother said, "even though there are times when I think we all are. I just happen to need a bit of her good sense, and besides I want to put a stop to this wretched scrubbing."

"Because you remember," my father called after her as she started for the house, "we don't have to come to any decision at all until long after haying."

## 29

Mrs. Gowan was clearly not up to wielding a rake to make haycocks in the summer of 1905. She was saving all her strength for making the loads, she said. She felt sure she could tread the hay quite as well as ever. Though she did not seem perceptibly older in any of her ways, she was far more frail, and there was an odd transparency in her face and in her eyes when she widened them. After my father had lifted her down from the carriage and we all ran to throw our arms about her in welcome, she was the embodiment, the incarnation, of complete happiness and safety.

"I can't believe it!" she cried, tossing her white head toward the left in her familiar, piquant gesture. "I really can't. I said to Mrs. McCarthy just this morning, 'Bridget,' I said, 'how could anything so wonderful happen to me, and three times running?' "

"What did Mrs. McCarthy say to that?" asked Ansie, seizing her valise in one hand and encircling her waist with his arm to lead her toward the door.

"She said good things always come in threes, Ansie. The

Irish have a great fancy for threes. I wouldn't know just why."

"*I* would," Mrs. Baxter said, coming from the side door at just that moment to greet Mrs. Gowan, perhaps not with our exuberance, but with genuine heartiness. "Not that I know a thing about the Irish, but as to the number three, I've lived with that most of my life. It seems made for parsons. They always have three points to every sermon. One, two, three."

My father laughed as he led Snow White toward the barn. We could see how proud and happy he was about Mrs. Gowan. Betsy Ross and Philadelphia had apparently gone for good out of her mind. Her real world here with us had become her all, only heightened and illumined, a dream come true. She laughed, too, at Mrs. Baxter.

"Mrs. McCarthy says the third time is always the best," she said as she walked into the house. "And I can well believe it with you children all so tall and fine and the grass as tall and fine as you are. Just right for the mowing."

The weather did its utmost toward a perfect haying season with long, bright days and warm, clear nights. During the few days between Mrs. Gowan's arrival and the cutting of the field we sat in the orchard in the afternoons, telling her of all our doings except, of course, the deferred decision, and listening to her tidings from the hospital.

Mrs. McCarthy was well and happy and, for the most part, quite clear in her mind. Whenever she roved about among her several worlds, she was, we must understand, always quite sure that she was wandering there of her own free will and only by way of diversion and pleasure. On St. Patrick's Day, when there had been a little party, she had danced an Irish jig as part of the entertainment. She had worn a wreath of shamrocks fashioned out of green felt for her by

Mrs. Gowan, a green apron, and around the ankles of her long white stockings some bows of bright green ribbon.

"You really should have seen her," Mrs. Gowan said, rising from her chair to impersonate Mrs. McCarthy a little breathlessly. "She spun this way and that way, with her hands clapping in the air like this, with her skirts whirling right up to her knees, and she sang, 'The green isle of Erin, oh, that's the isle for me.' There was tremendous applause for her. Bridget was just like a young girl in her dancing, but then she's only sixty-nine. That seems very young to me."

Mrs. Nesbit had actually broken her silence to send her love to us all and her thanks for the little glass saucedish which we had given her and which was her most precious treasure. And could Mrs. Gowan possibly manage to bring her back some fireflies in a little box with grass in it to make them feel more at home?

"She seems to have a queer fancy for fireflies," Mrs. Gowan said. "She will really talk about fireflies. They must be the special keys to unlock her special chains."

Mr. Wheeler had been chosen out of many men in the hospital to lay a new walk in the grounds. It was to be made of paving stones, and Mr. Wheeler was wholly in charge of laying each one, which he was doing with such pride and care that everyone was impressed.

"He's even got a name for his walk," Mrs. Gowan said. "It comes from all his studies about ancient Rome. He calls it the Appian Way, but there's another form of it which he fancies more and is likely to use when he talks about his work. I can't recall it just at the moment."

"Probably the Via Appia," my father said. "That's the Latin term for it."

"That's it," Mrs. Gowan said eagerly. "That's exactly it.

It seems that Roman emperors rode along it in their triumphs after great conquests many centuries ago. But because not many of us know Latin, he's willing to have it in English. It's wonderful what that walk means to Mr. Wheeler. He says he never imagined he'd lay a really Roman road. It's just his own, and he's hoping there'll be a sign made for it which will say *The Appian Way*."

"Wonderful!" cried my mother. "I'm so proud of Mr. Wheeler."

"And about the best of all," Mrs. Gowan said, "which I've been saving to the very last is Charley Bright. He's been made chief editor of a newspaper right in Augusta itself, and he plans to run a real column of hospital news. When the Appian Way is finished, he means to have a piece right on the very front page about its designer and builder with a photograph. Now what a triumph that will be for Henry Adams Wheeler!"

Mrs. Gowan still plaited her wreaths, though her hands were not so nimble as in the past two summers. She almost preferred on this visit to help my mother in sewing name-tapes, this year on Mary's things. She was not just now making large flags since they were heavy and cumbersome for her to handle, but she had made any number of small ones for the Fourth of July party at the hospital only a few days ago. Each guest had worn one pinned to a coat or dress; and each had expressed the intention of keeping it always.

"I do hope Charley Bright will have an article about your flags in his paper, Mrs. Gowan," Mary said.

The colour rose in Mrs. Gowan's cheeks. Her proud, rather tremulous smile encircled us all.

"To be quite truthful," she said gravely, "he's already planned that very thing."

30

Our plans for haying had been somewhat changed for this summer. With dry July weather, a little later than usual, hastening everyone on to his own cutting, the Johnsons with John and Charles were busy in their own upland fields, to Mrs. Gowan's regret for she had dearly loved the oxen. This year the doctor and my father had gone into partnership, each to help the other; and since the doctor had his own raking machine together with his horse which could be paired with Snow White for the hayrack, things could be accomplished more easily for both him and us.

Mrs. Baxter after a consultation with my mother reluctantly surrendered the Harvest Home Supper in the barn. They both decided that Mrs. Gowan after the treading of the loads would be much better off with a quiet supper in the house which would be as gay as possible, yet not quite so taxing for her. She did not seem to be too disappointed when she learned of our plans. So long as she could help make the loads she was content.

The great day dawned, still hot and clear in the late morning as my father and Ansie shaped the cocks in the wake of the doctor's skillful manipulation of his raking machine, which with methodical clatter and the rising and falling of its shining prongs left the cocks needing only a few quick strokes of the hand-rakes to be ready for hoisting into the rack. Mrs. Gowan watched from the orchard, ready in Mrs. Baxter's pink sunbonnet and a cool blue cotton frock of my mother's for her share in the afternoon's labour. Some menacing thunderheads gathering in the western sky made dinner a somewhat swift meal, at which Mrs. Gowan insisted on wearing her sunbonnet in order not to lose a moment when the treading should actually begin.

At two o'clock the horses were hitched to the lumbering grey hayrack which the doctor had left in the driveway. Mrs. Baxter forsook her kitchen, which was not precisely in order according to her standards, and we all clambered in to ride down to the field, bumping over the uneven ground, clinging to the stout side-rails, singing the Harvest Home Song. My mother rode to the field with us, wanting, I am sure, to keep an eye on Mrs. Gowan; but when she saw no apparent lessening of either strength or fervour, she left us to the treading and was glad to take over her task of gathering up with her wooden rake the strands of fallen hay behind the loads.

The thunderheads were still threatening near the horizon, but the sun above them remained hot and clear. It was a perfect day for haying, Ansie said. He only wished Tom were with us to enjoy it. He pitched with my father while the doctor saw to the progress of the horses from cock to cock; but he always rode back to the barn with us on the top of the loads, standing high in the air and clinging to the long handle of his fork. Mrs. Gowan, as she had done a year earlier, stood beside him, scorning the ease with which Mrs. Baxter, Mary, and I lay down in the hay. Sometimes she wavered a little, but she remained standing in her pink sunbonnet, laughing with Ansie as her voice broke or suddenly left her on the words and notes of the harvest song.

We made five fine loads in all. The tired horses lunged up the slope which led toward the open barn doors and the entrance to the loft into which, once the load had cleared the lintel and the heavy beam above the doorheads, the hay could be stowed away. They could rest when the weight of the rack had cleared the threshold, when its front stood solidly on the floor of the barn. We could rest, too, on the grass beside the rack while the men pitched the great forkfuls upward;

and Mrs. Baxter saw to it that we all had some cold swipes and the horses some lumps of sugar before we started back to the field in the empty, swaying rack.

After the fourth load was stowed away, my mother declared that she for one had had enough.

"I'm creaking in every bone," she said, "from just walking behind and watching all you Amazons. I'm for a good cup of tea, and I'm inviting you, Mrs. Gowan, to have it with me."

"Oh, please!" Mrs. Gowan cried. "Oh, please! The last load is always the merriest, isn't it, Ansie?"

Ansie sent my mother an entreating look in which I saw his promise that he would look after Mrs. Gowan.

"It's bound to be a high and heavy load, Mrs. Gowan," my father said. He studied the sky. "We ought to make six, but the rain's not far off. Don't you really think—"

"Be a good girl, Mrs. Gowan," the doctor said. "Enough is enough, you know."

"Oh, please, sir!" Mrs. Gowan cried again.

Perhaps my father and the doctor should have been more firm with Mrs. Gowan; but it is always harder to deny the old their hearts' desires than it is to refuse the young, who after all have years to weather their disappointments. Perhaps the two horses, no longer young themselves and already fagged, lunged more suddenly in their mighty effort to raise the front wheels of the last overladen rack across the high threshold of the barn. Perhaps Mrs. Gowan at the front of the load with Ansie and tired, too, had loosened her hold on his fork.

No one knew precisely how it happened, as one rarely does know. In my own confused memory, after Ansie had forced Mrs. Gowan downward into the safety of the hay and stood again upright, he caught the heavy beam beneath the loft squarely on his forehead. When he fell from the rack, he struck head first against the threshold. But as the doctor said, most kindly, it was probably all over before he hit that, too.

The storm did not come after all. It passed over to the eastward where others would doubtless be gathering in their hay. The twilight was fair and still.

Some hours later Mary and I sat together on the steps to the side door. Now and then people came with sympathy and offers of help, and, after the manner of the country, with food or flowers. We said thank you as we took their offerings, and they went quietly away. The stars came out one by one. Some fireflies glimmered above the grass under the orchard trees. I had never known before now how grief can make physical anguish, around one's heart, in one's chest.

Now and again we turned to look into the lighted kitchen. Mrs. Baxter's black teakettle was boiling on the stove. She had set some cups and saucers on the table. But mostly, as we looked, we saw that she was sitting between my father and my mother, holding a hand of each. Mrs. Gowan sat in the red rocking chair by the window. She was completely motionless, her hands folded in her lap, her pink sunbonnet, which no one had remembered, still on her head.

"Isn't there a thing we could do for them?" Mary whispered to me.

"I don't know," I whispered back.

Then I suddenly remembered. I went around to the front door, through the dim sitting-room, and up the stairs to our room. The little blue shoe from the ancient abbey ruins of Bury St. Edmunds was in its box there. I took it in my hand and went down the stairs, around the house in the darkness, and in the side door. When I gave it to my father, he smiled at me and closed his hand over it.

I don't know how long Mary and I sat together on the

steps. I remember mostly the sparkling of the fireflies and the silence in the kitchen. Mrs. Baxter had told us we could help just by sitting there, thanking people who came, and politely sending them away. It was late, I think, when she came to tell us that she was making some toast and cocoa for us and that my mother and father now wanted us with them.

Just as we went in the door, Mrs. Gowan looked at us. Her eyes were wide, but they were far away.

"Perhaps one of you children would answer the doorbell," she said in a frightened voice. "It's been ringing and ringing for a long time. I'm sure it's General Washington to see me about the flag. I don't want to keep him waiting out there in the thunderstorm."

A new sorrow swept and lined my father's face. Mrs. Baxter crossed the kitchen to the red rocker and put her hands over the listless ones of the old woman.

"I'll go myself to let him in," she said. "You and I will talk with him right now in the sitting-room while the others eat their supper. Don't you worry a mite, Mrs. Gowan. I've always wanted to meet General Washington."

FIVE · *The Return*

W*E DID NOT* have to decide between Augusta and Portland. My father and mother and I went to England in September after Mary had set forth for college in Massachusetts. My mother had set her heart on going back if only for a visit; and my father could not bear to disappoint her, he said. Moreover, his Pepperell congregation in a truly noble gesture of sympathy and affection had given us the journey as a farewell token of affection and good will, an act which lay warm and glowing in my father's heart.

Nor did he have to worry any longer about Mrs. Gowan; for a few days after our friend, the doctor, had taken her back to the hospital, she died quietly one night in her sleep. She had been quite clear and happy in her mind, Dr. Thomas said, when he came to visit us in August, only with the near past mercifully blotted out. This assurance was immensely cheering to my father.

Katie in her hat with the rakish cherries met our ship in Liverpool. She was still solid and strong, though her face was swollen with tears. The English countryside in early autumn was sunlit, grave, and quiet as we journeyed through the pottery towns and southward toward Cambridge. The cottage gardens were purple with Michaelmas daisies, and the meadows seemed more than usually filled with sheep.

"It must have been a fine lambing season," my father

said, "at least in the Midlands."

" 'Twas a prime one all over," Katie said. "Mutton's never been better nor less dear."

"See the churches, darling," my mother said. "I'd almost forgotten how lovely they are. And there are some swans on that tiny stream."

"I mean to fish all I can," my father said, feeling in his jacket pocket for his *Walden*.

"The vicar's full o' notions about that, sir," Katie said. "Last Sunday 'e told that very thing to me. I mean to say 'e's fair burstin' out with plans, an' not alone for fishin'."

## 2

My father had no intention of remaining in England. America was still his land of hope and promise. He stayed on through the winter only because his parents, now old and frail, cherished his nearness to them, and perhaps because Professor Bentley suggested some research in the university library which would be invaluable to him for a book he was writing if only my father could possibly help him out. Then in the spring when a chapel parish on the Suffolk border, not far from his boyhood home, lacked a pastor, he and my mother decided to tarry for yet a few more years, since after all there was the matter of currency to consider, even with the scholarship which Mary had won for herself at college.

Mrs. Baxter had solved the problem of Mary's holidays, just as she had solved most of our problems, whether in arithmetic or in the larger aspects of life, during our sojourn in Pepperell. Just how she managed to transform herself from a legacy to an independent existence we never quite knew, but she accomplished it without, she wrote us, so much as one "teeny twinge of conscience." By Christmas following our departure she had established herself in a home of her own, with Lilla, big with child, in her barn and a room set aside

for Mary as well as one for me when, and if, I might wish
to occupy it. She planned, of course, she said, to uphold the
Methodists by every manner of means except by living with
Reverend and Mrs. Shoemaker, who had six ill-brought-up
children and no standards whatsoever either of neatness or of
common sense. She carefully refrained in her frequent letters
from any mention of Primrose and Cowslip, and we all refrained from questions concerning their welfare or their fate.

When matters were settled, at least for the time being,
and my mother had transformed yet another chapel parsonage,
my father entered me as a day pupil at a Church school in
Bury St. Edmunds, to which I travelled daily by a wheezy,
one-carriage train. Bury had not changed a whit, though its
abbey gardens each year grew more lovely. The river Lark
still stole beneath the abbot's bridge and between its narrow
boundaries under the limes and the willows. My father rarely
missed a market day. There had not been time before we had
gone to America for him to study thoroughly all the antiquities, Roman, Anglo-Saxon, and medieval, newly housed in
the ancient Norman building in the Butter Market; but now
he could bend over them for hours. And since Mr. Read's
parishioners in Saintsbury had overwhelmed him at Easter
by the gift of a new bicycle, my father was the grateful
recipient of his old one, which, he told us, was far better
than any he had ever pedalled in all his life.

My school was like all not quite first-rate English schools
of fifty years ago, cold, precise, dingy, and thorough. We
wore pleated skirts and black stockings, dark-blue jackets
and white jumpers, and broad-brimmed hats of felt or straw
with streamers. We walked in queues whenever we went to
church or into the town, played outdoor games even in
bitter weather, ate indifferent food, minded our manners
meticulously, expected chilblains, a long winter, and icy water
for washing our hands, and got all in plenty. But since I had

the weekends in the parsonage with my mother's gaiety and my father's help on my lessons, I did not fare so badly. My knowledge of America, which I am sure I was not slow in scattering abroad, helped considerably in school to dim the fact that I was *chapel* rather than Church, like almost everybody else.

### 3

With his books and his deferred investigation of the Devil's Dyke, his Cambridge associations, his kind and devoted parishioners, and, above all, his thoughts, my father was contented in what he chose to term our *interim* in England. He held not only a singular respect for the considered thoughts of men, but a conviction as to their actual value to the corporate life of the world. To him an impure, unjust, or merely selfish thought or desire, whether or not it resulted in definite action, held the power to darken untold thousands of hearts and minds, quite unknown to one another and yet mysteriously linked together. Reflection and study, contemplation and worship were not, then, solitary pursuits to one who embraced them with understanding. Instead, they provided an invisible manna for the restoration and hope of one's fellow men.

He was not given to saying much about these beliefs except occasionally in his sermons, where they were doubtless not too clear to his Suffolk farmers, labourers, and tradesmen; but since they lay at the very root of his being, the place of their utterance, or even their utterance itself, was to him of relatively little importance. In the evenings while we sat together in his study, I with my Greek and Latin, my mother with an endless succession of baby jackets, or potholders, or scarves for the chapel sale, we would notice how often he dropped his books and went far afield in his thoughts. I used to wonder, I remember, whether they were in the steerage of some ship crossing the Atlantic, carrying courage and assurance there, or with Horace composing his odes on his Sabine farm, or on Walden Pond, or merely, like our own, back in Pepperell, when universals suddenly gave way to particulars as they are bound to do even in the richest, most dedicated minds.

My mother was of vast help to him in copying his pages on the Devil's Dyke as they were slowly completed, one by one, although the secondhand typewriter, which he had rented from a not-too-candid Cambridge stationer, proved of vast misery to her. Its *e* had an irritating way of inscribing itself far above the other letters, which mannerism conveyed a disturbed and tremulous appearance to her otherwise faultless typescript.

"If it were only a *zed* or a *y*," my mother said in despair. "And if only those wretched Iceni were Saxons. I've managed that bloodthirsty Boadicea by calling her *Boudicca*, which was her real name, I gather, but which I'm sure your father won't like. That doesn't help definite articles, though. All the *the*'s look as though they were scared out of their wits, and so does the *Devil* and his *Dyke*. Well, what does it matter? Your father's having such a wonderful time."

"Perhaps Mr. Brown, the saddler, could help," I suggested, distressed myself over the numberless elevated *e*'s. "He has all sorts of tiny tools."

Mr. Brown was immensely flattered over being invited for a consultation one day when my father was wandering along the Dyke; and, although typewriters were at an immeasurable distance from his trade, his fumbling with an awl and a screwdriver was successful beyond our hopes. Both the *e* and my mother regained their composure.

My father missed his morning and nightly chores. There was only a small patch of discouraged land about our parsonage in Heathwold, and our diminutive coal-shed was far from a barn. He rejoiced greatly when in the early spring of 1906 Mrs. Baxter sent us the news that Lilla had produced a beautiful calf, and—could we believe it—a heifer!

"It may even be the result of prayer without ceasing," she wrote in jubilation. "I haven't crawled into bed a single night for nine months without saying, 'No more bulls, please.'"

There was to my father's delight a lambing meadow not far away. The shepherd was a quiet, thoughtful young man, whose name was Giles Milsom and who, once my father had spent some chilly January evenings with him, in and out of his hut, began to come to chapel on Sunday mornings. He knew a great deal, we discovered, about the ageless history of sheep and fancied his job, like my father in his own youth, as being a small part of that history. Sometimes he came home with us after chapel for dinner. Then he and my father talked happily about linseed oil cakes for young lambs to supplement their mother's milk, about the danger of crude vegetables for ewes near their time, about the fact that the American Indians had known no sheep until the various colonists came from Europe, and about the endless centuries during which men had followed or led their flocks across the deserts and hills of Africa and Arabia in search of grass and streams. The shepherd was in no sense an educated man, perhaps barely literate; yet he listened eagerly while my father told him of Vergil's concern in the *Georgics* that the hard ground of the shelters be strewn with straw or dried fern lest the winter cold bring illness to the ewes, and how he warned the shepherds of that early time not to pray to the gods for healing, but instead to have courage to use their knives to cut into ulcers in spite of the pain, whenever quick surgery was necessary. One afternoon he asked my father to write down for him what Vergil had said so that he might read it at night in the pauses of tending his lambs.

"There's a young man whose thoughts travel far beyond his lambing hut," my father said.

4

My father never returned to his land of promise. During his second winter in Heathwold while he was helping Giles in the lambing meadow on a bleak January night—which, my mother said later, was perhaps what he loved to do beyond anything else—he became so chilled and exhausted that pneumonia was the result. He died only a few days later.

When I had finished school in Bury, I went back to New England for college, as he had wished me to do.

"There's something in America," he had said, smiling and flushed among his pillows, "that I can't find anywhere else, at least not to the same extent. I think it's a kind of respect for the human mind, for what it can and must become. Perhaps *hope* describes it better than any other single word. I'm not at all sure it's going to last. I don't like all this wealth and prosperity. Perhaps—we can't know—the hope for all men will be swallowed up in the greed of a few. And I've been thinking of what Tocqueville wrote about the danger to a democracy: that complacency and apathy can be even more deadly than actual corruption. I hope America will never become careless and indifferent to her particular ideal of freedom. I hope she won't forget what she really has meant and can mean to countless millions of people everywhere in the world. Anyway I want to go back and do my bit. Once I'm up and about again, we'll make real plans to go. Augusta will be ready for me next year, and there'll still be my work at the hospital, Dr. Thomas says."

Mary was teaching when I went back, and after four years I began to teach, too, first in the Far West and then, following some years of study, in a college in the Berkshire Hills. I am still there. My mother stayed on in England, through two wars, through tyranny and cruelty and sin which might have lessened even my father's lovely ambitions and tenacious faith.

Whenever I went home, as often as possible, to see her, we always journeyed to Bury St. Edmunds, across the heath land, by the Devil's Dyke, to the abbey ruins. The last time, twelve years ago, when she was an old woman, though still gay and buoyant, and I far from young, we sat by the river Lark in a late-summer twilight.

"I read somewhere lately in one of these new novels, which I must say I find hard to grasp and perhaps harder to respect, something which I think is very true," she said. "This man writes that shame is more acute than sorrow and much more difficult to bear. That's become quite a space-taker for me, even though it's not always a wholly comfortable one. I've had all manner of shames to bear, but I honestly don't think your father had ever a real reason to be ashamed of himself."

"I'm sure he didn't," I said, watching through a sudden mist of tears the girls coming across the grounds of my old school on the other side of the Lark. They were still in a long queue, still in hats with streamers.

"And don't let me forget when you pack tomorrow to give you that little blue shoe. It's a bit shabby, I'm afraid, from your father's carrying it about in his pocket. I've never quite been able in past years to give it back to you, but I daresay the time has come. Wasn't it right near here that you found it so many years ago?"

"Yes," I said. "In the abbot's kitchen among the stones and rubble."

"It was a sort of symbol to your father," my mother said, "of everything that he valued most. I won't pretend that I always quite understood just what that everything was, but I hope I had the sense to see that it was all that really matters."